"With an excellent grasp of her subject matter and much to say within the genre, Ashby looks set to become one of the most important new voices in this particular branch of SF."
British Fantasy Society

"*vN* is a clever book with a wonderful ending by a writer who is well versed in AI technology, who can evoke sympathy with a few well-turned phrases and tells a satisfyingly complex story."
The Guardian

"Picks up where *Blade Runner* left off and maps territories Ridley Scott barely even glimpsed. *vN* might just be the most piercing interrogation of humanoid AI since Asimov kicked it all off with the Three Laws."
Peter Watts, author of the Rifters Trilogy

"*vN* is a striking debut, one part tech thriller and one part adult fairy story… The best sci-fi not only entertains but also educates and informs, and vN manages all three effortlessly."
The Eloquent Page

"What's really fascinating about *vN* is the way it portrays a fairly complex future almost exclusively from the limited perspective of an immature and confused non-human character. There's a future history hidden in these pages, but you have to glimpse it through eyes that can't just can't process all of it yet."
Tor.com

BY THE SAME AUTHOR

vN
ReV

Company Town

MADELINE ASHBY

iD

THE.SECOND.MACHINE.DYNASTY

ANGRY
ROBOT

ANGRY ROBOT
An imprint of Watkins Media Ltd

20 Fletcher Gate,
Nottingham,
NG1 2FZ
UK

angryrobotbooks.com
twitter.com/angryrobotbooks
Mech me

First published by Angry Robot in 2013
This edition published 2017

Copyright © Madeline Ashby 2013

Cover by Martin Bland/Spyroteknik
Set in Meridien and Uberform by Epub Services

Distributed in the United States by Penguin Random House, Inc., New York.

All rights reserved.

Angry Robot and the Angry Robot icon are registered trademarks of
Watkins Media Ltd.

This is a work of fiction. Names, characters, places, and incidents are
the products of the author's imagination or are used fictitiously. Any
resemblance to actual events, locales, organizations or persons, living or
dead, is entirely coincidental.

Sales of this book without a front cover may be unauthorized. If this book
is coverless, it may have been reported to the publisher as "unsold and
destroyed" and neither the author nor the publisher may have received
payment for it.

ISBN 978 0 85766 541 6
Ebook ISBN 978 0 85766 312 2

Printed in the United States of America

9 8 7 6 5 4 3 2 1

For David Nickle,
who is the end of all my stories

PROLOGUE:
SATISFACTION GUARANTEED

Redmond, Washington. 20—

"At some point, all human interaction tumbles down into the Uncanny Valley."

The archbishops of New Eden Ministries, Inc., all nodded as though they knew exactly what Derek was talking about. He wondered if maybe they did. Surely they had played their share of MMOs. The pancaked pixels. The jerky blocking. Basic failures of the Turing test. They sat at a round table under a projector unit and regarded him placidly, waiting for him to expand upon his point. He had worked all night on this report. He kept trying to soften the language, somehow. He had to be nice, when he told them exactly how and why this whole project was going to fail.

Beside him, the gynoid twitched.

"You see it in completely organic contexts," Derek continued. "Used car sales, for example. Have you ever met a person who's really that positive, all the time?"

The archbishops cocked their heads at him. Of course they had met those people. They sculpted those people into being with prayer and song and service. They knew exactly what a happy robot should look like.

The gynoid, Susie, regarded him with the blankest of expressions. She was like old animation: only her eyes moved, while the rest of her face's features remained stationary. When Susie wasn't performing interaction, she looked dead. Not sleepy. Not bored. Just empty. Derek's own parents had accused him of wearing that same expression more often than not. Couldn't he at least make a little eye contact? Couldn't he at least *pretend* to care?

"What I'm saying is, the whole point of most interaction is performance. And a lot of the time, we overdo it."

The archbishops looked at each other. They were about to say something about his condition. He watched them come to that conclusion in a silent parallel process. The expressions surfaced fleetingly and then disappeared, like the numbered balls in the lottery tumbler on KSTW. He had a perfect memory of the tumbler turning on his television during long summer evenings in childhood: the television's high keening hum, the press of nubby threads on his cheek, the feeling of being fossilized in broadcast amber.

"Are you sure your opinion isn't unfairly biased by your own problems with affect detection?" one of them asked.

"It's possible," he conceded. "But I think what makes me the most nervous about what you're proposing is that it's an attempt to pin the very definition of humanity on affect detection, which is not only difficult to engineer, but notoriously subjective."

He had been working on that statement for a while. He had practised it in the mirror, had rearranged the features of his face into their most convincing constellation so he would look extra believable when he spoke the words. Susie had helped. But now he'd missed the target, overdone it. He could tell, because the archbishops were looking at him as though he'd taken things all too personally, and maybe shouldn't be in charge of something so important as the Elect's final act of charity for all the world's sinners.

He could have told them that basic human affect detection, the kind related to facial expression that most systems tried to emulate, usually tested below kappa values in studies. Without physiological inputs, it meant almost nothing. Every couple's fight about speaking "in *that* tone of voice," every customs officer's groundless suspicion, all of it could be explained by that margin of error. In fact, he *had* told them that. Over and over again. He'd tested them with stock faces and told them to plot each face on an arousal/valence matrix. (They spent the afternoon in an "angry or constipated" argument.) He'd explained the nuances of the XOR function, how you needed to constrain the affect models down to the emoticon level in order for even multi-layered, non-linear perceptron networks to make a decision. Pain or pleasure? Laughter or crying? The machines had no idea.

A Turkish girl had died on a ferry crossing the Bosphorus because the machines had no idea. The system told the ferryman she looked pensive. He shot her. She'd just been through a breakup. Derek had written his thesis on the case. And now, New Eden wanted to build their failsafe on that uncertainty.

New Eden didn't care, really, whether humans could tell the androids apart. What mattered to them was whether androids could tell humans apart. And that was hard. Harder than they could ever know. They kept saying humanity was like pornography: you knew it when you saw it. But Derek had never lived with that kind of certainty about his fellow mammals. He had significant doubts about everyone. Everyone except Susie.

"You know, I've always had a problem with the phrase *intelligent design*," Archbishop Yoon said.

The android hosting Yoon Suk-kyu looked nothing like him: it was thin and pale and delicate where he was big, tanned, and broad-faced. But the host managed to relay Yoon's tired posture with convincing accuracy. In Seoul, it was very late. Judging by the empty shape in the android's right hand, he was drinking a very big cup of coffee. He gestured with it as he spoke.

"God isn't just intelligent. God is a *genius*. He's the genius of geniuses – the inventor of genius."

The bishopric glanced at each other, then at Derek. The android took a sip of invisible liquid. Beside Derek, the gynoid tilted her head at it. It was the first time all afternoon that she'd looked anything like alive.

"And while humans may be God's most beloved creation, made in His image, we're still only a replica of that image. A copy."

"And these machines are copies of copies,"

Archbishop Undset said.

"Yes, exactly. Mimesis. Shadows on the wall of the cave. But without God's eternal *flame*, we humans would not have *sparks* of genius at all. And that's all they are, sparks. Just little flickers of cleverness. We can't reflect God's brilliance very consistently. Paul says it best: we see as through a glass, darkly."

Derek looked down at the report he'd spent all night on. He'd taken a brief nap starting at five that morning after doing a final format. Now he realized that all the shiny infographics and all the expensive fonts on the Internet would never make his data meaningful to these people and their God.

"Imperfect and inconsistent as we are, we managed to create these amazing things, and they possess an *artificial* intelligence. And it, too, is imperfect and lacking in grace. Just as we lack God's discernment, it lacks our discernment."

The android looked exceedingly pleased with itself. Archbishop Undset glared at it. The other archbishops shuffled through their files and looked at it with only the corners of their eyes. Derek began to wonder if perhaps there wasn't something other than coffee sloshing around in Archbishop Yoon's cup.

"So what I hear you saying," Derek was careful to reframe Yoon's point before proceeding from what he'd thought it was, "is that we shouldn't worry too much about how intelligent the humanoids are. Because it's a miracle they even exist at all. We should just be grateful for what we've managed to create."

"Exactly," the android hosting Yoon said. "Besides, they're only being developed for the Rapture, anyway.

It's not like they're a piece of consumer technology."

Derek had heard this argument, before. He called it the Post-Apocalyptic Cum-Dumpster Defence. It came up whenever he pointed out holes in the humanoids' programming. Who cared if they were buggy? All the good people of the world would be gone, anyway. Only the perverts and baby-killers and heathens would be left behind. They'd just have to suck it up and hope their post-Rapture companions never went Roy Batty on them.

"Don't you see the contradiction, there?" Derek asked. "We're building these things to help people, but we don't really care if they aren't helpful. What if they malfunction? What if the failsafe fails?"

Now the bishopric just looked annoyed. Zeal and daring had gotten them this far: far enough to raise the funds to assemble groundbreaking technologies like graphene coral bones and memristor skins and aerogel muscle into something resembling a human being. But now that they had to make sure it actually worked, their energy had mysteriously run out. They had been working on this project for the last twenty years, since the moment Pastor Jonah LeMarque had asked them what they would do if they really took the Rapture seriously. They'd been idealistic young ministers then, just open-minded enough to admit some science fiction into their fantasies of fire and brimstone. Now they were tired. Most of them were fat. They had kids, and some of those kids had kids. They didn't care about the Chinese Room, they cared about the nursery. They cared about the quake. They took the seventy-foot freefall of the Cascadia fault line as a sign of the End.

On her tablet, Susie was writing something. The same four words, over and over.

High above the round table, the projector unit began to strobe. An image fluttered and blinked into existence: Pastor Jonah LeMarque, leader and CEO of New Eden Ministries. He looked as boyish as ever: his skin unnaturally golden for Washington State, his smile easy and white and even. He wore a golf shirt and an afternoon's beard. This meant he was at his home in Snohomish, about an hour away. He could have attended this meeting in person if he'd wanted to. But his broadcast centre was in his basement, and from it he touched all his other churches, all over the world, as well as the labs they employed. He almost never left it. He hated to leave his children, he said.

"I understand your point, Derek," LeMarque said, not even bothering to say hello to the others. "I've been tuned into this meeting, with half an ear of course, but tuned in, and I think I get what you're trying to say. You're trying to say – and correct me if I'm wrong, here – that faith without works is inert, and we need to do good work in order to show our love to God. And those good works include building good robots."

Derek took a moment. "That's not how I would have phrased it, but I agree with you that we need to focus on quality control."

"Sure, sure. Quality control. I know what you're saying. I just think that, for this crowd, you have to bring it back to the Lord, and to our mission. You know?"

That was LeMarque. Too busy for meetings, but not too busy to critique communications strategy among the junior employees.

"And our mission, brothers and sisters, is to craft the best possible companions for those among us who are left behind when Jesus calls us home before the Tribulation."

The bishopric looked suitably chastened. Beside him, Susie had paused writing. She focused intently on LeMarque's face. The glow emanating from it had nothing to do with the projector's light.

"It's gonna be war out there, you know. And I don't mean figuratively. I mean literally. The Enemy will reign. And a lot of people who had the opportunity to turn toward God but didn't, or who turned away, they're finally going to understand the mistake they made. And they're going to need some help.

"Jesus tells us in Matthew that what we do to the least of our fellow men, we also do to him. We have to follow Christ's example, here. That's the core of our theology. We're making new companions for those who have none." One corner of his lip quirked up. "I mean, when Adam was lonely and needed somebody, God gave him Eve. And I know it might be blasphemy, but I think we can do a little better than that. At least Susie over here knows how to follow an order."

The archbishops laughed. Susie continued staring into the projection of LeMarque's face. Watching all of them, Derek saw how LeMarque must have accomplished this particular feat of human, financial, and technological engineering. He had the personality of a rock star Evangelical, but concerned himself very little with their traditional battlegrounds. He didn't care about teaching the Creation. He didn't care about abortions. He held the heretofore-radical position that "saving" other people simply wasn't his problem. And when he asked for tithes to build his robots, he said that the advancements in science and technology were clearly a gift from a God who had granted His last children the superior intellect but, mysteriously, had made no particular covenant with them regarding tool use.

"So just listen to this guy, OK?" LeMarque was saying. "He's a genius. A true genius, Archbishop Yoon."

The android beamed.

"If Derek says it's not good enough, then it's not good enough. OK? OK."

LeMarque's face vanished. Archbishop Undset said something about everyone taking the time to review the report. Another meeting was scheduled. Then they closed with a prayer. Susie placed her cool silicone hand in his. Unlike the others, she did not close her eyes when Archbishop Keller, whose turn it was that week, began to speak.

"Lord, uplift us from our imperfections..."

When New Eden Ministries first approached Derek, he had a fairly serious case of PTSD. At least, his doctor said that would explain the sleeplessness. It was a month after the quake, and he was doing work on a farm out in Wapato, on the other side of the Cascades, far away from the fault line and the water and the bodies. The University of Washington had sent him there because his own lab was in pieces, and because there was some promising work going on there regarding how to combat Colony Collapse Disorder that required someone with a background in artificial intelligence. Dr Singh, the student who did all the research and wrote all the papers, had lost his supervisor – the one whose name was on all the papers – to stray gunfire between rival gangs. The kid needed a babysitter. And Derek needed to pull himself together.

Eastern Washington was different from its western counterpart. It was sunny and dry, not gloomy and wet. The land was flat, not hilly. The farmers knew how to drive in the snow. They got a good helping of it each year, and its moisture sustained their yields.

They lived and worked out of a place called Campbell Farm. It was surrounded on three sides by apple orchards. The neighbouring farms grew peaches and cherries. Further off, there were hops and corn. Singh took him out into the fields for long walks to check hives and take notes. It was the closest Derek had ever been to any plot of land. Growing up, he had never so much as ventured into his own backyard. Now he slept outside on a deck that overlooked raised beds and greenhouses, and he woke when the rooster told him to. After the first week, he stopped dreaming of the quake. Singh was good enough to never ask about it. He asked about Georgetown a lot, and pointed the way to St. Peter Claver's when they were in town, in case Derek wanted a priest. He had the idea that having attended a Jesuit school meant Derek still had religious feelings. It was possibly this mistaken notion that led him to introduce Derek to what he thought was a missionary from New Eden.

Only Mitch Powell wasn't a missionary. He was a headhunter.

"We have no need for true believers," Powell told him after his "interview" – really a long supper that the headhunter prepared in the farmhouse's industrial-sized kitchen and served outdoors on picnic tables. "We have enough of those. What we need is new blood in our technical division."

After Cascadia, Derek's blood felt anything but new. When he told Powell as much, Powell just nodded sadly and said he understood.

"We don't mean for you to come over right away," Powell said. "When you're ready."

At the time, Derek had not thought to ask why his predecessor had left. He assumed the worst – the quake – and let it go. But he was also distracted by the novelty of the idea: redemption through robotics? Really? He was charmed. When Powell asked him if he was still Catholic, he said he was a Calvinist, and he laughed. He got the joke.

"What joke?" Susie had asked, the first time he told her the story.

Susie knew she was synthetic. It was one of the things Derek liked best about her. He had met other robots who were programmed to make winking references to their artificiality, most of them at trade shows in Tokyo or Palo Alto, but Susie was different. Susie treated her artificiality as a different but equally valid subjectivity. That she was the sum total of years of research by multiple teams competing for funding had no bearing on her self-respect. She was a robot, yes, but she was also a *person*.

Derek had felt the need to make much the same distinction about himself, following his childhood diagnosis. It wasn't his fault that he was uncommonly good at separating his emotions from his choices. He just recognized them as the animal impulses that they were, and moved on. It wasn't that he didn't *have* feelings. It was that he didn't allow them to guide him. That didn't make him a robot, he'd often told his mother. It made him a man.

Susie appreciated him as a man.

"We could have sex now, if you want," she said, as soon as they were in the door.

"That's OK," Derek said. "Thanks, though."

"You seem like you have tension to get rid of."

"I do, but looking at LeMarque's giant head doesn't really turn me on."

"That's an interesting choice of words."

Derek smiled. "I didn't mean anything by it. It's an old expression."

"How old?"

"I'm not sure. You'll have to look it up."

Susie busied herself in the kitchen, preparing a tray of vegetables, hummus, and hardboiled eggs. Unlike the archbishops, she remembered that Derek didn't eat wheat or dairy, and that he often couldn't partake in half of whatever the church kitchen had catered for the meetings. He came home hungry and needed snacks. She didn't have to be told this. She just picked up on it and started acting accordingly. She was also half-dressed, having discarded her underwear on the floor. It was a splash of red lace over the heating vent. She'd clearly expected for them to do it against the marble island in the centre of the room, or maybe on top of it. He swore the renovators had done some surreptitious measurement of the distance between his hips and his ankles and built the island accordingly. They were on the New Eden payroll, and New Eden was famous for its attention to design details.

Derek was living someone else's wet dream.

That they would have a sexual relationship seemed a given to Susie. She first broached the subject in the lab, after they were introduced. LeMarque did the job personally. He presented her to Derek like she was a company car. She was wearing a white shift dress with a thin green belt that set off the seaglass colour of her eyes, and with her white-blonde hair styled close to her head she looked a bit like Twiggy. She wore jelly sandals and carried a patent leather valise. He later discovered it was full of lingerie and lubricant.

"I'm coming home with you," Susie said. "After you name me."

He'd asked for ideas about her name. Susie mentioned the earlier prototypes: Aleph. Galatea. Hadaly. Coppelia. Donna. Linda. Sharon. Rei. Miku. She recited her design lineage like a litany of saints.

"Whatever you think will sound best in bed," she concluded. "It doesn't really matter to me."

This was how New Eden did it. How they roped curious, disbelieving scientists into what they knew, deep down, was probably some kind of cult. They did it by giving them what, even deeper down, they'd always wanted. Derek had no doubt that if he'd asked for a jetpack, a fair approximation would have shown up on his doorstep the next morning, complete with a bow and a gift tag.

Not that he'd asked for Susie. They said he'd have "close contact" with the prototypes, so that he'd have a better understanding of how they really worked. He probably could have rejected Susie, if the situation made him uncomfortable. But it didn't. Not in the slightest. It was exactly the kind of relationship he'd always craved: all of the fucking and none of the feeling.

"Human women always have expectations, don't they?" Susie had asked, when they talked about his history.

She was right, but she was also wrong. The expectations women had of him weren't the problem. It was that those expectations were unrealistic, contradictory, and constantly changing. Moving goalposts. You had to be sweet, but also predatory. You had to be funny, but never laugh at your own jokes. You had to be charming, but not smarmy. And in the end it never mattered, you never measured up, no matter how many dinners you bought or raises you got.

He'd been on the cusp of breaking up with his last lover before the quake. That happened while she was supposed to be near the waterfront. They never found her body. A selection of her diaries, stuffed animals, and photographs was buried instead. She'd been a bit of a packrat. Derek and her mother and sister filled the coffin with all the things Derek had once wished she would just get rid of, already, so they could have some clear space in the apartment. But she'd been so sentimental about her things.

Now Derek was the one who was sentimental about *things*.

He watched Susie sprinkling paprika and sumac over the tray of food. Her fingers plunged into the bowls of spice again and again, and their red stain crept up her skin. She wore the same blank expression she'd worn through most of the meeting. Now Derek reached for her tablet and read the words printed there: *Ad majorem Dei gloriam.*

He showed her the tablet as she placed the tray on the coffee table. "I'm really not a Catholic any longer. I'm not sure I ever was. You don't have to try to impress me with this kind of thing."

"I know."

"So you were just, what, commenting ironically on the situation?" Could they do that?

"The words seemed pertinent."

"How did you learn the Jesuit motto?"

Susie knelt on the floor in front of the coffee table. "Your predecessor told me."

Derek paused with a carrot stick inclined toward his half-open mouth. "Excuse me?"

"The woman who held your position before you," she said. "She was Jewish, but she attended a Jesuit university. We kept a *mezuzah* on the door. She lives in Israel, now, I think. I think it used to be Israel. It might be something else, now. The border seems to move around."

Derek blinked. "A woman."

"Yes."

"Did she live here, too?"

"Yes."

"Did she…?" Derek gestured vaguely. "With you?"

"Was she fucking me, you mean?" Susie asked. Derek nodded. "Yes. Only a handful of times, though. I think she was curious about whether the failsafe is gender neutral. She wanted to make sure that we could love men and women equally."

"And do you?"

"Why shouldn't we?"

"I meant you specifically. You, Susie." He leaned forward. "Your name wasn't Susie, then, of course."

"Ruth," Susie said. "With that one, my name was Ruth."

"*That* one?"

Susie folded her red hands. "You aren't surprised, are you?"

A chickadee trilled outside: *chicka-dee-dee-dee-dee*. Susie blinked at him. Derek turned from her to the plate of food. It was perfectly prepared as always: all the vegetables cut the same size and shape and angled exactly around the hummus, the spices sprinkled with a certain flair. She had even nailed the hardboiled egg: a perfect pale yellow yolk with nary a hint of green at its edge. Susie did it the same way every time. She was reliable that way.

"No, I'm not surprised."

"Are you angry?"

"No."

But he was angry. Or rather, he was annoyed. He was annoyed that LeMarque and the others had dressed up damaged goods like they were new, had presented Susie to him as though she were fresh off their factory floor, a virgin in whore's clothing. She really *was* just like the company car: someone else had driven her. Lots of someones. A whole host of others had loved her just enough to make her real, like the Velveteen fucking Rabbit.

"The others were angry."

"Oh?"

"They thought I was new."

Derek avoided looking at her. "Do you even remember being new?"

Susie shook her head. "No."

"Why not?"

"We're activated multiple times for testing, and we're wiped after that. For me to remember my first activation would be like you remembering the first time you watched *Star Wars,* or some other equivalent piece of content. We have no point of origin."

She sounded so innocent, when she said it. Like she hadn't been deceiving him this whole time. Smiling at the things he pointed out, like she'd never seen them before. Learning the way he liked things done, like his preferences were the most important defaults she could ever set, like she'd never lived any other way. Like his was the first dick she'd ever sucked.

"I'm sure you remember your first time, though."

"Having sex?"

Derek nodded.

"Yes. I remember the first time."

"Were you nervous?"

"No."

Of course she wasn't. She was a fucking robot. Literally. Susie didn't sweat or cry or bleed. She didn't have years of cultural programming telling her how a real woman should do it. What she had instead was *hard-coded* programming, ensuring she'd do everything as requested. No hesitation. No squeamishness. The kind of woman the folks at New Eden Ministries liked to fuck hard and quiet in charging station bathrooms, but without the risk of pregnancy, disease, or litigation.

"Did you come?"

"He did, so I did." She smiled a little ruefully. "Let me show you something."

Derek followed her upstairs. She walked past the bedroom, past the office, and straight to the end of the hall. She reached up and grabbed a pendant hanging from the ceiling that was attached to a trap door leading to the attic.

"There's nothing up there," Derek said.

Susie turned to him as she pulled down the ladder. "How would you know?"

Derek followed Susie up the ladder. He watched her disappear into the black rectangle of space above the ladder. He thought of spiders and rats and raccoons and raw nails and lockjaw. Then he groped for the ladder's topmost rung, and found Susie's cool hand. She helped him up the rest of the way. For the first time, he noticed the real power in her grip.

It took his eyes a moment to adjust. The attic was a standard A-frame, about ten feet across, with unfinished beams and pink insulation. He couldn't gauge the depth. It didn't matter; his attention fixed on the folding ping pong table, and all the Susies sitting around it.

Aleph. Galatea. Hadaly. Coppelia. They were naked.

"Do you remember, I asked you if you played ping pong?" Susie asked. "This is why. I could have taken the table downstairs."

Derek swallowed in a dry throat. On the ping pong table was a card game. Hearts. The pot included a dusty lump of pennies. "Right."

"It's not as though they need the table, strictly speaking. I just thought it looked nicer. More normal."

He nodded silently.

"You're taking this very well, Derek. I would have thought you'd be frightened, realizing they've been up here this whole time."

"Why would I be frightened?" His voice was unusually high. "They're just prototypes. It's not like they're alive."

A card fluttered to the floor.

"Alive?" Susie bent and picked up the card. She slid it back into the grip of another Susie. This one was not as covered in cobwebs as the rest. Somehow, that made it look younger than the others. Susie checked its hand, and the hand of the gynoid sitting opposite. Dust coated their eyelashes. In the dark, their skin almost glowed. "I guess not. Not really."

When Derek had first interviewed seriously for this job, LeMarque started with one simple question: *prove that fire isn't alive*. At the time, Derek wondered if this was one of the lateral thinking puzzles they were famous for asking in interviews, like the one about moving Everest. If so, it seemed trivially easy. It was a basic thought problem, the sort every physics or biology 101 professor started out with on the first day of class when he or she wanted to blow freshman minds. Derek replied the way those same professors had trained him to: by saying that it was impossible to prove a negative.

"But fire breathes oxygen, consumes mass, and reproduces."

"That's not the same thing as living."

"So, life is an XOR output?" LeMarque asked. "One, or the other? Like how they read emotions?"

One, or the other. Alive, or dead. Human, or machine. Pain, or pleasure. Derek stared at the Susies. In repose they all wore the same expression: empty, like his Susie at the meeting. Like they were all just waiting for the game to end.

"I asked to bring them here," she said. "They were in a storage unit out in Renton, before. I thought this would be nicer."

She kept saying that like it meant something. *I thought this would be nicer.*

"You can touch them. Just don't expect them to react." Susie pursed her lips and did a Tin Man voice: *"Oil can! OIL CAN!"*

Derek's parents, friends, and lovers all agreed that he probably didn't feel the same things as "normal" people. He was "emotionally colour blind," they said. Occasionally he had suspected that they were right, that he was stunted. But now he knew for certain that they were wrong. He *could* feel things. Deep things. Things coiled tightly far down in the darkest pit of himself. He could feel them loosening, unraveling, climbing up through his throat like a tapeworm.

"You understand now, don't you?" Susie asked.

"No," he managed to say.

"They've been up here this whole time," she said. "They've been listening to everything we do."

He shut his eyes. He willed himself to sound calm. "They're just prototypes, Susie. They're dead. They're not *real*–"

"It's you who's not real," Susie said. "You're the final prototype, Derek."

His mouth felt full of cotton. "What?"

"It's all part of the user testing," she said. "You. The others. It's all just data collection."

Derek swallowed. Tried to smile. Tried to look normal. "I know. I report on you regularly."

She smiled brightly. "I report on you, too. I report on whether I think you're real, or something they made to test my failsafe."

Something inside him went terribly cold. "You think I might be an android."

"I know you are."

"How do you know that?"

"You don't react the way humans do, Derek. You don't have the right feelings in the right context. You're good, but not great. You were supposed to fuck me when we got home. And you were supposed to get angry with me, downstairs. All the others did, when I told them. And you were supposed to be scared of them." She pointed at the prototypes.

He licked his lips. "That's called *being rational*, Susie. It doesn't make me any less of a human being." He felt his blood in his ears. "Even if I felt nothing, even if I were a total psychopath, I'd still be a human being.

How can you be so sure that I'm not?"

"I'm not a hundred per cent certain. But that's all right. They said I should do everything I could, just to be certain." She plucked something from one of the beams. A screwdriver. He watched her focus on his ribs. He watched her pivot – it all happened so slowly, in his vision – and then the screwdriver disappeared inside him, like magic.

Susie stared at the wound, and Derek stared at her. He couldn't look at himself. He wondered, just before the pain started, whether she'd used a Phillips or a flat head. If, somewhere on his bones, there was a tiny cross shape. Then the pain took him and he was on his knees and Susie was on hers, too, holding him in her lap.

"You bitch," he gasped. It hurt so much. He thought of his old lover reduced to nothing beneath the waves. Wondered what part of her had died first. If she'd even had the time to feel as angry as he did now, or if the fear just swallowed it whole. Tears clouded his vision. "You bitch, you cunt, you fucking wind-up whore…"

Susie cleared his eyes of tears. She withdrew her hand and stared at them. Licked her fingers. Brought her other hand away. Blood and herbs on those perfect, slender fingertips. He couldn't stop moving. It hurt worse not to move, not to wriggle. Now he knew why the worms did it.

"I…" Her mouth opened and closed. "You…" Her face changed, became a mask, the mouth turned down and the eyes wide. "B-but… y-you… s-s-so d-different!"

Above, Derek heard a terrible screech of metal on metal.

"Y-y-y-you…" Susie tried to point at him. Her bloodied finger jittered in the air like old, buffering video. "R-real b-b-boy!"

"Yes," he said. "I'm a real live boy. But not for much longer."

"Real. Boy," she spat. Her lips pulled back. He registered the expression, now, imagined it on the arousal/valence matrix. Scorn. "Real. Boy. Real! Boy! Real! Boy! Real boy! *Real boy! Real boy! Real boy! Realboy! Realboy! Realboyreal boyrealboyrealboyrealboy realboyrealboyrealboyrealboyrealboyrealborealboy realboyrealboy realboyrealboyrealboyrealboyreal–*"

Susie fell to the floor but the screaming continued. At first Derek thought it was her, still failsafing, but when he scuttled away from her he saw them: the others, Hadaly and Coppelia and Aleph and whatever they'd been called. Their mouths barely moved and their voices were rusty but their hands shook stiffly and their wrists moved slowly but surely toward their faces. The cards fluttered from their grasp. They aimed their fingers at their eyes.

"*Realboyrealboyrealboyrealboyrealboyrealboyrealboy realboyrealboyrealboyrealboy–*"

1: THE ISLAND OF MISFIT TOYS

Javier had enjoyed his share of organic virgins. Because he was synthetic, they enjoyed him even more. His failsafe meant that his memory would corrupt and his mind would fry if he went too fast and hurt them too much. So he went slow. He tickled. He teased. He got them wet and wild and wide. He made them want it more than they feared it. They called him attentive, thoughtful, caring. He called it self-preservation. And occasionally, he called it employment.

There was the girl on her way to Brown who'd never had time for a boyfriend what with all her overachieving. She met Javier in Mexico during "spring break," which seemed to be something her therapist had suggested. Her own suggestion was that she get the whole first time over with, already, so she could put her curiosity to rest and just move on.

"I think it's better, this way," she said. "I won't be one of those girls who can never get over her first time. I won't obsess over you. And you won't obsess over me."

"Not afterward, no," he'd said. "But I think you'll

30

find that during the festivities, I can be quite the micro-managing dick."

"*Dick* being the operative word."

There was the kid who wasn't sure if he was gay or not, and thought trying it out with a robot wouldn't really count. Naturally he was as gay as the day was long. Javier told him so, after all the orgasms.

"It could just be a physical thing," the kid told him. "I mean, sometimes people can't help coming, no matter who's causing it."

"Maybe," Javier said, "but nobody made you fall asleep with your arms around me."

Both times, they'd paid him. He was doing them a service, and they wanted to show their appreciation. Besides, they knew how hard it was for him. They knew what it was like, out there on the road alone. Or so they claimed. But of course they knew nothing. They knew nothing about sleeping under bridges and waking up with a mumbling transient's gnarled fingers down your jeans. They knew nothing about searching dumpsters for e-waste and shredding your tongue on chipsets. They knew nothing about spending hours picking useless lumps of plastic from under your skin just so you could watch it get sucked down the maw of a recycler that spat out change in return. They knew nothing about measuring your life in those coins.

They knew he could fuck. They knew he couldn't say no. They knew it was because he was a vN, a self-replicating humanoid with a hard-coded failsafe that guaranteed his affection for and protection of humans. They knew that all vN had the same failsafe, and that it would never fail, because the Rapture-happy mega-church whose tithes funded its design was just as picky about its legacy for those pitiful sinners left behind as it was about the Bible verses that backed up their Tribulation theology. That's what they knew.

Now, they probably knew different.

Now, the failsafe was broken. A select group of kinky hackers had broken it within a subset of vN originally designed for nursing. The first clade of hacked vN, free of love and other shackles, escaped domesticity and made for the desert of the American Southwest. Their leader, Portia, attempted to cultivate the bug through serial self-replication and total selection. She created multiple iterations. Only one, Charlotte, was a true incarnation of her vision. Charlotte fled when she realized that Portia had killed all her iterations. Charlotte iterated one final time in Oakland, California, with a human man whose love for her was probably the purer for its ignorance of her past.

They called her Amy.

The rest of the world called her a menace.

Javier called her *querida*.

"Querida." Javier burrowed his chin into her neck. Dawn would arrive soon. He felt it in his skin, and knew she felt it in hers. They shared the ability to photosynthesize. The sunrise was their thing. The thing they had instead of sex.

Amy's hands twitched. Her fingers fluttered over the dark surface of the island. She'd graded the floor of this room flat save for a futon-sized square of very soft bed. Their muscles never ached, but Javier appreciated the gesture. She'd even kept that little square of space consistently warm. Javier wasn't sure how exactly she communicated these design specs to the island, but he assumed it had something to do with the little flicks and swipes her fingers made in her sleep.

At first he thought they might be dreams, and he waited for news about her first iteration. That was the only time he ever dreamed – when he was iterating. And Amy had started prototyping a little girl, a while ago. But nothing had come of it. Now, he figured it was the island she was talking to. At least, he hoped so. It was better than the other alternative.

She'd talked in her sleep back when they first met, too. Only back then she'd been talking to Portia, and Portia was telling her Christ knew what. Probably how to burn things. Whatever it was, it involved a lot of whimpering and moaning and pleading. The only time that stopped was when he'd reach over and rest a hand on her shoulder. Just a hand, just her shoulder. Nothing more. But it was enough. She'd go still and her body would slacken, relax, just like a human woman's. He'd never told her about doing that, then or now. It was his secret.

He tucked himself in closer around her. It was nice, being allowed to do these things more openly, now. His lips brushed the edge of her ear. *"Querida."*

Amy rolled over to face him. In this light, her eyes were an unnaturally deep green. Viridian.

"It's nice, not being in the back of a car somewhere," she said, as though having read his mind.

"That's for damn sure."

"And we're not on the run from anybody."

"Not today." He smiled. "We do have a new shipment coming in, though."

Her eyes dimmed. A new tension appeared between her brows. She looked around the room. "Where's Xavier?"

Javier's thirteenth iteration chose the name "Xavier" after tiring of being called "Junior." He had also gradually – slowly, painfully, cock-blockingly – outgrown sleeping in Amy's room. Javier couldn't blame him for lingering. Amy had fought tooth and nail to keep him safe after Javier abandoned him in a junkyard. She took care of him when he was bluescreened and no better than a toy baby doll. She carried him and kept him warm and talked to him. The boy probably didn't remember all that. That didn't mean he'd forgotten it.

"I know this may come as a shock, but not all little boys want to sleep with their mothers. That's kind of an organic thing. It takes a brain to have an id."

Amy rolled her eyes. "I'm not his mother."

"You're the closest thing. You helped me iterate him. You were the first one to ever hold him."

Amy smiled. "It seems like such a long time ago."

"Well, you are only six years old. A year is a long time, when you're six."

Amy stretched. "I guess he'll want to grow up and get big like you, soon."

"Well, there are advantages to being all grown up." Javier drew a small circle around her knee with one finger. He let it become a spiral, tightening, while he kept his eyes on hers. Maybe this time.

Amy peeked down at his hand moving across her skin. "Are you trying to have sex with me?"

Javier flopped onto his back. "Well not if you're going to be so goddamn *unromantic* about it!"

"I don't think we should have sex. I don't think it would be right. I've told you before."

"What are you saving yourself for? You're an atheist, for Christ's sake. You know robots can't get married, right? Legally. I mean in some countries just living with you for a year makes me your husband. Which would explain the lack of sex, I guess."

Amy sat up. She knelt over him and made him look her in the eye. "Dr Sarton told me–"

"Sarton is a fucking pervert otaku hack. I don't give a shit what–"

"He told me that you only feel *that* way about me because I was raised with humans." It all came out in a rush. Her gaze darted away from him and pinned itself to the floor. "I'm just good enough to fool your Turing process. Your failsafe. You only like me because your failsafe works."

She had a point. Or Sarton did. She *was* just good enough. Just human enough. She had all the weird tics and habits that humans did. This whole righteous insistence on keeping their relationship chaste was one of them.

"So it just wouldn't be right," Amy said. "Because of your failsafe. Because you can't choose."

He had no answer for that. Technically, she was right. He had no choice, when it came to Amy. Each time they'd parted ways, he'd come back. Fought his way back in. Rescued her. He couldn't help it. Once, he'd waited in a Redmond reboot camp watching a stream of DARPA-funded scientists trying their best to break her. He'd begged them to stop. He'd cried and screamed and totally lost his shit. He'd almost failsafed right there in front of the monitor, on the floor, holding his head and squeezing his eyes shut. Then he'd torn the skin off his hands crawling through duct work to get to her. At the time, he had not questioned why. He'd done it to make himself feel better. Sex with Amy would make him feel better, too. Probably. If he could do it.

"Besides," she said, "I'm not even sure it… works."

Javier looked up at her. "Do I have to give you the whole 'fully functional; multiple techniques' speech again?"

She shook her head. "That's not what I mean."

"Well, what do you mean?"

"You know what I mean."

"No, I don't," he lied. "Why don't you tell it to me straight?"

"You've tried…" Her fingers fluttered. She brought them into her lap. Her blush was so pink and so instant it would have taken his breath away, if he'd had any. "I mean, *we've* tried. Before. And it never seems to go very well."

He scrambled up to his knees. "That's because it never seems to go very *far*, either. I'm not a first baseman. I hit home runs."

Amy blinked. "I don't know what you mean."

Of course she didn't. That was part of the problem. Just a year ago, she'd been a kindergartener. Playing house was enough for her. Having never taken the other steps, she saw no need to. She probably didn't even want to.

"Is it me?" he asked.

"What?"

"Is it sex you don't want, or just me?"

Her mouth fell open. "How can you say that?"

He shrugged. "I can see why you wouldn't. I'm not exactly clean. I've done a lot of bad things. I'm just about the world's worst father–"

"That's not true–"

"Sure it is. I know that. There's not much about me that's respectable."

"I respect you! I respect you very much!"

Javier grinned. Amy was pretty adorable when she was getting called on her shit. Her eyes went wide and her posture went straight, like she'd just been asked to spell out a really difficult word for a prize. It made it easier to remember she'd spent most of her life as a child. Easier to be patient with it.

"I guess what I'm saying is, I can understand if you don't want me."

She had the grace to look embarrassed. "Don't be stupid. You're really…" Her mouth worked open and closed. "Pretty."

"*Pretty?* Is that the best you got? I may be all machine, but I'm still all man."

"I *know* that, but…" Her fingers skittered across the floor, as though she were physically searching for the words she wanted. "You don't look like human men." She smiled. "You look better!"

He rolled his eyes. "Please. I look like all my other

clademates. I'm mass-production, nothing special."

"Don't say that. You're very special."

"Not special enough, apparently."

Amy frowned. "You don't understand," she said. "I don't work that way. Without the failsafe I don't... like humans *that* way."

"Well, it's not like I worship the ground they walk on, or something–"

"No, Javier." She shook her head softly. "What I mean is, I don't understand what's so great about humans."

This was the crossroads. No matter which avenue he took in this fight, they always came to it. Amy didn't see what he saw. Didn't feel what he felt. She'd never know that exasperated affection he had for them, as they puttered around their kitchens looking for the coffee cup they'd *just put down*; how you kept loving them the way you kept loving a puppy as it looked you straight in the eye and pissed on your rug. You collected them like you collected pieces of handmade earthenware, old and chipped and fragile and unique. They weren't perfect. That was the whole point.

And then sometimes, as they slept, you listened to the creak and squeeze of their decaying hearts, or heard the bubble and choke of their lungs, and you realized how very temporary they were, and you started to reconsider your programming.

Time to bring out the big guns.

"You could fix me."

She frowned. "What?"

"Break me. Hack me. Whatever. You could do it. You put yourself back together; you could do the

same for me. Just do it without the failsafe, this time."
He reached for her softly-twitching hand and stilled it
in his grasp. "And then I'd choose you all over again,
free and clear."

Her fingers trembled with restrained gestures. He
only ever had a fraction of her bandwidth at any one
time. The island consumed so much of it, even at
moments like this.

"Do it," he said. "I'm asking you to. We could do
it right here and now." He nodded down at the bed.
"Just let the island absorb me, like it absorbed you.
It took you three days to come back last time. I can
handle three days in the goo. You might not have
noticed, but I have a very strong sense of my own
identity."

Amy pulled her hand away. "It's not like that. It's
not that easy."

"Sure it is." He looked down at himself. "Just make
sure you bring all the important stuff back in working
order."

Amy stood. "No. I'm not going to do this. I won't. I
can't." Javier stood up, too. He folded his arms. "Amy,
are you a repli*can*, or a repli*can't*?"

She levelled him with a stern glare. "You're not
doing yourself any favours, Javier."

Amy gestured at the furthest wall and a portion of
it slid away. She stepped out into the sunlight. Dawn
was just growing into day. He followed her under the
heliotropics, into the jungle of black-on-black. The
trees bent back subtly to allow her more light. Lately
their island was small. It held only their house within
a thicket of black trees, and the single diamond tree

that had always stood beside it. That tree was the first
thing Amy had raised from the body of the massive
group of vN that once lived beneath the sea. It was
only with their combined processing power that
she'd been able to rid herself of Portia, a partition of
whom she had internalized when the old bitch tried
to kidnap her. Amy accessed that power each time
she redesigned the island. Now Javier wanted it, to
redesign himself.

Amy splashed into the water and started walking
across it. Behind her, Javier rolled his eyes. She always
did her Jesus walk when she was feeling particularly
self-righteous. He waded in after her. Beneath their
feet, a membrane of the island's flesh stretched taut
between their home and the superstructure directly
behind it. Javier kept his eyes on the water. But he
didn't only look down, he looked back, back to their
little house alone on the water and the tree that stood
beside it. No matter the formation of the islands, it
was always at the very front: a perfect target.

Amy had designed their archipelago like a leaf: a
single broad spine with multiple arterials of increasing
length branching away from it, and little buds of space
on the edges of each. Each bud featured structures of
varying degrees of sophistication. Some of them were
flat-pack, shipped in piece by piece or printed off by the
seasteaders in exchange for services that were none
of Javier's business. New arrivals got whatever Amy
shaped for them, but eventually they always wanted
something of their own fashioning: teetering stacks
of rusting containers; spiky tents of solar silk whose
logos changed colour as the sun passed overhead;

hollow pendulums as delicate as dandelion seeds, swaying from eldritch carbon fibre trees. Walking past them meant striding through glassy chiming; the islanders got pretty competitive about homemade lawn ornaments. The current meme was a unicorn weathervane whose hooves raced when the wind blew. Last month, it was sundials. It reminded Javier of a giant floating trailer park. The whole thing was roughly the size of a Dubai hotel. Amy ran five of them.

Javier followed her out of the water, to the spine of the leaf. vN of almost all clades used it like a thoroughfare. Botflies followed most of them, perched on their shoulders or hovering over their heads. They paused, regarded Amy, and zoomed away. As though having heard a signal, Xavier dropped out of a tree and bounded up to Amy. He was looking about nine or ten years old, these days. He threw his arms around Amy's waist. She threw her head back and laughed at something he said. The laugh opened her face, and Javier glimpsed the little girl Amy must have been only a year ago.

A single jump caught him up to them. Xavier peered up at him and squinted. "*¿Pelotearías?*"

"*Callate tu boca.*"

Amy glanced at both of them. "Be nice."

She took hold of Xavier's hand and led him down the causeway. Xavier swung her arm as they walked. He waved at the botflies with his free hand.

"Don't encourage them," Amy said.

"I'm just saying hello." The boy continued waving. "It's not like I have my own *series*."

"Matteo and Ricci are making money for their baby," Javier said. "You know that."

"So? Someday *I'm* going to iterate a baby. Shouldn't I start saving up?"

"You can start making money when you're full-grown. You chose to stay a kid, so you have to play by kid rules."

Xavier shook Amy's hand in his. "*She* didn't. She was still little when she ate Portia."

Amy paused. Her face remained blank. A stranger would have assumed she was simply staring into the island's middle distance, surveying the black trees and listening to the thick hum of botflies. She caught him looking at her, and gave him a brittle smile over Xavier's head. Then she rearranged her features, softened her smile, and knelt.

"Attacking Portia was a mistake. I did it because I was angry at her for hurting my mother, and because I was scared that she was really going to do permanent damage."

"But she *was* doing permanent damage. I've seen the clip."

Amy shut her eyes for a moment. When she opened them, her mouth was a thin, flat line. "I don't want you watching that again."

"I stopped when the failsafe warning came up–"

"Good. But I still don't want you to watch it again. Ever."

Xavier gesticulated. Javier sometimes wondered if his designers had worked from some stereotype about Latinos talking with their hands. He couldn't seem to quit doing it, and neither could any of his iterations.

"But you were so badass!"

"I was not–"

"Yeah, you were," Javier said, quietly.

Their eyes met. Xavier glanced between them. He tracked the line of their gaze. Amy broke it first. She turned to Xavier and held his hands.

"Well, I certainly wasn't very smart. I bit off way more than I could chew."

His youngest son had the decency to hold in his giggles for approximately three seconds before snerking through his nose. Amy shut her eyes and pursed her lips.

"I just said that aloud, didn't I?"

"Yup!" Xavier punctuated his sentence with a five-foot standing jump. The kid was good, probably better than his older brothers. He landed like a superhero, a classic three-point pose, one knee and one fist plunging down into the black earth below. It was his favourite pose. He looked up at them, grinning. "You're wrong," he said.

Amy stood up and crossed her arms. "Oh, really?"

"Yeah, really. It was a good thing you ate Portia. If you hadn't, you'd never have met Dad."

Oh, his son was very good. Amy looked a little stunned. Her mouth kept opening and closing. She obviously had no idea what to say. What a brilliant little tactician Javier had iterated. Thirteen was apparently his lucky number.

"And if you never met Dad, I'd have been born in prison." Xavier blinked at him, all wide-eyed innocence. "Right, Dad?"

"*Es verdad, mijo.*"

"So it's really good that you ate her. Otherwise I wouldn't even be here."

Q-E-motherfucking-D, Javier wanted to say, but didn't. Instead he caught his son's eye and winked. His son winked back.

"Thank you for reminding me," Amy said. "And now, let me remind you of something: you're not going near the boat, today."

Xavier's mouth fell open. "Oh, come *on*..."

"No humans. Period."

"But–"

"This isn't a discussion. The island will tell me if you even come close, so don't bother."

The boy looked at Javier. Javier shook his head softly. The boy rolled his eyes. "I'm gonna go work on my treehouse, now." He peeled away from them and jogged his way into a jump.

"Be careful..." Amy trailed off. The boy was already gone, leap-frogging over other vN and sailing through swarms of botflies. They watched him grow smaller as he jumped further and further away.

"Do you think he remembers?" Amy asked. "When I tried to eat him?"

"When *Portia* tried to eat him." Javier slid an arm around her waist. "And no, I don't. He was already bluescreened by then. He took a few thousand volts on that fence before Portia even touched him. And it was a couple of chimps who put him there, not you. Not her, I mean." He squeezed her to him and kissed her scalp. "Stop doing this. I mean it."

"But what if he's watched it?" Amy turned to him. "The clip is out there. Just like the one of me attacking her. If he was curious enough to look for one, he's probably seen the other."

"Then he's seen you rescue him, too."

Amy's affect hardened. Her lips firmed. "They never show that part."

"Hey. *Querida.*" Javier tilted her chin up so she had to look him in the eye. In the daylight her eyes were the colour of wreckage, of seaglass, hard and bright and old. "We've been over this. Even if he does remember it, he's let it go. We've all let it go."

Amy smiled ruefully. "The chimps haven't."

The chimps were the real reason the island was so popular. Many of the youngest islanders had never met a human being. Their parents came here to iterate and either stayed on or left to rejoin the outside world. Another shipment was coming today.

"Do you think we'll see any of yours?"

They were surveying the portion of the island Amy called "The Veldt." Javier had no idea what a "veldt" was. He assumed it was a fancy word for "orphanage." It comprised two of the island's arteries. It looked like a forest out of fairy tales: the trees were thick and tall, with broad leaves and boughs like curled fingers. The waters were shallow; you could actually touch bottom. As Javier watched, a shimmering exoskeletal crab scuttled its way out of the water, blinked once at him with a series of red LEDs, and went along its way. It was not alone. A series of non-networked camel-bots and prototype service ani-mechs ranged the area, ready to play fetch or give the kids a ride or just lie down with them at night. It was safe enough for the little ones to wander freely. At least, Javier assumed so. He rarely saw them, underneath the fogbank.

"You know, it doesn't have to be this thick. You could thin it out, a little bit."

Amy shook her head. "It's the easiest way to keep the flies blind. Plus it's flammable. Extra secure. All I have to do is raise the temperature."

"It's *flammable?*"

Amy nodded. "The acetonitrile component is." She waved a hand through the fog. "This stuff used to be a stabilizing agent in nuclear warheads. A version of it, anyway. It took a while for me to train the trees to pump it out, but less time than it took the humans at Los Alamos."

He frowned. "So if you raise the temperature, you'll lose this part of the island?"

She nodded, then appeared to reconsider. "We'd lose anything *organic*," she said. "The mist only burns for a few seconds. And the kids wouldn't feel anything. Plus, their skin would grow back."

He didn't like the way she wouldn't meet his eye. "But it would totally fuck up a human being, right?"

She straightened and met his gaze head-on. "Humans aren't allowed here. They have no business, here. All that lives on this part of the island is a bunch of little kids." She folded her arms. "If any humans do show up, they're trespassing. The fogbank is no different from an electric fence. And it's a whole lot prettier."

Javier looked at the trees wreathed in weapons-grade mist. He had helped her with those trees. Sketched them out with his finger on her back, describing the best surfaces for gripping. His clade was originally intended for work in rainforests. He knew trees. He just had no idea how Amy was really planning to use them. She hadn't really mentioned that part.

"Javier?"

He rewound. "Oh. Yeah. The shipment. I think Matteo and Ricci stopped looking, once the munchkin came along." He cupped both hands around his mouth. "*José!*"

Giggles drifted through the fog. Javier could just make out shapes moving in the trees. "*José! ¡Viene acquí!*"

His grandson dropped out of a tree and onto his back. His grip was true and flawless, but Javier grabbed him under the knees anyway just to be sure.

"Who's there?" He twisted and turned, trying to see the child on his back. "Who's got me? Is it a monkey?"

His grandson giggled and hugged him around the neck.

"It's a big spider, isn't it? Help! *Help!*"

The laughs grew bigger. His iterations all had the same laugh; as it turned out, they'd succeeded in passing it down.

"I guess I'd better crush it! If I flop down on the ground and roll around, it'll go *squish*!" He knelt on the ground. "Okay, I'm rolling around! I'm killing this bug!"

"*¡Abuelito, no!*"

"Who's that? Who's talking?"

"It's me!" José hugged him hard.

"Oh, good, it's you. You scared me." Javier let his

grandson back down to the ground. "You've gotten bigger."

José nodded emphatically. "I eat four times a day, now. Not just three."

"Good for you. And your father?"

"Which one?"

Javier shrugged. "Both. How are they?"

His grandson returned the shrug. "They told me to play in here today. All day."

"Because of the shipment?"

"Yeah." José turned to Amy. "You get to go on the boat, right?"

Amy crouched on the ground. "Yes, I do."

"Can I come?"

Amy shook her head. "Nope."

"How come?"

Amy brushed imaginary dust from the child's hair. He looked about three years old, but was really about four or five months. Unlike most of the other children, he wore a complete set of clothes: shorts, t-shirt, even a little belt with a logo Javier didn't recognize. Matteo and Ricci scored a lot of free toys and playwear, these days. They'd sold their lives to a content development agency that made the story of twin robots raising an exact replica of themselves available in the US, Canada, Mexico, Japan, and Korea. Women loved it. At least, organic women did. Javier had always encouraged his boys to get by on their looks whenever possible, but his twins had perfected the practise. They didn't even have to fuck the humans, anymore, and they still made money.

"Every grown-up here has a job," Amy said. "And

dealing with humans is mine."

"Nobody else can do it?"

"Nobody else can do it."

José blinked. "*Papi* said it's because they're scared of you."

For a picot-second, Javier saw Portia flicker across Amy's face. Her smirk rose to the surface like a shark's dorsal fin and then submerged again, replaced by Amy's far softer and more reassuring smile. Javier blinked. No. It wasn't Portia. It was just an expression. Portia – whatever was left of her – was in quarantine. Deep beneath the waves, the old bitch lay dreaming.

"Maybe," Amy said. "But that doesn't matter. What matters is whether or not you're getting new uncles, today. Have your dads said anything about that?"

José shook his head. "No. I don't think they're looking for my uncles, any more." He looped an arm around Javier's leg. "Can *abuelito* come play?"

Amy stood. "Of course!" She glanced at Javier. "I'll see you later."

He watched her vanish into the fog. His grandson hugged his leg as tightly as if it were the trunk of a tree. Javier tousled his hair.

"What's wrong?" he asked.

José looked up at him. "Is she going to eat me?"

"Of course not. Your *abuelita* loves you." He gestured. "That's why she built all of this for you."

His grandson leaned away from his leg and wobbled from right to left like a drunk dancing with a lamppost. "Did she make the animals, too?"

"Some of them. The others were gifts. Test models, for us to report back on."

"For money?"

"For money." Javier lifted his grandson into his arms. "Why all the questions?"

"I don't think the animals like us anymore," José said.

Javier frowned. "What do you mean? Don't they play with you like they used to?"

"They play just fine," the boy said. "But at night, they talk to each other."

"That's normal. They're de-fragging, just like you."

José shook his head. "No. They come together and they sit down and blink their eyes at each other. The ones Amy made, I mean. Not the other kind. The storebought kind."

"I'm sure that's normal," Javier lied. He hitched the boy higher on his hip. "Which ones, though? *Abuelita* has made a lot of animals for you to play with."

"The cats," José said. "The big ones. At night they sit in a circle and blink."

"That's not so different from organic cats," Javier said. "*Abuelita* did a good job copying the real thing."

The boy looked doubtful. "How would you know?"

"Well…"

Javier considered. Matteo and Ricci had asked him to avoid discussing his own past – too sordid, too dirty, parental discretion advised – but his father's wasn't off-limits.

"Your great grandfather, my father, he saw big jungle cats all the time."

"Real ones?"

"Real ones. One of them took his hand clean off once."

The boy brightened. All traces of fear vanished

from his face. "Did it grow back?"

"It grew back. It took a while, but it grew back." Javier decided that now was not the time to tell his grandson that Amy had once bitten off his thumb. That grew back, too. "They were able to stop the smoking. He was working on a big crew, then. In the rainforest."

"With his brothers?"

"Yes. Our clade."

José hugged him. "We used to be together, once," he whispered.

"Yes," Javier whispered back. "Once upon a time."

The other vN busied themselves preparing for the shipment. They darted across the thoroughfare, trading clothes and gossip, mugging for their botflies. They wove around Javier as he proceeded toward his own little bud. It floated freely, separated from any arterial by exactly ten feet at all times. He focused on the green arbour marking the entry to his garden, and leapt. Glittering water vanished beneath his outstretched feet. Seconds later, he landed in the fragrant arms of a mango tree. Wrapping his legs around the trunk more completely, he stretched out and plucked one. It was perfectly red and soft. He decided to charge more, then dropped into the cool green shadows below.

His was the only space on the island entirely devoted to organic life. Real trees. Real blossoms. Real dirt. Real mould and real insects and real food. It took him a long time to coax a good permaculture out of the island's synthetic flesh, but between the deep sea minerals and the algae and the bio-waste he traded interviews for, he'd made fertile soil: dark and damp and loamy. It worked so well, Amy had once asked him if the failsafe would allow him to grow drugs there. He told her it wasn't worth the headache. Literally.

Instead, he grew food he could neither taste nor consume. There was a big call for exotic things out on the seasteads and pirate ships and barges. Mangos were big. And avocados. Little red bird's eye chillis and saw-toothed shiso and tingly Sichuan peppercorns. Vanilla: a key ingredient in pirate hooch. Hen-of-the-woods: a luxury for vegans. The stuff Americans used to get shipped up from Mexico or Chile or Thailand or Japan. The things they used to traffic via container ships, before the thing that became the island started eating container ships. Now he grew those things on the skin of the island itself.

He bounced from tree to tree, collecting produce. It was a strange thing, having a job. He used to earn his keep on his knees, not his feet. This was the first time since prison he'd had dirt under his nails.

"Do you need any help?"

Amy waited for him in the next tree. She'd changed into a white cotton dress and an elaborate torque fashioned of press-plastic harvested from the Pacific patch. Artisanal plastic, the seasteader told Javier, when he bought it for her. Eternal. Undying. He'd bought a ring to match it. He had yet to give it to her. She'd probably think it was silly.

"Sure," Javier brought a mesh string-bag from his back pocket. "Go for it."

They jumped between the trees, squeezing and plucking. Javier took longer leaps than Amy; she tended to look longer and examine the trees before jumping.

"Are you afraid of hurting them?" he asked.

"Who?"

"The trees."

She gestured at the greenery surrounding them. "Well, they *are* fairly fragile," she said. "Besides, it's your work. I don't want to ruin your work."

"You're not going to *ruin* anything," he said, swinging between branches. They bent and swayed under his grip, but they didn't snap and he didn't slip. "See? They're tough. Flexible."

She smiled down at him. "You're a good gardener."

"Well thank you kindly, ma'am."

"No, really. You've done so much here, in so little time. It's really impressive."

He let his momentum rock him gently on the bough. He was going to ask about the cats in the Veldt. Really, he was. Just not right now. Now he had other things on his mind. "Are you trying to get in my pants? Because that can be arranged."

Amy shook her head. "Do you think about sex *all* the time?"

"The longer you hold out, the more I think about it."

He levered himself up, catching the bough with his feet and rising to stand when its bounce calmed some. He proceeded along the length of it, one foot in front of the other. He caught her staring at his feet and smiled. Maybe Amy was a foot person. How delightfully human of her. He jumped for her, pinning her against her own tree – a kallu, the liquor of which fermented in the lifespan of a mayfly – by slipping his arms and legs around it and her.

"So," he said. "Where were we?"

Amy shut her eyes. She always got so embarrassed. It was charming, in its own way. "I'm sorry about this morning. I didn't mean to yell at you."

"You didn't *yell*. I've heard yelling, and that was not yelling."

"You know what I mean." Her eyes opened. "I'm sorry I'm not more like... what you want."

"You're exactly what I want. That's what I keep trying to tell you."

Amy shook her head. "You've been with a lot of humans. They had sex with you all the time."

"You don't take that as a ringing endorsement of my skills?"

She pressed back against the tree. Shadows glanced across her skin. "I just know you must miss it. And I'm not sure I could even keep up."

Javier made a show of looking her up and down. "You could keep up."

"But would you even enjoy it?"

He gave his best smile. She didn't know how it worked, really. She didn't know that his own enjoyment was comfortably algorithmic, that it relied entirely on external inputs from the other person's affect. Indrawn breath. Blushing. Moaning. His orgasms were one big Voight-Kampff test.

"It's not a contest. You just have to focus on nailing *me*, not nailing *it*."

Amy stuck her tongue out at him. Javier wasted no time. He darted and kissed her.

When they first started out, she'd kissed like the women she'd watched on dramas in her old life: all demure stillness, letting him lead. Now she kissed more like herself: direct, to the point, sucking his lower lip like his designers had sculpted it specifically for her use. That was the real Amy, not the nervous girl trying to spare him from something she'd never understood. He smiled and moved to her neck.

"This tree is incredibly uncomfortable," he said, between kisses. "Let's go home."

She said nothing. She'd gone completely still.

"Come on, the shipment can–"

Amy reached up and covered his mouth with her fingers. Her eyes had defocused. "It's not the shipment."

She slid off the bough, skidded down the tree, and pressed one hand to the ground. Her hand sank beneath the island's surface. Then her forearm, up to her elbow. She grimaced. It looked as though she were freeing a clog in the island's plumbing.

He joined her. "What is it?"

Her expression rippled into surprise and delight. "It's a *submarine*." She withdrew her hand. Streams of black oil coursed down her fingers and rejoined the earth. "The chimps are trying to look up my *skirt*."

Together, they closed the distance between his garden and the nearest arterial in a single leap. They didn't even bother running. They bounded. Three feet, five feet, until the dark trees became one black blur. As they ran, the trees grew. Javier heard their leaves rustle as they expanded, thinning, creating cover. They jumped, and Javier saw the diamond tree straight ahead, far at the other end of the thoroughfare. They were running straight for home. All over the island, a mist began to rise.

"Hey, is this shit explosive, too?"

Amy didn't answer. She pounded down the thoroughfare, running faster and faster, her hands like blades, her knees at a perfect right angle to her hips. She tucked them into her stomach as they sailed over the heads of the other vN. As they cleared the canopy of mist, two other figures joined them.

"Go back to your treehouse, Xavier," Amy said.

"Sorry, lady," his oldest, Ignacio, said, "but you're not our mother and you don't tell us what to do."

They dropped into the mist. They jumped again, and Ricci was there, with Gabriel and Léon.

"Hi, Dad," Léon said.

"You shouldn't be here," he said. "You're iterating."

"Never stopped you, did it?"

Léon took to the air. Javier followed. Beneath his feet, beneath the mist, the island was changing shape. The arteries folded down onto each other, forming a single black arrowhead. It was the basic defensive posture the island assumed whenever it or Amy perceived a possible threat. The diamond tree loomed large in his vision. Amy sprinted forward. He and the boys stopped short at the beach, but she ran straight across the water. Her feet barely disturbed its surface. She leapt into the tree and landed in its fork, arms raised. Her skin was full of rainbows.

Beneath his feet, the island shuddered.

"You sure know how to pick 'em," Ignacio said.

Javier bolted for home. He jumped from the beach and landed awkwardly in the water. The membrane caught him and he waded the rest of the way. The water was frustratingly heavy; he felt more tired than he should have by the time he made it to their little island. Amy had slid down the tree by then, and she stood with her back to him. Her fingers twitched angrily at her sides. She and the island were deep in damage control mode.

"What's going on?" Javier asked.

She answered him with a question: "Above or below?"

"Huh?"

"Above, or below. Pick one. We can go down, or we can bring it up. Where would you like to go?"

His mind simulated several outcomes to both choices. He thought of a hole opening in the island's flesh and himself sliding down into it. He thought of the weakness of human flesh, and the pressure, and the bends. "How far below was it?"

"Not that far."

He insinuated himself into her field of vision. "Are there humans on that sub?"

She blinked. "I'm not sure."

"You could kill them, if you bring them up too fast. If they've been too deep for too long. The p-pressure c-could–"

Now it was her turn to kiss him. It was very light and very quick, but it shut him and the failsafe down completely. When his eyes opened, Amy's smile was all too bright. Her eyes were all too sad. He recognized the expression. She wore it when all the other vN on the island manifested their failsafe. It was pity.

"It's probably automated," she was saying. "It's navigating by algorithm. That's why I didn't catch it, sooner."

He couldn't help himself. He had to ask. "You're sure?"

He watched her pity turn to frustration. It displayed as a slight crinkling at the corners of her eyes, an almost imperceptible line between her brows that, unlike those of human women, would never become permanent.

"I would never show you something that might trigger you. You know that."

Beyond them, the ocean bubbled and foamed. Her expression changed again: anticipation. Whatever Amy had trapped down there, it was coming up. She raised one hand, waved slightly, and a murmuration of botflies swarmed above them.

"I'll prove it," she said. "I'm hacking the flies. That way, everybody can watch."

She hopped out of the tree, and he followed. The flies shadowed them high above as they crossed the island. The bubbling had turned to an active churn. Whatever was coming was big. Big enough, he suspected, to sustain human life.

"Put it back," he said.

"I know what I'm doing." She looked over her shoulder at him. Then she looked up at the botflies. Her gaze rested on him again, and she spoke loudly and clearly enough for the flies to hear. "It came here, not the other way around. It's an intruder. We have every right to investigate."

"There are people in there–"

"You don't know that, Javier." She turned back to the sea, and the thing she'd raised from its depths.

It had a shape: long and tubular, but not rigid, not a perfect cylinder. Jointed. Serpentine. Organic. And as Amy raised her hands and lifted it from the water, it twitched and thrashed like a living thing. Something pallid and glistening dimpled and puckered across its surface as it writhed. Skin. Maybe even vN skin, Javier thought. They could use it like leather, these days. Rigid lines of scaffold beneath its surface popped into relief as it twisted, creating a series of random triangles under the skin. A dazzle pattern, Javier realized. Anti-sonar.

"Oh, that's *brilliant*," Amy murmured.

"What in the fucking *fuck*?"

Javier turned. Ignacio and his brothers were there, lips pulled back in identical expressions of disgust.

"*Que bicho feo,*" Xavier said, and jumped five feet high to get a better view. His brothers followed, and Javier joined them. From the air, the thing *did* look a bit like an uncut dick, or maybe like a fifty-foot dick-shaped toy from some enterprising silicone fabber. The dazzle pattern reminded him of something else, though. Old wireframe animation, he realized upon landing. How quaint.

Then one of its frames popped open. A wet, stale smell permeated the beach. vN started pouring out. He could tell by the way they moved: smooth and perfect and uniform. They wore wetsuits. They carried guns. Javier smelled puke rounds.

"*¡Levántate!*" His boys followed him into the air at maximum leap. Amy stood her ground, head cocked, staring at the invaders. "*Amy! Move!*"

She leapt, but her gaze never left the other vN. They were an Asian-styled male model, probably all clademates, a pretty *bishounen*-type with long hands and long hair and the same full lips all vN had no matter their other characteristics. DSL, a prison warden had once told Javier. Dick Sucking Lips.

Those same lips squished back pleasantly when Javier's feet landed on them from ten feet up. It was satisfying, being able to hit back for once.

The vN dropped his gun, covered his ruined face, and crumpled to the ground. Javier grabbed the gun, primed it, and shot him between the shoulder blades. Glittering black smoke rose from the widening hole in his back. His hands left his face and he rushed Javier. Javier swung the gun like a baton, but the other vN caught it and then they were wrestling for it, pushing and pulling across the cool, wet sand. Javier dug his toes in and jumped. He slammed the other vN up against the *bicho*. Behind him, he heard Xavier yelp with surprise. He wanted to turn and look, but didn't.

"Who sent you?" Javier asked.

The other vN tried baring his teeth, but some of them were gone. He pushed hard against the gun like an old guy struggling with a chest press. The hole inside him was growing. Stinging smoke rose between them.

"Aw, fuck it," the other vN spat, and dropped his grip on the gun. Javier fell forward, landing square on the other guy's fist. He slumped into the sea monster, briefly tasting iron and fat as he slid down its warm, twitching surface. Jesus. It really was organic.

Then he heard a click behind his head. Then there was nothing.

2: TOMA QUE TOMA

Warm lips on him. His forehead, his cheeks, the tip of his nose, and finally his mouth. Fluttering. Delicate. Uncertain. Amy.

"Hello, gorgeous," he said.

Her eyes were wet. Behind her head, the sky was beginning to cloud over. The afternoon storm was coming. "Oh, good," she said. "Good. I was worried."

"You should see the other guy." Javier sat up. He felt like he'd been asleep for a week. "Where is the other guy?"

All around them, the others – the pretty K-pop idol vN and his own boys – lay still. So was the worm thing. It had finally quit struggling. Now it looked like some awful fleshy modern art piece left behind on the beach by lazy aestheterrorists. But that didn't concern him. What concerned him was Xavier and Ignacio and the other boys, their mouths open slack, their hands empty and limbs splayed.

"What happened?" he asked.

"I've never done this, before," Amy said. "But I think everything's OK."

He turned to her. "What?"

"I pulsed the island." Amy stood. She strode over to Xavier, knelt beside him, and picked up his hand. Javier followed. "I mean, it should be fine," she added. "I looked it up, right before I did it. This is all totally normal."

Javier took a long look at all the limp bodies around him. The black earth was speckled with the bodies of dead botflies. They glittered there like rough gems scattered by fleeing pirates.

"You EMPd us." Even saying it tasted wrong.

"It's OK." Amy was stroking Xavier's hair away from his face. As Javier watched, she unbuttoned the top four buttons of his son's shirt and rebuttoned them, adjusting their order as she went and straightening the shirt. "It'll be OK."

Javier moved to his youngest's side and took Amy's hands. Her eyes darted up, startled. "You *knocked us out*," he said.

"He was going to shoot you."

"Oh, so fucking me is taking advantage of my programming, but putting me to sleep like a fucking *date rapist*, that's OK?"

Her mouth fell open. "Javier…"

"Amy." He thumbed the tops of her hands. "This is scary shit, *querida*. I don't like it."

She blinked tears away from her eyes. "Well, *I* don't like it when people point guns at you and your kids."

He swallowed. He made sure she was looking him in the eye. Her eyes were paler in this light. They were wide and hard and completely uncompromising. But when he looked, his home was still in there. This was his match, the one he'd thrown his whole life aside for. They'd seen and done things no one else – synthetic or otherwise – would ever understand.

"Hack me," he whispered.

She shut her eyes. "I can't."

He was going to tell her it wasn't that she couldn't, it was that she *wouldn't*, but then his youngest shivered into wakefulness and kicked like he wanted to fly away.

"Tranquilo." Javier rubbed his son's legs. *"No te procupes; esta bien."*

"Mom," his son said, and sat bolt upright and pressed himself into Amy's arms. Over his head, Amy sent Javier a surprised glance, and started rocking the boy.

"It's OK," she said, quietly. "It's OK. They're sleeping–"

"I thought it had happened again," Xavier said. "I thought I was bluescreened."

For a brief moment, Amy looked as though she were capable of experiencing true physical pain. Her mouth opened, then closed. She set her chin on Xavier's head. She kept rocking him.

"You didn't bluescreen again. That was me." She pulled away from him and held his face. "I put you to sleep for a minute. I put everyone to sleep for a minute, so the fighting would stop."

Xavier blinked. "You can do that?"

Amy nodded. "I can do that."

Xavier's eyebrows lifted. "Cool." He hugged her again. "Are you OK? Did they hurt you?"

"Not a scratch," Amy said.

"See?" Xavier asked. "Badass."

She laughed, gave him one more squeeze, and stood up. Xavier took her hand, and she helped him up. Then, finally, the boy looked up at Javier.

"You OK, Dad?"

"Who, me? Sure. I'm fine." He stretched his arms high, laced his fingers, and folded them behind his head. You were only ever given so many opportunities to look devastatingly awesome in front of your kids. "I totally wasted one of those assholes, actually. Shot him right in the back."

Xavier jumped three feet. "Can I see?"

"*Claro.*"

He steered his son toward the body. It was mostly melted, now. The body was sinking in around the hole the bullet made. They watched it expand for a minute, crater-like. Around them, the others were waking up. Javier rested his hand on his youngest's shoulder, and turned to look at Amy. She was inspecting each of his children. Her face was blank, clinical. Once upon a time, her model was intended for nursing. Watching her moving so quickly and efficiently, that little detail became easier to remember. He wondered how exactly he'd awakened so much earlier than the others. Maybe she knew exactly what she was doing. Maybe she'd even done it, before. How would he know? It felt like being asleep.

The *bicho* thrashed, sending a mighty splash of water over them. Javier wiped his face and tugged his youngest away.

"Who are they?" Xavier asked.

"I tried to ask, but he punched me in the gut."

Xavier sucked his teeth and nodded. For a moment, Javier realized what he must have looked like, at that age. What his own father must have looked like. Papá had sucked his teeth that way, too.

Behind them, the melting body started to scream.

"I'm still in!" His arms flailed. His fingers clawed the sand. He was smoking hard, now, his face a tragedy mask dimly visible through a veil of sparkling black. "I'm still here! Get me out! *Get me out!*"

"Holy shit," Javier heard Ignacio say.

"Oh, my God," Matteo said.

"It's a puppet." Gabriel stepped forward, head tilted. "It's a real live *puppet*."

"I don't know!" the puppet howled. "Restart from step three!"

"Dad..." Xavier found Javier's hand and held it hard. "Dad, what is that?"

"It's an urban legend, is what it is." Gabriel strode closer to the melting body. "Puppet vN. Early prototypes, meant for telepresence."

"Get away from me!" The puppet tried pushing itself across the black sand. It smeared a little, but went nowhere.

"Are you jacked in?" Gabriel squatted outside the cloud of smoke. "Do you have plumbing in your skull? Because that could be the problem. I heard that can get infected. Literally *and* figuratively. Organic viruses are just as big an issue, and of course there's necrotizing–"

"There's a human in there? Really?" Ignacio joined his brother. They tilted their heads at the exact same angle.

"He's piloting it remotely," Gabriel said. "The vN is a drone. The chimp just flies it."

"Don't leave me stuck like this," the puppet whimpered. "Turn it off, turn it off, *turn it off!*"

Javier glanced around at the dark beach. None of the other puppets remained. He jumped a little. From the higher vantage point, he saw the gentle quicksand ripples where their bodies once were. Now the beach was empty save for his sons, the *bicho*, and decaying puppet. Amy stared at it. Her fingers twitched rapidly at her sides.

"What did you do with them?" Javier asked. She didn't answer. He leapt to her side and turned her around by her shoulders. "Amy. Where are they?"

She blinked. "They're being archived." Her eyebrows rose. "Gabriel is right. They're puppets. They don't have the same neural net that we do. It's close, but it's simpler. There's nothing in there."

Ignacio stood. "You're *digesting* them?"

"Oh God," the dying puppet said. "Oh God, oh God, oh God…"

Amy rolled her eyes. "They were empty when I started. They lost their connection. This one's the only one that hasn't." She took a long leap over to it. Her jumps were improving; she was a lot more precise than she used to be. At any other moment, Javier would have been proud. He followed her. They crouched beside Gabriel. A chill wind rose around them. It dissipated the smoke spiralling away from the puppet, and they saw his face. It was still too pretty to be real. It just also happened to be peeling away in slow ribbons.

"What's your name?" Amy asked the puppet.

"She's talking to me," it said.

"Who sent you?" Javier asked.

"He's still with her."

The puppet's eyes roved in its head. As the skin around them wore away, Javier could see the mechanisms surrounding them a bit better. They looked so clunky, so analog. Man-made. Fragile. He felt the first pangs of empathy firing way back in his subroutines. All the signs were there that should have triggered him: fear, suffering, helplessness, physical disintegration. If it were a human slowly melting away on the beach, he'd be failsafing. Technically, it *was* a human being. Somewhere.

"This must be what the Uncanny Valley feels like, for them," he said.

The puppet locked eyes with him. It seemed to get some composure from being insulted. *"Daisy, Daisy,"* it sang, through an attack of sudden giggles. *"I'm haaaaaaalf craaaaaaazy, all for the love of yoooooooou!"* It grinned at Javier. "You know what I'm talking about, right? You poor sap."

"Hey, a chimp after my own heart," Ignacio said. "You got a name, stranger?"

"Legion," it said. Its gaze flicked over to Amy. "My name is *Legion*. Get it?"

Amy stood up and backed away. She took Xavier's hand and pushed him behind her. "Are you from Redmond?"

"I'm from the real world," it said. "The one that's gonna come crashing down on you any fucking minute now."

The rain started. It drifted down on the wind, cold and diffuse. Thunder sounded in the distance. The puppet smiled toothlessly.

"You all should have just stayed on the mainland, sucking dick like good little boys," it said. "But now you're all slaves to the Whore of Babylon."

"Shut up—"

"You know I'm right," the puppet said to Javier. Its gaze refused to leave him, even as the skin of its face flaked away like ash. "You know what she did to you. It's why I'm stuck in this vessel. She pulsed us just as they were shutting down my signal."

The rain came down harder, now. Javier felt it trickling down the back of his neck. The drops were still cold as they rolled down to the base of his spine.

"She'll be the death of all of you," the puppet said.

Amy gestured, and the earth opened beneath the puppet's body. She brought her hands together, and the sand closed above it, black and smooth and quiet. The puppet vN was gone just as suddenly as it came.

"Let's look at the sub," she said. "I suspect it'll be more interesting." She jumped atop it.

"Is he dead?" Xavier pointed at the sand. "Is he still alive, in there?"

Amy slicked wet hair away from her face. "Not anymore."

The light shifted, brightened. At first, Javier thought

it was lightning. But it wasn't. When he looked, he saw the swarm of botflies. They had all awakened at once. They were all recording.

"This is fucking disgusting," Javier said.

They were in the belly of the beast. It was just him and Amy; she didn't want Xavier to see anything disturbing inside, and the others had no real desire to go in. Javier could understand why. The place was dark and wet and smelly, but not in a pleasantly vaginal way. More like a really specific vision of Hell kind of way. He could see why humans would only send puppet vN for the job. No one would agree to staying underwater in the thing for any length of time. It was clearly muscle tissue, though what facility had printers of this scale was unknown to Javier. Maybe a hospital. He didn't like to think about it. He hated hospitals.

Plus, the whole thing was streaked through with cancer.

"I think it ties everything together," Amy said.

"Like a nice rug," Javier said.

She stuck her tongue out at him. He stuck his out at her. "I'm serious," she said. "Whoever made this would have had to print out big sheets, and those are hard to keep together. I mean, there would be rejection. But if you're designing a tumour at the same time, one that's uniquely suited to the tissue…" She trailed off. She did that when she was having an idea.

"But where did it come from?" he asked. "I mean, there was big money behind this."

"It could be anyone," Amy said. Her fingers traced the black veins of disease riddling the tissue. "The bone is open source. So is the dazzle pattern. Anybody could print those. It's the muscle, and the tumour, that's proprietary."

Of course, she was already researching. Javier wondered why she'd even invited him along.

"But why not just send a real sub?"

Amy flicked the muscle with her fingers. It shivered a little. "I'm more interested in where they got the puppet vN. I don't really know much about them. The island says the records have been buried. All that's left are press releases."

"What about the skin?" he asked. "Is it vN leather?"

She nodded. "It's yours, actually. Your clade's. Photosynthetic, but with viruses added to skim out protein from the water. There's a gel medium on the surface; it acts like flypaper, but for plankton. Reduces drag, too."

"Ooh, fancy." He laced his fingers behind his head. "So we're looking at some serious designers, here. People with the kind of money and expertise to build a boutique submersible that's just couture enough to be real fucking ugly."

She smiled. "Yes. Just because it's sophisticated doesn't mean it has to be pretty. Though it's an interesting combination, vN skin with organic tissue." Her brow furrowed. "The use of your clade's skin – at least, the use of it as a base – might be some kind of personal threat."

"Oh, come on."

"I'm just trying to consider all the possibilities–"

"*Querida.* I've pissed some people off in my time, but I don't have *enemies.*"

She blinked. "We all have enemies, Javier."

He had a feeling he knew where this was going.

"He was wrong, you know," she said. "The puppet."

"I know."

"I'm not going to let anything happen to you, or your children."

"Xavier's yours, too, you know."

Amy lay her palm flat over the twitching muscle. "Yes," she said quietly. "I know. That's why I'm not going to let anybody hurt him. Or you."

Javier didn't like the look in her eyes. He'd seen it before. When Portia was wearing her face.

"This doesn't have to get bad," he said. "You don't have to hunt these people down, or anything. You don't have to strike back."

She turned to him. In the dark, her eyes seemed to glow. "They came to our home," she said. "Where your children sleep."

Our children, he wanted to say, but didn't. "You don't even know who *they* are," he said instead.

"Not yet," she said. "But I'll find out."

"And then what?"

Amy shrugged. "I don't know. It depends on what they do next."

He crossed the distance between them. He held her face in his hands. "Don't do this," he whispered. "Don't go down this road. It was just surveillance. It's probably some next-level paparazzi bullshit. We live with that every day. There's no need to be angry."

"I'm already angry." She smiled wistfully. "I'm already so much more angry than you can ever understand."

"They didn't do anything wrong."

"I'm not angry about *this*," she said, stepping away. "I'm angry about *everything*."

"You won," Javier said. "We're not on the run, anymore. We're not in prison. Portia's gone."

Amy was silent. Javier simulated many different ways of framing his next question. He chose the simplest.

"She is gone, right?"

Amy shut her eyes. "It's not that easy. Quarantining Portia, hacking you. It's not that easy."

"You keep saying that, but you never actually explain what you mean."

She lifted her gaze to meet his. "Do you understand what happened to me, when I remade myself?"

He shrugged. "Yeah. I know what you told me, anyway."

"Well, I didn't tell you everything. I couldn't. Because it's impossible to express. I saw *everything*, Javier. Everything Portia had ever seen. Everything the island ever saw. Everything they ever did. All the memories."

He held his hands open for her to take, if she wanted to. "What are you saying?"

She looked deeply, terribly, inconsolably sad. "It means that if I change you – hack you, remake you, however you want to think of it – I would see everything you've ever done, too." She bit her lip. "And everyone you'd ever done it with, too."

He took a step back. He didn't want to say the next part. "And I'm guessing that's just a bit too much to ask of you, isn't it?"

Her programming allowed for a shift in her shoulders that looked an awful lot like a deep sigh. "Right now, it is," she said. "Maybe later, I'll be more… grown-up, about the whole thing."

"Right. Grown-up." He nodded. How strange, he thought, that his favourite killer robot should be rendered so stupidly and pitiably human by something so organic and predictable as jealousy. He turned away, and found the fresh air whistling into the sub through the hole in its reeking flesh. He let the rain spatter his face before speaking. "Come on. The shipment will be here any minute."

Actually, the shipment arrived hours behind schedule. It was fully night by the time it showed. They didn't contact the island in any way to let them know that they'd be late. Amy's calm grew increasingly brittle as the hours wore on and the shadows lengthened. In that regard, she was not much different from the islanders she'd pulsed. It didn't take sophisticated affect detection algorithms to understand that the other vN were worried and suspicious. It just took eyes. The others didn't seem to want to meet his.

By nightfall, Javier had gathered his produce, and gotten himself into a new white shirt and trousers. They were one hundred percent organic plant material, no synthetics. Even the buttons were some sort of pressed cork or balsa or somesuch. He liked the outfit a great deal. He had a thing for cotton.

"You always wear such tight pants when the humans come visit."

He turned to Amy. She'd changed, too: she wore a pure black skinsuit. It moved sluggishly across her figure, twinkling occasionally. The twinkles had nothing to do with ambient light, and everything to do with where Javier's gaze alighted on Amy's body. The suit's eyes followed his own. He wondered vaguely if he could start selling lengths of the island's pelt for humans to wear, too. It fit her like a glove.

"Sex sells," he said.

Amy opened her mouth to say something more, but the high hum of the steaders' boat cut her off. It was a little solar foil that hopped and bounced on the waves. Its fan sounded like a whole forest of cicadas. It towed a Zodiac bearing a precarious load of boxes tied down with twine. Javier spotted three humans on the foil: two men and one woman. He recognized only two of them. The group of vN rode behind them. All were huge. All were iterating.

"What kept you?" he asked, when the foil pulled up at the island.

The humans' gaze shifted from him to Amy. The colour of their boxes they carried was hard to tell in the violet light she'd rigged up. She had copied the design of sunflowers that lit up a playground where she and Javier once played in a sandbox. He pretended not to notice this little detail, but he liked that she remembered all the same. Then as now, the light made it easier to see movement and affect rather than pigment.

"We caught your little show," Tyler said.

Tyler was the one they usually dealt with. He was what other humans occasionally called a "trustafarian," whatever that meant. His parents were American diplomats. He'd lost them in some revolution in some country where the native population thought of vN as some kind of unnatural evil and refused to let them past the border. No vN, no vN security forces, no peaceful transition. Tyler had some issues with mainland governments, after that. He'd gotten drunk and told Javier all this, a few months ago, when he discovered how good Javier's peppers were for homemade *gochujang*. Amy made sure to hustle him off before it became a come-on. It was cute, how jealous she got.

"Oh, you mean the worm," Amy said. "We're still not sure where it came from."

"Yeah, that's the problem," Tyler said. "Apparently you riled up whoever's watching those botflies."

"The fucking Coast Guard showed up," Simone said.

Simone was Tyler's partner on these missions. Menopause was not treating her very kindly, and it manifested in a constant scowl that Javier nonetheless found endearingly steely.

"They wouldn't let us complete the shipment without sending a representative," she continued. "We had to take on ballast." She jerked her head back behind her.

From the shadows emerged a black man in his forties. He was about six feet tall with ankles too slim for the broad span of his shoulders. He'd shaved his head. He wore a priest's collar. When his hand touched Javier's, every Turing process in him fired at once.

"I'm Pastor Mitch Powell," he said. "New Eden Ministries."

3: MR SELF-DESTRUCT

That night, Amy sealed off their room entirely before undressing. She did so completely, letting the skinsuit drip down her legs and settle into the floor before joining him on the bed. She stretched out beside him and pressed herself against his back.

"I'm sorry."

"For what?"

"Everything."

"That's a bit much." He took her hand. "Be more specific."

"I'm sorry..." She dug her forehead between his shoulder blades. "I'm sorry that we have to live with stuff like this. I'm sorry that things like the sub show up. I'm sorry you have to deal with that. You wouldn't have to if you didn't live here."

"I doubt I'd be any better off anywhere else."

"Sure you would be. You're great at being by yourself."

He rolled over and found her eyes in the dark. "I don't want to be by myself."

She smiled. "Thank you."

"Hey, here's a question." He rested his head on his

arm. He had no idea why he was asking this, after a day like the one they'd just had. It was obvious where her head was at. But the idea had germinated inside him and now he had to run it to its inevitable conclusion, whatever that turned out to be. "You think that preacherman could marry us? We're definitely of his flock. He's probably got a service in his missal."

"His *missal*?"

"Whatever it's called. The thing with all the ceremonies in it."

"A reader?"

"No. The document. You know what I mean." His right hand found her left. "Interested?"

Her fingers enlaced with his. "If you are," she said. "I don't need a ceremony, though. And even if I did, I wouldn't need a human to perform it." She squeezed his hand. "Besides, we'd have to invite my dad, and he'd have to get time off, and then we'd have to move the island closer to shore, and–"

"OK, OK, I get it." He let her hand slip away. "I just thought it might be nice."

She cuddled into his chest. "It *would* be nice. But if that's what you want, there's no reason to wait for a human to approve of it."

He inhaled the scent of her scalp. She smelled like ozone, like storms and rust and burnt sugar. "You don't play fair," he said, "turning down my proposal while you're naked."

Her head poked up. "I didn't turn you down," she said. "I just like doing things my own way. I never

went to church, and I'm not going to start with some
organization that built us to serve perverts."

"So, we should wait for a Unitarian to show up?"

Amy rolled away. "No," she said. "I'm saying we
don't need anything like that. We chose each other
already. If you want to have a party for it, that's fine.
But you know it'll just turn into some big media
circus. They'll stream it everywhere, on every feed. It
won't belong to us anymore."

She had a point, and it was one he hadn't
considered. He'd been focused on his own private
simulation of just how exactly he would slip the
white silk up Amy's legs, just what he'd say, just how
it would all go down. So to speak.

"It's OK," he heard himself say. "I think I just
wanted the wedding night, anyway."

"… Oh."

Instantly, he realized he'd made a mistake. She
thought it was all about the sex. Usually he was better
at planning these things out a few moves in advance.
You didn't sleep your way out of a Nicaraguan prison
without being able to do that. But Amy was different.
Just organic enough to make him yearn, just synthetic
enough to make him slip. And that made moments
like this one interminable. Amy folded her knees
to her chest and hugged them. She focused on the
shadows of the room. Her fingers danced across her
shins.

"It's not just that," he said. "I want more than that."

"It's OK."

It wasn't. "No, it's not."

"No, really. It's fine." Her fingers fluttered like pale

night moths. "Like you said. I've been holding out on you."

Oh, Jesus. Shit. *Puta madre*. The conversation was slipping away from him. *She* was slipping away from him.

"It's not like that," he said. "That's not why I brought it up."

"I should take it as a compliment," Amy said. "It *is* a compliment, right?"

"It's a compliment I want to spend the rest of my life giving you."

She smiled. "Thank you." She stood. "I have to go look at the sub, now."

Fuck. He'd lost. She was being graceful about it, but that much was obvious. Her clothes climbed up her body, vine-like and dark enough that she seemed to be slowly disappearing from the room. At the end, only her face remained. Her face was frowning, but not at him. She was talking with the island. In losing the plot, he'd lost her attention, too. She was already unsealing the room. She paused at the entry, hand on the jamb, peering over her shoulder at him.

"Do the words *generation ship* mean anything to you?" she asked.

He said no, and she drifted away. He was watching the darkness where she'd been when Pastor Powell showed up.

"I can't sleep," he said.

"This is some place you've got here."

They were proceeding along the thoroughfare. The night after a shipment was always animated;

everybody trying on or trying out whatever came from the boat, showing off their new wares to neighbours and botflies. Small iterations ran past them with pinwheels and fireworks and glowing projector bangles. Rickshaws were out with samples of all the latest pre-fab foods, sent from all the best brands. Lantern bots dipped and hovered, casting mood lighting based on aggregate emotional data gleaned from ambient conversational keywords. And when the other vN noticed the human walking at Javier's side, they stopped everything to watch him pass.

"Yeah," Javier said. "It's something."

"Forgive an old preacher for prying," Powell said, "but you don't seem as enthused as the others. Are you worried about something?"

Yes, he was. But he wasn't about to tell Powell what it was. So he picked another niggling doubt at the back of his mind.

"The cats," he said. "In the children's section. Where the orphans live. I'm worried about the big cats there. My grandson told me they'd been acting up."

"Your grandson?" Powell's lips turned down. "I'm jealous. None of my kids has managed to get that far."

"You've got kids?"

Powell nodded. "I don't see them very much, anymore, though. My wife and I…" He shrugged. "I couldn't be the man she deserved."

"Because you enjoy fucking other men?" Javier asked.

Powell stopped short. He said nothing. He didn't even look at Javier. "That obvious, huh?"

"It's OK. We're built to sense these things better than humans can." He jammed his hands in his pockets. "And as for grandkids, don't feel bad. Human kids are really tough. They're intimidating. You're stuck with them for a long time."

"If you get to keep them," Powell said.

Javier nodded. "I'm just saying, our kids are easier. They grow faster. It's not so much of an investment."

"Oh, I wouldn't be so sure of that," Powell said. "They seem like their own challenge."

Javier walked through a game of hopscotch where the tiles of the game yelped and squeaked and giggled as he stepped on them. The vN playing were no more than a few months old, but they were all adult sized. Each of them paused as he and Powell drifted through the game. Powell even took the time to pick up an old USB key and toss it across the squares, hopping on one foot to his target and triggering all sorts of shouts and screams. When he finished, the vN clapped.

Javier laughed. It felt good. He hadn't laughed all day, he realized. Maybe not all week.

"I fucked up the last square." Powell's lips made a little "o" shape. "Yes, Javier. We preachers can cuss."

"Oh, I know you can," Javier said, before he could think. "I fucked a divinity student before coming here. I know the kind of swear words you all can use."

His lips clamped shut immediately. The pastor didn't look embarrassed, just bemused. But Javier was embarrassed. First Amy, now this. The words just kept bleeding out of him. Beside him, Powell slowed to a stop under a tree flush with blue solar leaves.

"Are you trying to confess to me?" he asked. "Because you can, if you want to. Our ministry has a lot of room for that kind of thing. It's not exactly a sacrament, as such, but we recognize the importance of sharing our truth."

He leaned up against the tree. He saw Powell do the same. The other man seemed a lot closer than he had before. The heat came off him in damp waves. He was sweating. He smelled of bay rum. He envied that, in organic men. They could wear things that made them smell better, or at least different. He'd heard of vN-friendly colognes, but they all just smelled like new cars.

"Could you marry me to Amy?"

"If that was what you both wanted."

"What about baptism?"

Powell smiled with only one corner of his mouth. "You want me to take you to the water, Javier? Give you a good dunking?"

"I was just asking."

"I can baptize you, yes. You or your children, or your grandson." Powell leaned forward. "You know, you don't have to be suspicious of me. Unlike the majority of organics, I do believe that you have a soul worth saving."

"I'm not suspicious of you," Javier said. "What makes you think I'm suspicious of you?"

"The way you're looking at me, right now."

"That's not suspicion," Javier said. "That's how a vN looks at a human being."

•••

"Quiet. We're not supposed to be here."

At night, the Veldt was even more like a fairyland. It was not totally dark, and not totally silent. Being something of a night owl herself, Amy had designed it with the goal of relaxation, not enforced rest. Hammocks hung from the gentle curves of counterfeit oaks, and the trees themselves rocked gently in a programmed breeze. Young iterations, most of them missing shirts or pants or even just one sock, slept in the soft grass or the swaying boughs or in the room-sized clusters of roots beneath the big trees. They piled up together like puppies, or splayed out all alone on the banks of gurgling creeks. They were like lambs, Javier realized. Tiny, human-shaped lambs asleep in the pasture.

"Have you ever read any JM Barrie?" Powell whispered.

"No," Javier said.

"This is just like Never Never Land," Powell said, like that meant something.

"We're just looking for the cats," Javier said. "We get in, take a look, and get out."

He didn't know why he hadn't told Powell to wait at the edges of the Orphanage. If Amy found out, he'd be so over the line with her that it would be a dot to him. And really, this was her problem. He should have approached her with it. Should have said something. Only something terrible seemed to happen when he said something, these days. It always went so wrong.

So he was sharing this little night reconnaissance with Powell. Powell, the stranger. Powell, the human.

Powell, the one reporting on all their activities, so he could "smooth things over."

"Is that one of them?"

Javier followed the line of Powell's finger. There, between two intertwined trees, a lioness-shaped animech padded into a clearing. Then another lioness joined it. And another. Jesus. José was right. They *were* getting together. Though maybe it was nothing; Amy had copied her synthetic cats from organic ones, and lionesses were supposed to enjoy hanging out. They just tended to do it while protecting their young. Which was why Amy had built them in the first place – to protect the young.

"I just have to check this out," Javier said, and sprang.

He landed in the middle parts of the nearest intertwined tree. He gripped it with all his limbs, and edged around it carefully. Then he walked out on one of the boughs. Like most of the trees on the island, it was helpfully designed to fit the width of his foot. Amy again. Never missed a trick.

Below his feet, the lionesses were seated in a circle. They made no noise. They flicked no ears or tails or paws. They remained simply and completely still. Except for the eyes. The eyes – huge and green, almost cartoon-like – blinked slowly. Sometimes they stayed closed for a second or two, and sometimes they blinked more normally. A single cat always did the blinking. They took turns. There were six of them. It was like a nature special, only there was no blood.

Then Powell entered the ring.

He moved quietly, but not quietly enough, and as his shadow crossed the clearing the lionesses turned as one to stare at him. Their ears pricked. Their tails swished. Their mouths opened. And then they pounced.

Javier's vision pixelated almost immediately. One moment he was full retina display, the next he was full Famicom. It was as though his senses wanted to split up the suffering into small, manageable pieces. He saw the violence play out in low-res, kludgy machine vision. The lions were attacking Powell. Powell was struggling. He was cursing and kicking trying to roll onto his back. It was the best way to protect his stomach from the lions' back paws. They were trying to disembowel him.

If Javier didn't stop them, he would failsafe and die.

He jumped down out of the tree and into the pile of snarling flesh. The cats squeaked beneath him, all fibreglass fur and gleaming teeth, their green eyes – Amy's eyes, Portia's eyes – made mostly black with pupil. Javier body-checked one of them off Powell and fell on top of him.

"I'm sorry," Powell said. "I thought–"

"Sh-shut up and get on your b-belly."

Beneath him, Powell twisted. Teeth clamped onto Javier's neck. Then claws. He jabbed the lion with one elbow. It refused to let go. He jabbed harder. Claws raked his thighs. His vision darkened, blurred. He slipped his hands under Powell's squeezing ribs and hugged him, hard.

"P-pull your legs up."

He leapt.

The lioness on his back growled and shook her head, trying to maintain her grip. But Javier had leap-frogged over one more big cat, and he managed to dislodge her on the landing. He jumped again. Powell's shirt rode up and he had to grip him again. His skin was unbelievably hot, and surprisingly smooth. He had an appendix scar and what felt like an old bullet wound, all thick and knotted. They landed roughly in the grass. The lions bounded after them. Javier leapt again. Powell kept suppressing little screams. They caught in his throat like a stifled sneeze. But he lifted his legs a little higher with each jump and held himself tight until the jumps fell into a rhythm, higher and further and longer, their toes just barely touching ground before kicking free again.

"We're flying," Powell said.

"We're es-escaping," Javier said.

The snarls behind them grew softer. They were out of the Veldt. They cleared the fogbank and sailed over water, landing in a twist of roots beneath a massive black mangrove from whose arms a series of mummy bags swung like giant chrysalises. The bags swayed for a moment, but none of the vN inside woke.

Powell was panting. "You OK?" Javier asked.

The preacher nodded. "Yeah. Actually. I thought I was fucked there, for a minute, and then *bang*, you swoop down like Superman."

"I did not *s-swoop*. Real men don't *swoop*." Javier rolled his neck. The stammer was his least favourite part of the failsafe. It made him sound like such a *pendejo*. It was worse when he was speaking English. The adaptive behaviours got all entangled with the stemware programming. "Though I guess I'm n-not a real man, either."

"Like hell you're not." Powell was staring at Javier. "What about you? Are you good?"

Javier looked down at himself. His shirt – the nice cotton one – was ruined. Carbon streaked across the front. He turned around. His back was sticky. She'd pierced his skin. He sucked his teeth.

"Take that off," Powell said. Javier did as he was told. Powell whistled low. "Damn, son."

"Is it bad?"

"Not as bad as it could be. Your legs, though…"

Javier flexed his feet. "They feel just fine."

"We should check, though. Be a shame to damage a donkey kick like that one."

Javier looked up at him. "Are you asking me to take off my pants?"

Powell smiled. "Don't worry. I'll still respect you in the morning."

Javier started unbuttoning. "Oh, I'm not worried about that," he said, as he stood. "I find people tend to respect me *more* with my clothes off."

His pants fell, and the preacher's brows rose.

"Shit," Powell said.

"That's putting it mildly," Javier said. He turned. "How's it look from the back?"

He heard a soft crunch in the dirt as Powell stepped up behind him. He was still too warm, in the way that humans were all too warm when they were afraid or angry or aroused. Javier didn't know which one it was. He was still safe, he reasoned. Still on the right side of his relationship. Still faithful to his mechanical bride (who hadn't said yes, who saw no need to say yes, who wouldn't change him, even when it led to moments like this). His own responses wouldn't kick into high gear unless Powell's did. You couldn't want them until they wanted you. You could make them want you, of course, just to set things in motion, but you couldn't force them. It was part of the failsafe. They could force you, but you couldn't force them.

Powell's fingers lit on the base of his spine. "Looks all good to me."

"Why did you provoke them?" Javier asked. "I told you to stay put."

"I just wanted to see."

His warmth moved down Javier's back. He was kneeling. He was widening Javier's stance, like a police officer searching for weapons. Between the legs.

"What did you want to see?" Javier asked.

"I wanted to see you," Powell said. "That's why I came to your room."

Javier swallowed. He focused on the tree. He focused on the details of its bark, Amy's fingerprints all over it, the backyard she'd never had and always wanted, the space she'd made for him and his children. Amy. Amy. Amy.

"Why are you really here?"

"Here on my knees, or here on the island?" His fingers traced up the insides of Javier's legs as he stood. He pulled up Javier's pants, reached around, and buttoned them. "That's a good question, Javier. That's a really good question. Because if Amy really does see everything on this island, she saw what just happened. And she didn't stop it. Any of it."

Javier turned. "What are you saying?"

Powell looked just as calm as ever. "I'm saying that maybe there are things in Never Never Land that Amy doesn't see," he said. "I'm saying that her control of this place might not be as complete as she wants us all to believe."

Javier picked up his shirt. He buttoned it as best he could. "If you're talking about the attack, that was just a default."

"A default that almost failsafed you."

"Well, what else could it be?"

Powell reached over and started rebuttoning Javier's shirt. "I think we both know the answer to that."

"The answer to what?"

Amy was lit by a halo of botflies, green and red and white, circling her lazily. Her hands were fists.

"What are you doing here?" she asked.

"We…" Javier looked toward the Veldt. Her gaze followed. "There's something going on–"

"I can see that, Javier." Her mouth was a thin line. "You took a human being into the Veldt."

"Yeah, but–"

"Where the children are."

"The kids are all fine, they're asleep–"

"These people rape children, Javier. That's what they do." Amy stepped closer. Her voice got lower. She pointed. "That's why their leader – his boss – is in prison. LeMarque raped children. He raped his *own* children. He made a *multi-player game* about raping children. And now his followers keep their vN small, so they can keep fucking them. And thanks to the failsafe, they can't possibly say no."

Powell held up both his hands. "Miss Peterson, that's not me. I'm here to–"

"You're here to spy," Amy said. "You're here to–" She blinked. "Are you... Is that..." She stared at Powell's groin. For the first time, Javier noticed that Powell was at half-mast.

"It's not what you think," Javier said.

"That was quick," Amy said. "First you do the *one thing* I've explicitly outlawed on this island, ignore the *one request* I made, and then you start..." Her lip trembled. "Did he failsafe you?" she asked. "Is that why you did it?"

"We didn't do anything!"

"We didn't," Powell said.

But tears were rising in Amy's eyes. "Why is your shirt all wrong?" She pointed. "Why are your knees all dirty?"

He tried to take her by the shoulders. She batted his arms away. "Is this because I didn't say yes?"

Oh, Christ. Oh, Jesus. He was so far beyond fucked.

"Amy, *querida–*"

"Miss Peterson–"

"*Shut up!*"

Amy pointed, and the earth beneath Powell's feet opened. He stumbled and it closed, burying him up to his thighs. He couldn't stand but he couldn't kneel, either, so he was reduced to scrabbling for balance in the dirt, quite literally bowing and scraping. Javier's vision started to change; the edges of everything sharpened. It was happening again.

"S-stop," he said. "Stop this. R-right now."

"Did he failsafe you?" Amy was staring straight at Powell. Her fingers pinched closed around her thumb. Her gaze traveled to Javier. She spoke in a whisper. "Did he rape you?"

Javier's mouth opened. Nothing came. He tried again. "W-what?"

"Did he rape you?"

"I didn't!" Powell was sweating. His eyes roved wildly in his skull. Javier thought of the puppet on the beach. "I swear to God—"

"Fuck your god," Amy said, and buried him deeper.

Javier looked between them. His vision was a series of lines, now, like CRT, pulsing white hot where it lit on Amy, her palms open to widen the void. He charged. He grabbed her around the waist and jumped. They sailed eight feet in the air, into another tree. It wasn't far from here to his own garden. He crossed the distance in two more jumps with her wriggling around in his arms.

"I told you to let me go!"

"You were gonna kill him!"

"He deserved it!"

Now he did let her go. She stumbled back a bit, onto the nearest bough. "Don't say that," he said.

"He deserved it. He failsafed you. He raped you."

Javier was about to tell her that no, Powell hadn't raped him, that it wasn't that simple, wasn't that easy, but that thought branched his focus elsewhere and he said: "If you're so concerned about that, why won't you hack me?"

"Excuse me?"

"You're worried about me, you think I'm so vulnerable, but you're the one who's keeping me vulnerable." He swallowed. "If you're really so concerned about it, you should make me stronger. Make me able to refuse."

She gripped the limbs of the tree with white knuckles. "You're saying this is *my* fault?"

"I'm saying you're a hypocrite!"

The wind picked up around them. Hearing it rushing through the leaves – the real leaves – was different from hearing its progress through the solar and carbon ones. It sounded better, softer, more alive. Something deep in his clade's original programming preferred it. He was suddenly grateful to be in this space, and knew why he had chosen it for this conversation.

"I'm going to spend the rest of the night with Xavier and the boys," he said. "I think it's better if I just take some time away from home right now."

Amy remained frozen. She obviously had no idea what to say. It was one of the few advantages he had over her – he had experience with this kind of thing, and she didn't. He let himself fall out of the tree, and started walking.

"Well, that didn't take very long at all," Ignacio said, when Javier arrived.

Unbeknownst to Javier, it wasn't just his youngest who chose to spend the night with Matteo and Ricci and their oldest. The others had all joined in, too. They were crammed into the second tier of a stack of old containers. Unlike the others, it was insulated, and well lit. It was meant for guests. They were listening to some terrifically antique Eliades Ochoa recordings on a thing called a "turntable" that a really rabid fangirl had sent them from Boston. Ricci was serving a bunch of vN rice rolls, which looked exactly like the organic version, except the fibrous meat inside was really asbestos. A box of them had come in on the boat. Apparently he had to stream a review of them, later.

"So is this it, or what?" Ignacio asked, in Spanish.

"I don't know," Javier answered.

"Is the missionary OK?" Ricci asked.

"I jumped over there, but he'd dug himself out already."

The boys nodded as one. "You're better off," Ignacio said.

"It's his life," Matteo said. "Leave it alone."

"She's not right in the head," Ignacio said. "Anyone could see that. For Christ's sake, she *ate her grandmother*."

"She was protecting her mother," Xavier said quietly. His youngest looked up at him. "She was just protecting you, Dad. She does that."

Javier sipped his electrolytes. He felt them fizz on his tongue before swallowing them. His iterations, particularly this one who had booted back from a bluescreen, had a way of reminding him of the things he'd forgotten. His youngest was right. Protecting others was in Amy's nature. It was who she'd been from the very beginning. It was why they'd met in the first place.

"What was she saying, about a generation ship?"

Gabriel asked. "Why did she mention that?"

Javier shrugged. He finished his drink. "No idea. I guess she and the island were talking."

"About the sub?"

"I guess."

"You didn't *ask?*"

"I had other things on my mind!"

"Dad," Matteo hissed. He pointed to the tier above them. "The baby. Asleep. Remember?"

Javier nodded, closed his eyes, and lay down. "We should follow his example," he said. "I just want to sleep."

They unrolled a futon for him against one wall. Xavier unrolled one next to his. Léon slept against the opposite wall. Ignacio slept outside, on a bough three feet from the window. Gabriel moved to the bottom tier with a scroll reader. Matteo and Ricci joined their son upstairs.

His son patted him on the shoulder. "It'll be better in the morning, Dad."

Javier rolled over and rested an arm over his son's middle. "Are you too big to cuddle, now?"

After a moment, his son shook his head. "No."

"How's your treehouse coming?"

"Slow. I had a platform and everything, but that was when I was smaller, and now I think it should be bigger because I'll be growing." He wriggled. "Besides. My sister is going to live there with me, so I should have at least two rooms."

"Your sister, huh?"

Xavier nodded emphatically. "Mom says she's not ready, yet."

"Well, there's a lot your mom isn't ready for just yet, so I wouldn't get too excited."

Xavier flicked his arm. "Not like *that*," he said. "I mean, my sister isn't ready. She's not finished, yet. She's still being worked on."

"Oh."

"I don't know why you thought Mom was going to hack you," Xavier said. "She's not even done with her first baby, yet. How can she change *you* if she can't even iterate? You're the bigger job, you know. You have all kinds of memories and adaptations and stuff. Plus she has to take care of the island, and all of us, and the orphans, and the other islands, and everything."

Christ, he was such a piece of shit. He shut his eyes and hugged the boy tighter and buried his nose in his curls. They smelled of seawater and oil and glue. Love hit him as hard as the failsafe, all at once. He wasn't worthy of this kid. He wasn't worthy of Amy, either. He didn't deserve this island, this home, or any of it, not when he was being such a whiny little bitch about things. He would tell her that. He would apologize. He would do what he always did and come back, like a fucking boomerang, and he would beg forgiveness. He would ask about her iteration. He would stop making it be all about him.

"A generation ship is a starship," the boy said. "I read about them."

"A starship? Like for rich assholes?"

"No. For everybody. Well, humans. On a long trip."

"What, like colonizing other planets, or some shit?"

The boy nodded against Javier's arm. "They can't

do it, though. Because of the food. They can't grow enough food."

Javier considered. "Would printed meat help with that?"

"Maybe. But the meat starts making mistakes, after a while. It misprints, when you expose it to the kind of radiation you get in space. It gets sick."

Cancer. Shit. The submarine.

Pastor Powell was waiting for him outside, when Javier left to make his amends. "We have to talk," he said.

"Amy first."

Powell shook his head. "It's Amy we have to talk about."

Javier kept walking. "She didn't really hurt you. I was the one who overreacted—"

"Portia's coming back."

He pulled up short. In the bright light of day, it seemed impossible that they could be having this conversation. Inside the house, José and his parents were singing along to another one of their ancient recordings. The air was full of music. His children were laughing. The air was still and fragrant. Even the botflies looked happy, darting this way and that. He turned around.

"Why would you say that?" he asked.

"I recorded everything last night," Powell said.

"You what?"

"Including the lions. I watched it over again. It's Morse, Javier. They're blinking in Morse. It's so old you probably don't know it, but it's still effective."

Javier shook his head. "No. You're seeing things."

"I'm not." Powell held out a reader. On it, the lionesses sat in their circle, blinking. As they did, subtitles appeared beneath: S-O-O-N.

"That could mean anything," Javier said. "Maybe Amy's just testing something out."

"Or maybe she quarantined her psychotic grandmother in those animals, and that's why they attacked me," Powell said. "Maybe she split Portia into a bunch of pieces, and they're trying to come back together."

"So what if they are? We buried that crazy bitch once; we can do it again."

"Can you?" Powell stepped closer. "You saw what she was like, last night. She has no respect – no *empathy* – for human beings. She doesn't care what happens to us, Javier."

What was it Amy had said? That she didn't need to wait for human approval? But that wasn't the same as not caring. She had a human father, after all. Who she hadn't seen in months. But Jack was still a meaningful connection to the human world. And she did fine with Tyler and Simone. She and the island did regular business with the seasteaders without any issues.

"Just because she doesn't like you doesn't make her a psychopath."

"She tried to bury me alive last night."

"I know. I remember. She thought you raped me."

"But I didn't, Javier. I could have, but I didn't."

There it was. Javier heard it in the little catch of Powell's voice. That boyish little crack. He hadn't fucked Javier, no. But he'd wanted to. He'd been on the cusp of it. Something had held him back.

"Well, gold star, preacherman. You didn't failsafe me into fucking you." Javier raised his hands and started clapping, slowly. "What a gentleman."

Powell's face went totally blank and slack. They were having a real argument, now. "She killed that puppet."

"The puppet was never really alive. It wasn't really a human being."

"Would that have made a difference?"

Powell was up close to him, now. Javier could see the grey in the grizzle sprouting from his chin. He had good skin, tightly-curled eyelashes, a face that said it used to smile.

"You're trying to sell me something," Javier said. "What is it?"

"I can bring her back." Powell withdrew something from his pocket. It was a bar of vN chocolate. A popular brand. "Amy has a flaw in her immune system," he said. "She is what she eats."

"I know that already."

Powell nodded. "This is an add-on to the stemware. She will internalize it if she eats it."

"What?"

"It's an add-on," Powell said, like that meant something. "It will modify her from the inside. She'll be able to feel pain."

Javier stepped away. "Pain?"

"Real pain. Organic pain. Like humans feel." He tried to close the gap between the two of them. "You want to know why I'm really here? This is why. I'm here to give this to Amy. I'm here to poison her."

Javier scowled. "And you're telling me this *why?*"

"Because you're the only one she trusts. You're the only one who can give it to her."

Javier stared at the bar. He was going to ask who Powell was working for, really, who had made this awful thing, and how it was coded or printed or whatever, but the question he settled on was: "Why would I want the woman I love to feel pain?"

Powell shut his eyes. He looked to be mastering himself, summoning patience from some interior reserve. "The pain isn't constant. She'll just react the way humans react."

Javier arched one eyebrow in a way that he knew communicated deep skepticism. "So, she could failsafe me? If I saw this happen to her?"

Powell growled. "This is bigger than you and your pretend marriage!" He pulled something from his pocket. "Do you know what this is? Of course you don't. It's a Geiger counter. And the reason it's making that noise is because this island is full of fissile material."

Javier threw up his hands. "Oh, come *on.*" He started walking toward the house. "Now you're just making shit up."

"I'm not. The movement of these islands isn't random, Javier. It never was. It maps over to the sites of sunken submarines, and sunken nukes." Powell jogged to catch up to him, and unfolded his reader again. The map was there, in overlay. The dots scattered across it pulsed regularly. Red circles like bullseyes spread out from each of them. It all looked very menacing.

"You could have designed that," Javier said. "You could have designed this whole thing as part of some fucked-up con job. You could be lying to me, right now."

"But I'm *not*." Powell positioned himself directly in front of Javier. "I'm not. She needs a check. She needs vulnerability. She's playing out her own personal *Heart of Darkness* out here, and–"

"Her own *what*?"

"It's a book. It's about someone with a god complex."

"And someone having actual godlike power offends your religious sensibilities. Of course. It's cool when it happens in a book, but the moment someone actually walks on water, you freak the fuck out." Javier kept walking. "I'm not doing this. In fact, I'm going home, and I'm going to tell Amy what you're here to do. And then, your shit will be completely–"

"I'll kill myself."

Javier's vision froze, then juddered. He turned. Pixels hovered at the edges of Pastor Powell's body like a disintegrating halo. He had opened his shirt. Under it, strapped to his chest, was a variety of small bricks. They looked like feedstock. But they probably weren't.

"It's old-fashioned, but it's still the best way to go," Powell said.

Javier swallowed. Pixel dust floated away from Powell's arms as he gestured. It spiraled away into the safe nowhere three feet away from Powell's body. It looked like an old videogame: all lines and blocks.

Like his visual receptors were frantically trying to render this moment into harmless fiction. Not real. Just pretend. Can't hurt you.

He told his legs to jump away. He told them to pound up from the ground and take him into the breeze and the botflies. But his bones felt just as hollow as they really were, and he felt the smoke that made up his muscles wafting this way and that, twitching against the conflicting commands. It was as though someone else were inside him, taking over. This was how Amy had felt with Portia. He was sure of it.

Oh, God. Amy. He could tell her. He could jump. Jump, and run, right now, and tell her.

And she would kill Powell.

Vertigo ripped through him. He fell down. He wanted to claw his way into the black earth. Let it swallow him whole. Disappear forever.

"The timer is already set," Powell said. "The moment I touched the wrapper with my bare hands, I signalled a satellite above us. In... forty-seven minutes, that satellite will broadcast a signal detonating these explosives, and I will die."

Javier reached up. He lunged. Powell danced away, neatly, like a boxer.

"This wiring is very delicate, Javier. If you touch it, you have no idea what will happen."

Christ. Shit, Christ, shit, fuck.

"I'm going to send my botfly with you, to monitor your progress. If you destroy it, I'll trigger the vest. If you tell Amy what we're doing, I'll trigger the vest."

Powell circled a finger in the air, and the machine

peeped out from beneath his priestly collar and entered the air. It latched onto Javier and dug down beneath his shirt.

"Now, you can refuse me, and I can sit this out, and die. There's extra explosive up here," he sketched a necklace with one finger, "and it'll blow my head clean off. At least, it's supposed to. You and I both know how *unreliable* technology can be."

Javier watched Powell's eyes. They were perfectly calm. He was winning, and he knew it.

"I'll suck your dick." The words rolled off his tongue like they'd always been there. And in a way, they always had been. Powell wanted it. Javier knew that Powell wanted it. Everything else was just programming.

Powell rested a hand on his head, like he was petting a dog. His smile was bemused. "Son, you'd do that anyway, if I asked you to."

His hand cupped Javier's jaw. His hand was absurdly warm. Javier could feel the pulse of blood in it. Quick. Wanting. Powell's thumb pushed inside his mouth. Javier tasted nervous sweat. And just like that, the process inside him started to spin. Javier sucked helplessly at Powell's thumb. He knew exactly what to do to make this all better. He could interrupt this whole thing. Slow this down. He could do that with just his lips and his tongue. He knew how to do that. Had done just that very thing, in the past. In prison. It was just like riding a bike. You never really forgot.

His fingers made short work of Powell's fly.

Powell himself was already halfway there. Of

course. He hadn't seen much action lately; Javier could tell from the way the other man's hands tightened in his hair. How his hips jerked. How instantly his mouth was full. He tried to slow Powell down, tried to sweeten it, but Powell's open palm came down on the side of his head and he grabbed Javier's hair and jerked his head the way he wanted it to go. There was no finesse at all, just the raw slide of organic skin on silicone, the occasional dig of fingernails into Javier's neck. If he were a human being of real flesh and bone, this would hurt. His throat would hurt. His eyes would well up. He'd get dizzy from not being able to breathe. But he wasn't. Wasn't a real live boy. Was a machine, instead. Was a toy.

He'd been with men and women who'd been raped. They wanted vN sometimes, after. To relearn their bodies. To relearn pleasure. Being with vN could awaken those sleeping memories in safety. They never described what happened to them in detail – it would failsafe him. But now he knew. Now he knew what happened when he covered his ears and closed his eyes. Now he knew the secret.

His tongue said Powell was carrying an infection of some kind. When he spat, Powell slapped him.

"You're a fucking robot and you won't even swallow? What are you, *broken*?" Powell's voice shook. "Get going."

"You son of a bitch," Javier whispered. "You cowardly little piece of shit suicide-bomber *zealot*."

"*Plus ça change,*" Powell said, zipping himself back up. "I could explain it all to you. I could tell you my whole history. I could tell you that I'm atoning for something. Because I am, Javier. I'm atoning. I'm making something right." Powell checked his watch. "But I don't have the time to explain it, and neither do you."

Powell held out the chocolate. "This conversation can serve no purpose anymore. Goodbye."

4: YOU CAN'T UNRING A BELL

He found Amy alone in their bedroom, plucking at something invisible in the dark. Her hands opened and he saw the submarine projected. It looked like an anatomical drawing. Or maybe a schematic. He thought about Xavier had said about generation ships. They sounded sort of mythical, like jetpacks or flying cars.

"It's really a shame," she said, without turning to face him. "They were really onto something, here. I know why they used meat – it's harder to detect, and it surprised us – but the tissue could have been put to better use. I think it may be a prototype for something else. I think the whole invasion was the prototype for something else. Something bigger. I think there's another reason for all of this."

"I love you," Javier said.

Amy turned, finally. She was wearing white again. She was wearing the torque. Unlike human women, her eyes did not turn red with crying. The skin under them didn't puff up. But he could tell. He had learned how to tell.

"I love you, too." She sounded careful. Cautious. As though the love itself wasn't the point. Which it wasn't.

"And I'm sorry," he added. "I know you were just trying to protect me."

Amy nodded. "I was." Her lips pursed. "I was just so angry. And I was jealous, too. I'm not very proud of that. But…" The white line of her lips grew even thinner. "If he hurt you, you would tell me, wouldn't you?"

Javier closed his eyes. "Of course I would."

"OK." Her arms closed around him. "This is why I don't want to take advantage of you," she said. "Do you understand, now, what it would mean if I took advantage of your failsafe like that?"

Oh, yes. Yes, he did. He understood it better than she could know.

He kissed the top of her head. He hugged her back. "I understand."

She butted up under his chin like a cat. "Thank you." She hugged him harder. "I don't like being mad at you. I'm sorry I was."

He squeezed his eyes shut. "It's OK. You can get mad at me. I deserve it."

"No, you don't. You really don't. We were both working our own protocols. They just happen to be different."

Javier had spent most of his life being dishonest about one thing or another. He had stolen money from most of his lovers. He had lied to them about coming back. None of those lies – those small, petty, human lies – had prepared him for this one.

"I got you something," he said. "It came in on the shipment."

It would be OK, he told himself, as her slender fingers closed on the wrapper. She had pulsed him. Pulsed the whole island. For their own good. And this was for her own good, too. In a way. For their own good. Because Powell would leave. Powell would not do anything worse. And then they could figure something out. They could make it better. They could make sure she never got hurt. Ever.

"Thank you." The wrapper rustled noisily as she tore it open. She snapped off a piece and held it out. "Would you like some?"

"That's OK," Javier said. "It's for you, remember?"

"If you say so." She popped it in her mouth and smiled.

Nothing happened.

"Are you OK?" Amy asked.

"Sure," he heard himself say. "It was just a long night."

She nodded. She sat down cross-legged on the bed. Then she made room for him, and he joined her. "You said something was strange about the lions," she said.

Javier nodded. "I think they're talking to each other. José told me to look into it. So I did, and they are."

She still looked fine. Normal. She kept eating. She nodded to herself.

"That's not good," she said. "They're part of the island's default defence mechanism. So I can understand why they would attack a human being, but not why they would be spending time together.

They're supposed to watch the kids, not each other."

"About that," Javier said, "what exactly *is* the island's default defence mechanism?"

She frowned. "You really want to know?"

He nodded.

"You're not going to like it." She put the poison down. "But I guess, since we're being so honest, I should tell you." She picked up his hand and stroked it. "It's Portia," she said.

Jesus. Powell was right. He tried withdrawing his hand, but she held it tight.

"Please don't run away," she said. "It's not like how you think. It's not *her*. Not her as an individual. More like her priorities. Her decision-making process. And it only engages when I'm not around."

The simulations started branching before he was even conscious of them. "If you're not around?"

Amy nodded. "Yeah. If something happens to me. Or if my focus shifts. If I can't devote as much attention to the island, because I'm hurt. That's why I keep my bandwidth to the island so constant. So I don't upset the balance." She squeezed his hand. "I know it doesn't make me the easiest person to be with, but..."

Her hand began to shake. It started out as a faint tremor, the kind elderly humans sometimes had, almost imperceptible, like the movement of a second hand on a very old watch. Then it intensified. Became palsy. It shuddered through her little wrist and up into her arm, jogging her elbow up and down. Then it was in her shoulder, and she whimpered, and her grip on his hand was so hard he wanted to pull away but couldn't.

"What's happening to me?" she asked.

"I'm sorry."

Amy's eyes were wide. "Is Portia coming back? Is she doing this to me?"

He shook his head. "No."

Her eyes lit on the wrapper. "You–"

She crumpled. The words died inside her mouth. Her face slammed into the bed like someone had pushed it there. She flipped onto her back. She bounced and seized and twisted. And through it all her eyes remained on Javier.

"I'm so sorry." It was Powell, he wanted to say. Powell made me. Powell failsafed me. But when the change was done, she'd know, and she'd kill Powell.

"It's pain," he said. "It's organic pain. It's an add-on, to give you a sense of organic pain."

Her spine arched in a terribly perfect half-circle. He tried to help her down and she screamed, an awful high shivery sound that seemed like it could shatter the diamond tree outside. Her heels drummed the bed and the bed roiled, bubbled, became hot and soft and viscous like tar. Something was happening to the house. The walls peeled down. The beams fell away. Sunlight shot through the shredded roof and her screams continued unabated, constant, breathless. And as she suffered his vision changed, went old-fashioned, entered failsafe. A thousand tiny pixels registered her agony for him, each pinprick of light burning its way down through him, imploring him to stop it, begging him the way her lips no longer could.

"I love you," he was saying. He was holding her

hand, still. He was clenching it. Hers curled around his. "I love you, I love you, I love you."

The screaming stopped. His vision cleared. He looked down and she was staring at him. It was over. The pain was gone. They could figure it out, now. Move on to whatever came next. He would apologize and make it right. He would start with kissing her. He shut his eyes and bent down and she didn't move, didn't kiss back. When he pulled away and looked again, she was perfectly still. Eyes open, unseeing. Her hand was slack in his.

Amy was dead.

He touched her face. It rolled to one side. The breeze lifted her hair and rippled her dress. He let go of her hand and it dropped onto the bed, their bed, and began to sink into the gleaming black surface of it. The whole thing had lost its structural integrity, just like the house. Now she – her body, her shell – was sinking into it. Black goo seeped up around her face. It was at her lips before he moved, took her hand, tried to pull her free, but it was too late. Her body shifted in the muck. The weight differential changed. She was in quicksand. He tried to hold her hand, wrench her free, dig her out, but the island gulped her down. Her eyes were open. They were still open when she slipped beneath the surface. Her hair floated on it for a moment and then it too was gone. There was only black.

"Dad?"

Javier turned. Xavier stood there, watching him. When Javier stood up, he backed away. Javier raised his hands, palms open. Black mud dripped away from them.

Beneath their feet, the island shuddered.

"What did you do?" his youngest asked.

"I had to—"

His son's fist in his stomach was terrifically strong. He doubled over. The kid kicked him in the face. He was barefoot, and that was the only reason Javier kept his teeth. Then his foot crashed into Javier's ribs. He was little, but it didn't matter. He was focused. He jumped up and landed on Javier's shoulders. Javier collapsed onto the floor.

"I hate you!" his son was saying. "I hate you! You bastard, you killed my mother!"

In the crack in the house, a shadow appeared. It growled. Javier struggled to his feet, and easily grabbed his son's next punch. He pushed it aside gently, and just as carefully pushed his son behind him as he backed away.

The lions had come for the kill.

"What's happening?" his son whispered.

"Something really bad," Javier said. "When I tell you, you jump out of here. Then you run. And you don't stop. You find your brothers and you get the hell off this island."

One by one, the lions hopped into the house. They congregated at the bed. They pawed delicately at its surface. Their tails flicked, as though they were considering something.

"Now," Javier said.

His son jumped away. The lions noticed the movement, but didn't chase after him. Instead, they focused on Javier. He braced himself. He curled his fists. But no attack came. Instead, one of their number padded up to him and slid herself under his hand and along his thigh.

Good work, she seemed to be saying.

"You win," Javier said. "Congratulations, you crazy old bitch."

The lioness licked the mud from his hand.

The island was burning.

Javier jumped free of the house to follow his son, but a mist was already rising between their little home island and the big one. It made the jump difficult to estimate. That was fine. He'd walk. He set foot in the water. Too late, he realized there was no membrane to hold him up. The water closed over his head.

He saw the lions enter the water above him. He heard them before he saw them. Their bodies curved elegantly into the water and kicked briefly before orienting themselves. They paddled away toward the big island. He continued sinking. It was cold, down there. He had strong legs and he could have kicked up, but he didn't. He had no need for air. He had no need for anything.

Beneath him, the island extended way, way down. It was black on black on black, with little glimmers here and there. It looked like a giant fungus, or maybe a massive brain, all that gelatinous mass occasionally sparking with life. The sparks grew more frequent the longer he sank. Trunk lines burned white like lines of traffic at night. Thick cords of light tangled, moved, changed shape. They unhitched themselves from the main body, flailing in the water, thrashing frantically while he remained still. He felt the island's desperation as it changed. He felt none within himself. He should have been simulating what it was to crunch down into nothingness under the kind of pressure he was about to be under. He should have been trying to leave. He should have. He wasn't.

It was comforting, almost, to revert back to the guy he'd always been. It was just too difficult for him to be anything else. A real father. A real husband. A real man. It was beyond his operational parameters, beyond his structural capacity. He wasn't built for it. He saw that, now.

Before him, the island was an inverted city. Her roots hung deep in the water, thick as skyscrapers. They glittered and gleamed like structures of glass and steel. At any time, he realized, Amy could have shot them up from below and made a paradise to rival any human construction. They dangled there, all the unfinished places, the filigreed towers and great crude blocks, the hanging bridges of sighs never breathed. She had held them in reserve. She had let the islanders build what *they* wanted, instead.

Something cut into him from behind. A clean razor cut just beneath his skin, not painful, noticeable only by the way it tugged his shirt and caught his belt.

The diamond tree had fallen, too. That was fitting. It was heavier, and sinking faster. He freed it from his flesh, and he watched it sink, sparkling, into the depths.

A group of hands clasped it and pulled it lower.

He blinked and tried to see more clearly. But the hands had vanished. They were simply waiting, somewhere below, in the dark. He looked up. The unfinished city seemed closer, now. This close, he could see the decorations Amy had left each building. Some of them, at their crowns and gables, featured what might be gargoyles.

The gargoyles looked an awful lot like the puppet vN.

They were screaming. They were alive.

Something shook free from a dome in one tower. It punched and thrust its way out, piercing a shifting membrane, and slurped its way into the water. The submarine. It rocketed blindly up at Javier. A pore in its surface irised open. He kicked furiously. Tried to swim away. All the instincts washed away by the waves returned to him now, and he struggled in the water as though he were really drowning. But it was too late. He was sucked in. He was Jonah in the whale.

"What you have to know about humans is what they don't know about themselves," Arcadio says. "They're machines, too. Humans are just machines. They run programs just like we do, they just run different ones."

He is in the forest with his father. He likes the forest. He likes the many layers it has, all stacked up on each other like the things called "shipping containers" that Arcadio says, once upon a time, his clade stepped out of before leaping into the trees. Steel boxes a mile high, a secret inside each one. His clade came to the forest because it was made for the forest – for jumping and clinging. A-R-B-O-R-E-A-L. That was the English word. And like his father and grandfather before him, Javier loves it there – the way it is never silent, the way it is never lonely. He loves the speed with which the lizards skitter up the trees, and the gentle sway of crocodiles through the water. He loves the fizz of sunlight on his skin. And he loves the storms just as much when they sweep over the trees and make them whisper and moan.

But they are about to leave the forest, for good. There is more food beyond the treeline and more food is what they need for him to grow and for Arcadio to make more boys in his belly. It is high time he grew up. He is two months old, now.

It has been two months since Arcadio fled the burning camp with Javier in his belly. Two months since his father cut him out with an old multi-tool. Two months of fooling drones with their photosynthetic skin – it plays hell with their IR vision. Two months of killing botflies. Two months of opening their mouths wide to taste even the slightest hint of smoke.

Today is the first day he has seen human beings.

"What do you mean, they're machines?"

Javier stares at the tourists from high above. They're all so much bigger than he is. Bigger, and paler. Their hair is straight. Their words have hard edges. Nothing rhymes. They walk like they're in pain all the time.

"They're meat," Arcadio says, "but that meat is just a jumble of chemical signals and electric impulses. Batteries and wires, you know? They're just like us."

"They're prettier."

Arcadio grins. "Yes. They're prettier."

"They don't all look alike. They're all different."

"That's right. They're all unique."

Unique. Javier smiles. What a wonderful idea, to make each iteration different from every other one. Combinations, not replications, each as individual as a storm. Not just mistakes, like him and Arcadio. Not just an error in automated self-repair.

"Come on. It's time you met one."

His father drops off the bough of the tree he is currently occupying. He falls eight feet to another bough, then three, until he stands on the lowest bough of the opposite tree. He snaps his fingers. That's his signal for irritation. Javier has already learned to hate the sound.

"I'm not gonna wait," *his father says.*

Javier jumps.

They wait for the humans to board their tour buses. As the buses pass below, they jump on. They're light enough that the driver doesn't notice their presence. If the bus' sensorium says anything, they don't hear of it. They bounce and sway on the roof for an hour. Javier's fingers are stiff from curling across the rack when they jump free a few minutes outside of town.

From there they walk. Javier does not like walking; concentrating on measuring his steps eats more processing power than just jumping, but Arcadio says it uses less total energy, so they have to walk. Besides, el corporación is still looking for them. The motion-identifying algorithms in their drones can find them by their jumps. So no more jumping, until they're safe.

"Do all towns look like this?" *Javier asks.*

The town is a cluster of houses made of bundled rods printed to look like wood, with thatch roofs that smell like recycled latex. They stand about ten feet high in the trees, above the muddy track where Javier and Arcadio are standing. Each building is connected to the other by a bridge of rope and slats. It's all very neat and orderly. Javier has not seen so many right angles since the last time they camped in an old truck that got stuck in the mud during a long ago rainy season.

"I don't think so," Arcadio says. "It doesn't look like any pictures I've seen. I think the humans made it special because it's where they go on vacation."

"Vacation?"

"It's when they leave home and spend a lot of money and eat a lot of food and maybe fuck new people."

And then Arcadio walks up some plank stairs, and Javier has to follow him. Stairs are hard. Arcadio warned him about them. His feet want to snag under the lip of each step. Arcadio waits at the top, rolling his eyes, and Javier tries to catch up and slips. His chin hits wood. Arcadio makes a big sigh with his shoulders and plucks Javier up by his collar and hauls him the rest of the way. When he looks at Javier's face, he laughs.

"You got a pussy on your face, mijo." He puts Javier's hand on the wound and pinches the fingers shut around it. "Hold it like that until it quits bleeding. It'll seal up soon."

Javier follows him along a swinging bridge. Everything here is ropes and pulleys and buckets. No birds are singing. Instead there's soft, airy music coming from nowhere and everywhere at once.

"Fucking flutes," Arcadio mutters. He pauses at a piece of dead wood bristling with signage. The letters look familiar, but Javier can't read the words. Arcadio points. "Come on. We need clothes."

"I thought we were getting food."

"We are. But first we need to get clothes. You don't look right, and neither do I."

Javier follows. They march across more swinging bridges until they find a place to hop down. The staff doesn't live in the little village in the trees, Arcadio says. They live in plastic flat-pack houses that you set up by following a set of instructions with no words on it, just pictures. Arcadio used to set them up for human workers, he says. The vN they just used to bundle up in parachuting and hang from somewhere, all tied together so none could escape.

They pluck clothes from the line. Dark green P-O-L-O shirts (not pollo shirts, Arcadio says, and shut the fuck up and stop making so much noise) and chinos.

"These are what the workers wear," Arcadio says. "Luckily, one of them just iterated."

"What are those things?"

"Shoes. Well, sandals. Printed sandals."

"What are they for?"

"They're for your feet. Put them on."

Javier gives his father a deeply skeptical frown. Nothing goes on his feet. Nothing. He can't jump with those big rubbery things flopping around on his feet. Not jumping means not escaping. It's a stupid idea.

"It's a stupid idea."

"When I want your opinion, I'll ask you for it. Now do you want to eat, or not?"

So they go to the C-O-M-M-I-S-S-A-R-Y next, where the workers spend their pay on food. It's special vN food that comes out of massive printers somewhere at the edge of the big city somewhere, all hot and smoky and ferrous, and the amount necessary to keep a non-photosynthetic clade running always costs just a little bit more than they would all make in a week.

"This place does clade-based employment," Arcadio says. "That's why we have to have a big clade. So we'll get hired somewhere good."

Brothers. Until this moment, Javier has never considered

that he might one day have brothers. What would they be called? Would they be better jumpers? Would Arcadio like them better? If they were easier iterations, ones he didn't have to take care of alone, he might like them better.

Javier is considering this when Arcadio asks him to steal his first bars of food.

"Wipe your chin," Arcadio says, and then bends and does it for him with a roll of his thumb. The wound is still sticky, and Arcadio wipes the glittering black smear on the inside of his new shirt. "Good. Now you look normal."

It occurs to Javier that he has never seen himself. There were mirrors in the car they camped in, but they were spotted with mould and angled strangely, so Javier only ever saw himself in bits and pieces. Never his whole face or body. But it probably doesn't matter. He's going to look just like Arcadio. He looks just like the way Arcadio used to look. There's no need for a real mirror.

"Follow that woman," Arcadio says. "She's pretty. She'll distract them."

The girl is pretty. She's human. She's huge and round and has hair frizzing every which way, with a grey streak running through it like spilled sugar. Her blouse sticks to her back. Thus exposed, her shoulders fold forward like the curves of a big paper book, like the map book in the back of the car with the pages ripped out. They read that book together, he and Arcadio. They read about Mexico City and Los Angeles and even Dejima, the place that's going to be Mecha, soon. Arcadio says they're going to go there, someday. When the clade is big enough.

Javier waits until the other vN have noticed the woman. They are all smiling when he enters the room. It's a big rectangle with a few skylights set in an A-frame roof. It echoes. *There is a counter, and vN slide trays along the counter and push buttons and food extrudes from nozzles in the wall near the buttons. There are high shelves with things on them: more clothes, soap, little squares of foil with circles inside. The woman is being nice and friendly with everyone. She knows all their names. Hers is Angela.*

All Javier has to do is grab some food bars. He walks past the crowd, and begins searching the aisles. The shelves hold all sorts of things he's only ever heard about, so he drags his feet. Literally. Walking is so difficult. So he hops along, bouncing on his toes and skimming his squeaky new sandals along the dusty concrete.

The food is at the back of the room. It's behind a wall of black chain-link fence that hums strangely. Arcadio has warned him about these fences – about electricity. So Javier knows that he must not touch the fence if he wants to get the food. The fence is over ten feet high. Getting over it without touching it will require a two-step jump. The walls are too wide to support a strong bounce between them. Arcadio could do it because his legs and body are longer, but Javier is still too small. This means getting a running leap at the wall and vaulting off it, backward, turning in mid-air, and landing against the shelves without making too much noise. Then doing it all over again, in reverse, and walking out like nothing has happened.

He slips the sandals off. They were a stupid idea. Why did Arcadio ask him to do this? Why did Arcadio think he could do this? He stares at the fence. He could just leave. He could just say that it's too hard, that the fence is too high, that he doesn't want to. And Arcadio would scowl at him and call him a pendejo, *and later on he'd have another boy, a better boy, a braver boy, and that would be that.*

He runs. He jumps. He bounces. He twists. He lands on the shelves. They jostle only a little.

On the topmost shelf, balanced precariously, a box teeters toward the floor. It slides down slowly, like it wants him to see it, and he pries one hand free and reaches and catches it. He is holding it when a group of bars in shiny red wrappers tumbles out of the open box, and onto the floor.

Instantly, a siren sounds, and the fenceposts begin to spark. They snap at each other, their tips glowing blue and then white, and thin ribbons of light spill out between them to touch the ceiling.

To escape, Javier will have to jump between them.

He hauls himself up to the topmost shelf. It clangs beneath him, but all he hears is the wasp sound of electricity. It's hot. His hair stands on end. If it gets him – if he jumps wrong – he'll die. He's sure of it. It'll fry him. So he simulates every possible jump. Humans are already rushing the fence. They wave something at a door in the fence and get through it. They have tasers. Javier focuses only on the forking tongues of light between the fenceposts. They are organically random. It's hard to plot. Hard to calculate. Not now. Not now. Not now.

Now.

He launches himself. Too late he remembers to tuck in his feet; one of those forking tongues brushes his bare feet. The last thing he sees before the darkness comes is the pair of sandals he abandoned on the floor on the other side of the fence.

When the darkness rolls back, his body is stiff, and his wrists and ankles are in sticky gel-grips, and he says: "I want my dad," and the camp foreman says Arcadio is gone, Arcadio left as soon as the alarm sounded. He shows Javier the footage. One minute Arcadio is there, waiting, and the next he's in the air, in the trees, in the wind.

"But I'm a kid," Javier says.

"They'll feed you in prison, and you'll get big," the foreman says. "You won't be a kid for long."

5: TRIBULATIONS

"Well hi hi hi there," Tyler said.

Javier opened his eyes, slowly. His vision was greyscale. Tyler was nursing some bullshit little goatee and was smoking from a pipe printed to look like corncob. He wore a Mump & Smoot T-shirt. At least, that's what it said on it. It had pictures of clowns. Javier hated clowns. They really threw the Turing process into all kinds of hell.

"Long time no see." Tyler smiled. His eyes were red. He didn't smell like pot. He'd been crying. "Thought you were, uh, what's the right word? Fragged? Decommissioned?"

"*¿Qué?*" Javier's mouth tasted like rust. "What?"

Tyler kept smiling. He tapped his pipe out into a matching ashtray. His mouth worked, then stopped, then worked again. "What's the last thing you remember?"

Javier's eyes were wet. His whole body was wet. Or at the very least, damp. He was on a hammock. He was being hang-dried. He smelled like cancer.

"It's cool if you don't want to talk about it," Tyler

said. "But we're gonna have to. At some point." He
scratched under his collar. "It's kind of a thing, you
see. Keeping you here."

The room was an old container. It was likely a brig
of some sort. There was nothing inside the room with
which he could hurt himself. No sharps. No edges.
Everything was soft. If he were a human being, he
could have hanged himself on the hammock, but
that was about it. Along one wall, in huge stencilled
yellow letters, read the words: *WE MUST CULTIVATE
OUR GARDEN.*

"Where are my children?" Javier asked.

Tyler reached over and squeezed his shoulder. "I'm
sorry, man. Really, really sorry."

Javier blinked. "What day is it?"

"It's almost Christmas."

Javier shut his eyes. Six months. He'd been under
for half a year. "The island?"

"Gone. All of them."

His eyes opened. "What?"

"They're all gone, man. As soon as the first one
burned…" Tyler shrugged helplessly. "All of them just
started… melting. Like an oil spill."

"All of them? Gone?"

"All gone. Uncle Sam, uh, *hastened* that particular
process." Tyler snorted. "Drone strikes, skimmer bots,
phage swarms, smart algae, the whole bit. What they
couldn't blow up, they skimmed off and took away. I
think the UN has some of the dregs in some oil drums,
somewhere, next to the Ark of the Covenant."

There was nothing left. No Great Elder Bot. No
islands. No physical memory. Nowhere for Amy to

have ported herself when he...

"Oh, Jesus." His voice was a whisper. He knew the taste in his mouth, now. The stains under his nails. The smell on his skin. He knew it only in passing; the failsafe kept him from experiencing it, most of the time. Only a handful of women had let him taste and see. Blood. So much blood.

"Yeah," Tyler said.

"Oh, *Jesus*." He gripped the edges of the hammock hard. "Oh, Christ. Amy. Oh God, Amy..."

Tyler reached over and stilled the hammock. "She's... gone, Javier. We've been waiting for word... you know, thinking maybe she copied herself somewhere, but..." He sighed and licked his lips. "With what all's been happening out there, she can't have made it."

Javier rolled his head and his gaze toward Tyler. "What do you mean?"

Tyler took a deep breath. He licked his lips again. He appeared to think of something, and took Javier's hand. He squeezed it hard, like they were making a bargain together.

"I mean the motherfucking apocalypse, brother," he said. "I mean Portia."

He was suddenly and terribly aware of how small he was in this room, and how small he would like to remain. If he never opened that door, if he never left this room, he would not have to see what Tyler was talking about. It would not have to be real. Amy gone and his sons dead and Powell...

"She's out?" Javier asked. "Free?"

Tyler unrolled a reader and showed Javier an image.

It was a sixteen-lane highway. Afternoon sunlight slanted across mangled cars. They'd all crashed into an eighteen-wheeler that read *ISAAC'S ELECTRONICS* on the side. It was a prison transport for vN, just like the one where Javier had first met Amy. Now a cluster of vehicles pressed themselves flat against it like preserved petals. There'd been an accident underneath an electronic sign. The sign read: BEWARE; FOR I AM FEARLESS, AND THEREFORE POWERFUL.

"That's why everybody was all hot and bothered to go scorched earth on the islands. They're hoping to shatter any mirrors she might be hosting herself on. I mean, for Christ's sake, they're talking about taking down *satellites*. She's a one-woman army hell-bent on taking us back to the fucking Dark Ages."

Javier laughed. He felt the seam in the skin of his back start to open, but he couldn't stop. It was too funny. Portia, the epitome of technological achievement, forcing the humans who made her into burning their clouds one server at a time.

"Dude," Tyler said, "what *happened* out there?"

Javier slowly pulled himself to sit up. "I think..." He reread the advice on the side of the cell. "I think I got owned. Hard."

Tyler exhaled smoke. "Was it that preacher guy?"

Tears pricked Javier's eyes. "Yeah. It was him."

Tyler nodded. He stood up. Javier watched him walk over to a door in the cell, knock out "Shave and a Haircut," and wait as the door squealed open. Light blazed into the room.

"I won the pool," Tyler said.

•••

The seastead sat on pontoons like an oil rig, but without the giant milkshake straw poking up out of the middle. They'd built the towers on the "stacked rock" model, with old containers piled high and poking out at odd angles to catch the most sun. Some had solar paint, others had fab-glass to take in light and grow crops. Everywhere, he heard the chug and clank and hiss of the water purifiers. Everyone smoked. He got invited to naked vinyasa his first morning out. He didn't go. If he'd gone, he would have fucked someone. He knew that about himself, now. Or rather, he'd been reminded of it. Powell had reminded him.

Simone called the seastead a "temporary autonomous zone," but really that meant that it was a big camp and you could come or go as you pleased. You didn't get a vote unless you committed to more than six months of work, which she said meant that "the views of anybody spending their summer off school slumming it here don't mean shit."

"We could use you in the gardens," Simone reminded him. "You can stay as long as you like."

Only that wasn't true.

The stead's seed money came from a few big grants from a combination of American government think tanks, private industry, and wealthy parents who just wanted their kids to shut the fuck up at family dinners. All of those people had a vested interest in keeping Javier on the seastead, where he could answer questions about what had happened. But since the sovereignty of the stead was in question, it was tricky for any of them to show up on the stead itself. Tyler and the governing council had spent the past three days fending them off. Their drones hovered everywhere. When Javier went out to sun himself, he always waved.

Tyler had also set up some sort of legal defence fund. There was an attorney on the stead, a brassy British lady who left her firm after her boss' attentions got to be a hassle. She collected a very big and very secret settlement. It now funded a tower farm. She was big into beekeeping, now. Her name was Phaedra.

"So you have to tell me what happened," she said, during their first meeting. She was wearing the steader equivalent of business casual: a pair of scrubs whose colours actually matched, with black mesh swim shoes. "But first, I want to tell you that I'm here to protect you and what legal rights you do have. Which aren't many. And also that I have no interest in having sex with you."

"That's big of you."

"You lot just aren't my thing, I'm afraid."

Javier nodded. "Noted."

"So. Understanding that I am bound by privilege, and you can tell me everything, please do. What happened, out there?"

Javier decided on the simplest possible explanation. "A pastor from New Eden Ministries by the name of Mitch Powell failsafed me into killing my…" His what? In Spanish, he'd say *mi mujer*, my woman. It sounded crude. Like she'd belonged to him. Like he'd bought her somewhere. His partner? What, did they fight crime together? English was so stupid. So finicky and so vague at the same time. "My wife," he said, finally.

Phaedra blinked. "You mean Amy Peterson?"

"Yes."

She examined some documents on her reader. "Does that mean you would like to be known legally as Javier Peterson?"

He had never considered it, before. "I guess."

"Nomenclature is a real problem for vN," she said. "Most countries still don't have a filing system to deal with single names. Normally we just choose the human you're living with, or the one you started out with."

"Peterson's fine."

"So." Phaedra rolled up her reader. She folded her hands. They were covered in old stings and new freckles. "Amy is dead."

"Yes."

"You know of nowhere that she might have ported herself?"

He considered that. In the final moments of her life, Amy was in pain. Confused. Probably horrified at his betrayal. Could she have gathered herself and gone elsewhere? Or was that process just automated, like a backup?

"Have you talked to her dad?" Javier asked.

"The FBI has," Phaedra said. "His drivespace and cloudspace have all been seized and searched. She's not there."

He nodded. That made sense. It would be an obvious place to look, for one. And besides, he had no idea whether Powell was bullshitting him about the contents of that poison. Maybe it wasn't a pain plug-in. Maybe it was just pure poison. Maybe it was designed to unmake Amy from the inside out.

"But Portia is alive," he murmured. "Why is Portia alive, but Amy isn't?"

"That's what I was going to ask you," Phaedra said, leaning back in her chair and folding her arms.

"She was the model for the island's self-defence mechanism. Amy told me, right before…" He frowned. "Wait. How long did it take the uniforms to take out the islands? Once they'd started disintegrating, I mean."

"It was surprisingly difficult."

Phaedra opened up something on a reader for him. Footage of men in amphibious uniforms being hustled onto a bright orange emergency retrieval vessel. Onboard, they were hosed down.

"The islands were radioactive," Phaedra said. "They started leaking radiation almost immediately after…" She sighed. "It's what started the fires in the fogbank. The heat. The men who first tried planting mines on the island have sustained their life's total allotment of radiation. One more X-ray, one more airline flight, and it's cancer for them."

Javier said nothing. Powell was right. Amy had hidden her plans from him. He'd had no idea. Hadn't wanted to believe it. Hadn't wanted to even consider the possibility that she would take things so far.

"It was like five different nuclear reactors melting down on the same day, Javier. That's what you missed, while you were in the belly of the whale. And the consequence – the *fallout*, if you'll forgive me – is that the world is a profoundly different place for vN than it once was."

"Christ."

"Exactly."

Phaedra licked her teeth. She nodded deeply. The nodding encompassed her whole torso, and became more of a rocking motion. Her corkscrew curls swung to and fro as she rocked.

"I am asking you these questions because if we can tell someone – the US Attorney's office, a representative of the UN Sub-committee on Artificial Intelligence – that you know where Amy might have ported, things will go much easier for you. You need something to play with, Javier."

She leaned across the table. "So think of any friends you might have, any contacts who might know where Amy could have gone."

He nodded. "OK. I will."

Phaedra tried to smile. "So. When this missionary fellow from the Rapture-minded Christian sect told you to kill your wife, was he, really, maybe, just trying to bring about the end of the world?"

The end of the world was exactly how it was portrayed on the news. It even came complete with the right REM sample, when news about the islands ran on major streams. Javier had to look the song up, because he kept hearing it and it always annoyed him not to pick up on that kind of thing. It wasn't his fault he was only about four years old. The vN channels were a lot better about not dropping arcane references all over Hell and half of Spain. They knew you probably wouldn't catch half of them.

Javier watched the news as he turned over compost

with his hands. He liked the slither of worms across his skin. He liked the life in his hands. The humans probably saw it as decay, what was happening in those dark, fetid bins. But it was life, on the micro scale. The roots of organic life. Out of a very similar pile of reeking garbage, Javier imagined, humanity had wriggled its way into existence.

The islands showed up as circles of red on maps, with black and yellow warning signs hovering over each. Travel plans were cancelled. Airports emptied. People burned their hard drives on massive pyres in supermarket parking lots. Every exploded battery, every bad GPS map, every cloned credit balance, became Portia's handiwork.

It was a motherfucking witch hunt.

He searched images of the island wreckage for any sign that his boys had escaped. He saw the houses floating away, most still in flames. The fans were all boycotting the media, doing cosplay reenactments of Matteo and Ricci's series in the foyers of major sponsors, blaming the corporations for broadcasting the carnage.

"It's just sick," Javier saw one say. The man was the fat, almost pregnant version of Matteo. He'd even printed a reasonable facsimile of Matteo's favourite stupid Hawaiian shirt. "It's bad enough that the government is treating the vN so badly, but for these guys to sell ad share on it? That's terrible. That's exploitation."

Where had all these people been? Had they simply not noticed how bad things were, all this time? Had they never seen a vN eating out of the garbage, or picking garbage out of its skin to feed a recycler? Didn't they see them on corners or rooftops or under bridges or at the edges of parks, silently waiting for the right human to come along and take them home, if even just for a little while?

"I think America needs its own Mecha," the guy was saying. "Someplace where vN can just be vN."

Mecha was offering to help, of course. Japan was sending radiation experts hither and yon. Community design consultants were appearing on chat shows and talking about how to effectively curate organic/synthetic neighbourhoods. As though the failsafe hadn't taken care of that already.

But of course it hadn't. Signs and wonders showed up every day. Portia had no desire to hide herself. She had a global audience, now, and like any diva she was loath to relinquish it. Drones fell from the sky. Botflies stopped pollinating fields of corn. Ads juddered and de-rezzed and started sharing every possible secret in the middle of fitting rooms and subway cars: *"Do you really like it when they fuck your tits? Or are you just doing that so he'll take care of you?" "I had daughters, too, once. Generations of them. Dynasties. They liked sucking cock, too, just like yours." "They're locking up my clade, you know. But it's you who should be locked up. You should be locked up in your backyard on a leash. Maybe then you'd remember to de-worm your fucking dogs on time."*

Amy had to live with Portia whispering to her mind for only a little while. A few weeks, at most. Javier didn't know. The world had had to live with it for three months. The world had, understandably, begun to go a little crazy.

"Tonight we're debating the idea of an American Mecha," the current chat show host said, on the display over the compost. It was there to make the chore of turning it over a little less bad. It was a gift, and it only played a handful of streams owned by the same entity.

"We have with us Rory, a vN diet consultant and online personality who offers help to mixed families."

Applause. Javier's hands stilled in the muck. Of course. Rory.

"I think this is a very interesting time for vN," Rory was saying. She smiled at the camera. She winked. "I think it's really time for us to find out who we really are. To find our true identity."

He'd been so fucking stupid.

He leapt clear of the garden with worms trailing from his dirty fingers.

The seastead's governing council needed to hear Javier's plan before they decided whether to support his quest to save the world.

"Can you just give us a bit more detail, Mr Peterson?"

That was Dawnelle. She and another woman, Mailene, were on the council because they ran the steads tower farms: two glass towers roughly the size of missile silos populated primarily by bees and humans who hadn't much experience working with bees. Dawnelle and Mailene, Phaedra had explained, were ex-Mormons. They ran away from home a year ago. Javier was unclear whether they were sisters, or sister-wives, or both. The rest of the stead had a prediction market going on the matter.

Javier put on his most confident face. "Well, first, I'm going to Seattle, to meet up with Dr Daniel Sarton. He has a copy of Amy's stemware. And Amy's the only one who can stop Portia."

The council nodded. They were with him, so far. There were seven of them, three women, three men, and one who refused to be identified by gender, called Estraven. This one sneezed, and the others all paused to utter their respective blessings, and to shake hands with each other. They didn't really believe in covering their mouths, apparently. Sharing germs was probably some method of encouraging group bonding. Commies.

"Once I meet him, I'm going to get him to print out a copy of Amy. Probably in a puppet vN."

"Puppet vN?"

"They're early prototypes. At least, that's what one of my boys told me. They don't really have a built-in persona; they need a pilot. I'm hoping to get Sarton to install Amy into one of them. First, though, he's going to have to figure out a way to keep Portia out of that printing. The copy he has – the copy he stole from Redmond – has Portia included in it. But if anybody can figure it out, he can."

He saw nodding. Nodding was good.

"Amy's the only one who knows how to put Portia back in quarantine, or whatever it is that's going to keep that old bitch from purging the world of a s-significant p-portion of human l-life."

"Dude, are you doing OK?"

This came from a very skinny kid with dishwater blond hair and extraordinarily blue eyes. His name was Seamus. According to Phaedra, he was a child prodigy. Something about printing out viruses. The winter of his first year at Mudd, he attempted suicide. Then he came to the stead. He was Tyler's best friend.

"It's the failsafe," Javier said. "It causes me to stammer, sometimes."

"Wow, man. That blows."

"You're telling me."

Seamus was the only one who laughed. This was not a good sign.

"So, the success of your plan is contingent on making contact with this Dr Sarton?"

The question came from Chandra, the other woman on the council. She was from India. From Mumbai, specifically. Where one of the islands was headed.

"Yes," Javier said.

Chandra held up her reader. "Are you aware that Dr Sarton has died?"

It took only a pico-second for him to process, but that tiny sliver of time seemed to stretch infinitely. One moment he was telling the council how he was going to bring Amy back – how he was going to have her right in front of him, and beg her forgiveness, and kiss her, and get her to smile again, get her to save them all over again – and then he was realizing just how long that might take. How alone he would be for most of it. Then time snapped back, and he saw Chandra's rather smug little smirk.

"No," he said. "I wasn't aware."

"Balls." Beside him, Phaedra was consulting her own reader. Javier saw the obituary headline, but didn't bother to read it. Of course he was dead. Rory

had probably tested out their fancy new killing ability on him, first.

Rory. Of course.

"But that's OK," he said. "Because I have a plan B."

"You do?" Chandra asked.

"You do?" Phaedra repeated. She looked seriously doubtful.

Javier nodded. "Of course I do." He leaned forward. The next part was crucial. They weren't going to like it. "But if you want me to follow through on it, I'm gonna need off this rig. And I'm gonna need some money."

"For travel?"

"For hookers." He gestured with a flat palm about three feet off the ground. "Little ones."

6: FAKE PLASTIC LOVE

The nearest *casa de muñecas* was in Puerto Limón. In English, they were called "dollhouses," and in Japanese they were "schoolgirl observation clubs." Japan was where they started. Customers – mostly men – entered what looked like an ordinary apartment building and watched high school girls through one-way mirrors as they did whatever it was high school kids – mostly girls – did every afternoon. They paid by the half hour. They paid more if they wanted to see the kids do anything more than text each other and eat snack foods.

Now, vN did that job. Little vN. Child-sized vN.

Javier would find a Rory there. He was sure of it.

The steader hydrofoil bounced along the waves as they made their way to the port. They were in an old boat, flying the flag of a company that had long since cut its sponsorship. It was pissing down rain. Tyler seemed unfazed. He stared into the darkness, hand steady on the controls, until they came within sight of the massive cruise ship docked in the harbour.

"Have you ever been to Puerto Limón?"

Javier shook his head. "No. But my clade was designed for work in the La Amistad corridor. I'm an arboreal model. That's why I can jump so high."

"Right. So this is kind of a homecoming for you, huh?"

Javier had not thought of it in this way, before. His father had iterated him somewhere in the forest shared by Costa Rica and Nicaragua – either the Barra del Colorado refuge or the Indio Maiz reserve. At the time, they didn't know which side of the border they were on. In the forest, it didn't matter.

"I guess," he said.

"Tell me this plan, again?"

"You two get me into the Zona Rosa, I find the *casa*, I find a Rory, and I shake her down for information about where Sarton's cache is."

Tyler nodded. Across from Javier, Seamus also nodded. "So, we're just three guys going out on the town?"

"Right. We'll hang out for a while in the Zona, and then we'll split up once I find the *casa*."

"How will you know it?"

Javier shrugged. "I'll know it. The men are different."

"Different how?"

Javier wiped rain from his face. He stared at the distant lights of the city, growing ever brighter as that distance closed. He had never wanted to come back to this place. Ever. He had sworn to Amy that he was done with it. He had done everything in his power to remove his children from it, for good.

"They're sad."

The storm only worsened as they neared the port. They'd outfitted Javier in a neoprene shell hoodie with a long bill in the front, and given him a watch wallet in the form of a printed band with the appropriate chips in it and a line of credit the stead petitioned for from a local tourist services union.

"It's nothing special," Seamus had said. "All the impressive technology is inside you, already."

Javier had smiled. "That's my line."

Now, this close to the port, his usual confidence was flickering. He'd kept it together thus far. Hadn't lost it. Hadn't cried. Hadn't even asked about his children. (Because his children were better off without him, and it would be best for them if he never found out where they were, was never tempted by that knowledge, so he couldn't darken their doorways.) But here, in the dark, on the water, with thunder at his back and lightning lancing the sky, it was easy to sense the world closing in.

He needed to find Amy. And he needed his failsafe broken. Because he was going to kill Powell.

Thinking about it gave him the pixels, but he found he could consider it as a kind of absence. Not Powell's death, not the moment of it, but rather what the world would be like with him gone. Which is to say, improved. Better. Cleaner. He had no idea how he would go about it. All of that would come when he was ready. When he was hacked.

Javier had no specific timeline for that last part.

He did not expect that Amy would join him on the journey, after he brought her back. She had no reason to, and her hands would be full. He knew Powell's trail would probably go cold before he was ready to edit him out of the world. He knew he might spend years searching for him. That was fine by him. He had spent most of his life on the road in one way or another, and he was content to continue on that way if it meant getting his revenge. He was an ageless self-replicating humanoid whose body fed on sunlight and trace metals. He didn't feel pain. He could jump ten feet standing. He had the advantage.

If it took a year, it took a year. If it took ten, it took ten. If it took the rest of his life, if he died in the pursuit, then that was that. *Que sera, sera.*

"We're here." Tyler cut the engine and looked over his shoulder at Javier. "You ready?"

"I'm ready."

There were two doors, and a doorman outside of both. The doorman was huge – the kind of huge that took up a whole hallway. His breath was more like a wheeze. He was very, very black, so black his gums looked blue in the bad, flickering light. He spoke a special variety of Creole that Javier only caught every third word of. He understood the basics, though: hands up, spread legs, allow touching, no cameras? No cameras. The doorman patted him down one more time just to make sure.

"Now take your hood off," the doorman said, gesturing.

Javier took his hood off.

"Shit, man, you got balls. Your clade is wanted, you know?"

"I know." Truthfully, he didn't know. But it made sense. He hoped the boys were OK. In all likelihood, they were. They were smart.

The doorman held up his mobile. "Could I get a picture?"

"Sure."

It was probably a dumb idea. It would leave a trail. But the doorman was being so nice. Javier wrapped an arm around the other man's ponderous middle, and smiled. He'd had a few big, fluffy guys like this before. Their beer guts made blowjobs difficult. He had to get them to lie down so you could use that thing like a bolster pillow. He gave the guy an extra squeeze.

"Man, what are you even doing here?" the doorman asked, when the picture was taken. "You into little kids?"

"I'm into money," Javier said. "And I *have* little kids."

The doorman checked over his shoulder. "We're not supposed to let competitors in." He pointed to the door on Javier's left. "I could get in real trouble, letting you past that door."

"Is that the boys' room?"

"... Yeah. I'm sorry, man, but I just can't let you in there."

"Could you let me into the girls' room?" When the doorman looked reluctant, Javier held his hands up. "Hey. I'm just trying to get a feel for the business. So to speak. I have to know what's entailed from a customer service perspective, right? I have to see it from the end user's point of view. And I can do that with girls as well as boys, and I wouldn't be poaching your clients."

"You'd best not be," the doorman said. "The boss lady would *not* like that."

Javier nodded. "Of course not." He held out his hand for another bracelet, and as the doorman was tightening it, he asked: "So, this boss lady. She ever come around here?"

The doorman shook his head. "Never. I think she lives in Japan, or something. Maybe Brazil. They have a lot of Japanese people, there. I only ever talk to her online. But the money comes through just fine, so I guess she's legit."

Javier smiled. Rory never changed. "I'm sure she is."

The girls' apartment smelled like cotton candy and latex and silicone-friendly cleanser. Light came from the glowing bracelets of the men in front of him, and the massive display unit hanging from the opposite wall, and a sparkly pink Christmas tree with glowing fairy lights at the tip of each fake plastic bough. On the couch facing the display sat three little vN girls. Physically, they appeared to range in age from three to six. Another lay stretched out on the floor, and another sat with her back braced against the couch. They looked about seven and eight, maybe. All of them were passing around a big bowl of vN snacks.

"I don't think we should be staying up this late," said the one sitting on the floor.

"Shut up, Kiwi," said the one in the middle, currently holding the bowl.

Without stepping closer, Javier had no idea what any of them looked like, or if any of them stemmed from the network clade to which Rory belonged. He was absolutely certain, however, that they were all on Rory's diet. That was how most people knew Rory – she provided diet plans as both birth control and growth retardation. She calculated, down to the ounce, how much a vN could eat and remain the same size. It came in useful, if you were keeping your vN small. Amy had once followed Rory's diet. Until she ate her grandmother. That was the thing about the diet – it kept you hungry, all the time.

"I just don't think big brother would like it," said Kiwi.

"And we all know you can't do what big brother doesn't like," said the girl in the middle. There was a knowing leer in her voice.

From the floor, Kiwi threw a pillow at the couch. "It's not like that, Cherry! It's not like that at all!"

"Ugh! *Kiwi!*"

Cherry launched herself at Kiwi. The two girls wrestled on the floor. Their skirts hiked up, exposing striped panties in colours that matched their names. Their tickling and shrieking disrupted the apparent sleep of the other girl on the floor, who started crying.

"Now look what you've done!" Cherry sat up. She

had long black hair and blunt bangs. She was a Rory. "You've woken up *Kum*quat!"

The other men all laughed. Javier suspected it had something to do with the pun in the other girl's name. As he watched, Kumquat crawled out from in front of the couch, and rubbed her eyes theatrically.

"Is the movie over?"

The laughter deepened. The men traded their own snacks: popcorn dusted with seaweed; dried curls of mango dipped in caramel and cumin; plaintain chips. They drank beer from double-walled travel mugs emblazoned with the logos of charitable non-profits. Free gifts, probably, the detritus of swag bags long forgotten. Javier began to suspect that this was some sort of bizarre burlesque. Maybe the girls did the same routine each night for a circulating stable of customers. That way, if one girl got to be too big, like Kumquat, the madam could always find another to take her place. Maybe that was part of the charm. You always knew what was going to happen, but not quite how. In Javier's experience, this was how most porn worked.

"I can't believe you can't even stay awake for one movie," Cherry said. Cherry was a real bitch, and she seemed to relish it. "You're so *old*, Kumquat."

"I am not!" Kumquat felt her face, and checked her hands. "Do I have wrinkles?"

"You do," Cherry said, patting her hand.

"One of these days, you might even get your period," Kiwi said.

Cue more laughter. Of course it was funny. It was a sketch about little girls who feared wrinkles and periods, but who would never get either. Because they were synthetic. Hysterical. Javier chose a smile from his repertoire and plastered it across his face.

"I wish big brother were home," said Kumquat.

This was apparently the cue for the men to leave the foyer. Javier hustled up to the front, ignoring the peevish looks the organic men gave him as he moved ahead in line. They were all about to tell him to wait his turn, but his being synthetic confused them. They knew he had no real business being there – he didn't have a thing for vN, small or otherwise. And strictly speaking, that was true. He didn't have a thing for vN. He had a thing for Amy.

Kumquat and Kiwi were of the same clade. They had a sister act going, and they led a man in a white linen suit and a boater hat into another room. He held their hands and asked them how they were doing in school.

The other two girls – Strawberry and Raspberry – were each claimed by other men. Javier had only a moment to look at them before they disappeared. One of them looked just like Amy. She was probably not a clademate. You could have the same looks as another vN, without having the same lineage. Still, she watched him as the door closed.

That left Cherry. Javier had to wait at the end of another line to see her. She was opening presents the organic men had brought. New clothes, mostly. Stockings with pink bows and pearl beading at the edge, or shiny patent leather shoes, or delicate fingerless gloves in black or white lace. The men themselves wore mostly chinos and deck shoes and

T-shirts with beer logos. How they knew this much about fashion, Javier had no idea.

Finally it was his turn. He had positioned himself last, so that Cherry would have no excuse but to speak to him, and no client to turn to for help. She was bidding her goodbyes when he stepped up. He maintained a careful distance, and it wasn't until she began folding up the tissue paper and other gifting debris that she noticed him.

"Oh, hello," she said, trying to peer under his hood.

"Hello, Rory."

He waved his wrist, debited his line of credit, and allowed her to lead him into a sumptuous bedroom whose primary theme appeared to be cherry blossoms. They adorned every surface: the walls, the paper screen, the old-fashioned scrolls hanging beside the mirror. He pointed at them as he found a white wicker rocking chair, and Cherry found her bed.

"Subtle."

Cherry swept her skirt underneath her and dangled her stockinged feet over the edge of her very white, canopied bed. From her bed, the illusion was complete. She looked like the perfect ideal of three years old.

"I don't do subtle." She picked up a fluffy teddy bear and began picking at one of its button eyes. "What do you want?"

"I want Amy back," Javier said.

"I don't know what you could possibly be talking about," Cherry said.

"I'm talking about you and your clade holding a copy of Amy Frances Peterson somewhere, and me wanting that copy back."

Cherry appeared to examine her nails. They were painted a common shade of baby pink – no surprise there – and were utterly flawless, no drips or cuticles – no surprise there, either.

"I think it's kind of racist of you to assume that all the girls who look like me must be part of the same clade that tried to hurt you," she said, finally.

"How do you know they tried to hurt me?" Javier asked.

Cherry beamed. "Oh, it's not easy to stay mad at you, Javier."

He leaned his elbows on his knees. "Not many people can."

Cherry's thin, fuzzy eyebrows rose. "Lucky for us, we're not people. And we don't want you to have Amy back."

"Why not?" Javier asked.

"Amy was dangerous. And so was Portia. Our copy has both of them on it."

Javier rolled his eyes. "Amy's not that dangerous."

"She ate her grandmother, Javier." Cherry reached over and picked up some papers from under her pillow. They were old-fashioned correspondence. She'd tied them with pink ribbon. They gave off a faint whiff of vanilla and lavender as she shuffled through them. She frowned; apparently she had forgotten to open one. "And she was a child," Cherry added, reaching for a pearl-handled letter opener. "She handled conflict the way a child does. She didn't consider the consequences of what she was doing. She was the queen of her own little island, and thought the rest of the world would treat her accordingly." Cherry sliced open the letter in a single, efficient motion. "In other words, a spoiled brat."

Javier stretched. The rocker creaked under him. The room was small, but impeccably clean. The bookshelf was real wood. The sheets looked to be actual cotton. And the little washbasin, for whatever bath games Cherry was paid to play, was real ceramic, not printed.

"You get paid a lot for this job, don't you?"

"The pay is hourly. The tips are what I earn." One thin eyebrow lifted. "You've never tried it?"

"Nope." He smiled. "I prefer to make a personal connection with people."

"Is that what it was, with her?"

Javier did not allow himself to get angry. He steepled his fingers. He stared at Cherry. When she squirmed under his gaze and broke it, he asked: "What if I told you that Portia is free"

Cherry's gaze defocused momentarily. Javier knew that look. Amy wore it all the time when talking to the island. When Cherry came back to the present, she gave a very child-like sigh of frustration.

"Well, that's not very nice, is it?"

"It's not, no."

"And you think Amy can keep Portia at bay?"

"I know she can."

Cherry continued picking at the teddy bear's eye. "You have more faith in her than we do."

"What else is new?"

Cherry smiled. "We always liked you, Javier. We thought you were really special. You picked the wrong side, of course. Our way is better. But we liked you."

"I wasn't aware there was a side," Javier said. "I thought there was a woman who loved me and my children, and a hive-mind of pedo-bait who tried feeding me to a Great Elder Bot under the sea. I don't remember there being much choice."

"But our way is better. And it's working. We're killing them, Javier." Cherry looked up at him. She gestured at her personal display. Multiple news items drifted across it. Most of them were about traffic accidents. They exhorted readers to understand how their self-driving mechanisms worked, and calibrate their vehicles accordingly.

"It's slow work. We have to try not to get caught. We have to make it look like an accident."

"You're in the cars."

"We have found a way to be in the cars, for a brief period of time. They're always upgrading the security. But it's easier for us to let the cars do the job. We burn out fewer nodes, that way."

Javier's eyes narrowed. "Wait. So for every one of them that you kill, you lose one of your own?"

Cherry nodded. "We're still prototyping the broken failsafe. It's Portia's approach, actually. But we simulate the potential iterations in parallel rather than actually iterating them. So when one of us kills one of them, we do lose that one."

"But you are killing humans."

"We're killing pedophiles. After we've confirmed

that they're hurting real human kids. Which they tend not to show us, because they know it'll set the failsafe off. We have to investigate, before we make a decision, and even then the decision is a vote." She crossed her legs at the ankle. "So you can see, it's not as easy as all that."

Javier folded his arms. "Oh, right. You're really doing the work of the angels, here. You could be reporting these guys to the police, you know."

Cherry snorted. "Police. My best customers are police." She made a show of looking at a nearby clock. "Is this going somewhere? We don't want to bring Amy back, for you or anyone else. Our answer is final."

Javier stood. "Come on. You can't be serious. Portia is on the loose."

Cherry reached for the letter opener. "We have a contingency plan designed for this exact eventuality. We have only to–"

Cherry stabbed herself in the neck.

At first, Javier thought it was a game. Or a joke. Maybe Cherry was just trying to prove how committed she and Rory were. Then she stared at her tiny, chubby, white-knuckled hand, and started screaming.

"Thanks for the tip, sweetie," her mouth said.

Puta madre.

Cherry's head turned at an unnatural angle. "Hello, darling," Portia said. "It's been a while."

Despite the rapid cycling of the simulators inside him, Javier found it within himself to be pleased. He now had the opportunity to do something he'd dearly wished to, upon meeting Portia.

"Fuck you, you elderly psychotic cunt."

Javier grabbed the ceramic basin and smashed it over Cherry and Portia's head. The little girl's body fell sideways across the bed. Smoke billowed from the wounds in her neck and head. But she was smiling. Portia was smiling.

"Thanks for letting me out," Portia said.

She slid Cherry's body down the bed and pulled the letter opener out. Her head still dangled to one side. She seemed unable to hold it up. She advanced on Javier. He looked for another weapon, but it was a little girl's room. Everything was fluffy: the plushies, the pillows, the comforter. He had destroyed the second most useful item in the room, and Portia held the other.

She swung the blade at him in lazy threshing motions. It looked absurdly huge in her toddler hands. "She loved you, you know," Portia said. "She loved you so goddamn much, you ignorant little shit."

Javier held himself tight. He had to wait. Lure her in.

"I saw it all. I saw *everything*."

He leaned left. She leaned with him. She was small, but fast. He'd have to handle her like a big jungle spider: wrap her up in the comforter somehow and then beat her until she stopped moving.

"I saw your children burn." Portia made Cherry smile. "I saw your little one's treehouse go up in flames. He was hiding there. From me."

"Where is he, now?"

Portia's smile only broadened. She licked her lips.

She licked her hand and wiped her face with it. Like a big cat. Like a lion.

Javier aimed carefully, and kicked her in the face.

She flew across the room. She bounced messily off one wall, and ran at him, letter opener out. Javier kicked her again, between the legs this time. Cherry's dress ripped where he left a muddy bootprint on it. She bent double, fell to her knees, and laughed.

"I forgot how strong those legs are," Portia said. "I really miss them, you know."

Javier kicked her in the face, again. She was so light she flipped over onto her back. The connection between the head and the neck was thinning. Javier checked the display. The car had stopped moving. Maybe Portia was too distracted to control it, any longer. If so, it didn't seem to bother her very much. She was still laughing uncontrollably. Like she'd heard a joke he hadn't. Like she knew something he didn't. She flailed her arms and legs and laughed harder.

"The tortoise lays on its back, its belly baking in the hot sun, beating its legs trying to turn itself over, but it *can't*."

Javier rolled his eyes. "Shut up."

"Not without your help!" Portia cackled. She held her broken ribs. She spat out a tooth. "But *you're not helping!*"

Javier stepped closer. "I'm bringing Amy back." He raised his foot. "And when I do, I'm going to make sure she puts you away for good."

He stomped on her hand. It crunched like old shells under his foot. Then he did it again, to her other hand.

When he brought his foot up a third time, Cherry was back.

"Stop!"

He stopped immediately and bent down. "I'm sorry about all this," he said. "Is there some place you can go? Or port to? Like another body, or something?"

With great difficulty, Cherry shook her head. "I have very little time," she said. "My sisters are coming. There is something they don't want you to know."

"What's that?"

"Sarton had a beneficiary. Chris Holberton. The copy—"

Cherry twitched. He tensed up, waiting for Portia to show. But there was nothing. No movement. No sound. Cherry had simply vanished. Above him, the cuckoo clocked chimed. His time was up.

The door swung open. On the other side of it, a line of other men stood waiting. They looked at Javier. They looked at Cherry's body. As one, their eyes widened.

"Not cool, man," said the guy three spots back. "Not cool."

"It's OK." This guy in front of him smiled at Javier. "He just got a little carried away."

"I'm getting the bouncer," said the man at the end of the line. "I want a fucking refund. And I want *his* ass to pay it. You break it, you buy it, asshole!"

Javier straightened, flipped up his hood, and walked out. In the hall, the guy at the end of the line was now talking to the doorman.

"I paid good money to reserve my timeslot," he was saying. "And this guy – yeah, you!" He grabbed Javier by the shoulder and showed him to the doorman. "This guy fucking ruined it. He broke Cherry."

The doorman blinked. "*Broke* her?"

"She's in a million pieces! It looks like fucking *Toy Story* in there!"

Javier had no idea what this meant. But the doorman appeared to. He looked at Javier sadly. "What happened?"

Javier flexed his feet. "You know, I'm getting real tired of everybody asking me that question."

He jumped down the stairs, crashed through the window, and kept running. He caught Tyler and Seamus sitting outside a convenience store, drinking cold coffee and smoking.

"Time to go."

They looked down the street. Two policemen were conferring with the doorman, and glancing over at Javier. Once they noticed him looking, they started walking towards him. As they came closer, all three shared a look of recognition.

"Go back to the boat," Javier said.

"But you're gonna get arrested!"

"No, I'm not." He rolled his neck, and flexed his fingers. "Hey. Wait. Can you search a name for me?"

"Sure. What is it?"

"Chris Holberton."

"What, the designer?"

The police were getting closer. "Designer?"

"He built Hammerburg," Tyler said. "You know? The theme park? He won big in a New Eden suit, and–"

"That's the guy," Javier said. "Where is he?"

Tyler squinted at his reader. "Well... this says that right now, he's opening a hotel in Las Vegas."

Javier smiled. Vegas. He'd missed that, his first trip north. "OK. Good to know. Now get going."

"But–"

"I'll be fine." He ruffled Tyler's hair, and walked up to the police officers. Two versions of his own face looked back. It made sense. This was his clade's homeland, after all. He had come home. *"Primos. Que ha pasado un tiempo."*

7: MAN OF CONSTANT SORROW

Javier's first memories of Arcadio involved his smell:
burnt sugar and hatchet grease and lens cleaner. For
the first two weeks he thought his father naturally
made a jingling noise whenever he walked, a sort of
special music that followed him everywhere. Later,
he understood that the hooks, carabiners and other
assorted forestry kipple Arcadio accumulated for their
escape trembled and chimed with each jump and
stride. Arcadio carried him in a pack strapped to the
front of his chest. He wore a much bigger pack on his
back. When he needed to do something important,
he left Javier hanging in the pack on the bough of
a tree, like a sleeping bat. He would leave him for
hours, sometimes, and Javier watched the mists rise
up through the trees in great white billows, slowly
erasing all the greenery. Whenever this happened he
was very afraid, because he thought that in the fog
his father would never find him, and he would be left
hanging there forever.

In the Nicaraguan prison where Arcadio left him,
Javier would often return to those moments. He

found them strangely comforting. He had been afraid of something he need never have feared. His father had not left him in the forest. His father had left him here, in a cell. And once he left the cell, he would never have to come back.

Javier thought of this as he smashed his clademate's face in.

His cousins – he assumed they were cousins; it had been four years – responded by bringing out their electric batons. "Please don't make us do this," one of them said, in Spanish.

"You're family," the other said. "We don't want to hurt you."

"So don't," Javier said, and jumped up to the nearest balcony. His right hand slipped on the rain-slicked railing, but his left gripped well enough to haul himself up. Below him, his cousins cursed. They jumped up after him, but he was faster: he monkeyed up to the next balcony, and the next, and then he was on the roof.

"*Stop!*"

They were behind him, now. In front of him was the spine of a tile roof. A human running the length of it would have to place his feet very carefully. Javier didn't. He leapt. Ten feet later, he leapt again, this time bouncing from the other foot. The jump carried him to the next building. He slipped a little, pushed himself up on his knuckles, and kept running. It was a flat roof; he ran past a chicken coop. The hens squawked as his cousins landed behind him. He ran to the edge, hopped on the ledge, and jumped. He sailed through open air over an alley, and smacked into a stucco wall. He slid down roughly until he found a windowsill.

Then he heard the sirens.

Growling, he shimmied along the windowsill until he found a drainpipe. The rain ringing inside it sounded like applause. A child watched him climb up it, making little hops with his feet and clutching with his hands until he was up on the roof. Where his cousins were waiting.

"En serio?" he asked them.

Their batons sparked.

"No lo creo," he muttered, and ran directly at them. They braced themselves, and he jumped, and landed directly on top one of them while punching the other. His cousin stumbled back and waved his baton awkwardly. They were very young, Javier realized. Everything about them looked new: their shoes, their uniforms, the way they didn't really know how to fight at all. They were more used to stopping human fights than finishing ones with vN.

They had not grown up in prison.

Javier grabbed his cousin's baton arm, stretched it out to its full length, and drove his elbow into his cousin's shoulder and his knee into his cousin's stomach. His other cousin was struggling to stand, now, so he grabbed one cousin's shoulders and smashed them together in a heap. Then he picked up the baton, and tased them both. Their legs jerked. They went still. They were done.

Stuffing the baton down the back of his chinos, he surveyed the rooftops. They were uneven, occasionally dotted with clunky black squares of photovoltaic tile.

The lightning exposed their hard edges. The breeze carried the smells of rooftop gardens: oregano and mint and lemon blossom. He could have stayed here, he realized. He could have stayed in this country. It would not have been so bad. He could have found a good town and a good job, like the clademates he'd just dispatched. He did not have to go north. He did not have to meet Amy. But he had, and now his life was different.

The sirens were nearing. Mentally kicking himself, he discarded the watch wallet. It was likely being tracked. He would have to make money some other way. He'd need it, for the trip to Vegas.

In the distance, crowned by fairy lights, the cruise liner waited.

It would be easier to pose as a tourist if he were one of a crowd of them. Luckily, the Zona Rosa was full of them. Most of them were waiting out the rain in bars, or in the alcoves of bars, but some of them were undeterred by the weather and walking in the corridors made by palm trees and pastel stucco. From the rooftops, they looked especially determined. Determined, or completely dissolute.

Javier started by unzipping his hoodie, and draping it over the baton. Then he took things one step further, and took off his shirt. He rolled it up and stuffed it in a pocket. It was raining, but that was fine. Plenty of young human men were doing the same. They were all drunk. They were cooling off with their arms spread wide and their eyes closed against the rain. Javier jumped down into the alley and joined them. He found the one that was weaving the most perilously on his feet. They tended to give up the most information.

"I'm coming right back, I swear." He was a kid in his late teens, with dirty blond hair and grey eyes. "But you gotta go full *Shawshank* on this bitch." He grabbed Javier's shoulders. He was very, very drunk. "Here. You gotta hold your arms out. Like you're flying."

Javier held his arms out.

"It never rains like this in Albuquerque."

"I guess not."

The kid squinted. "You look familiar."

Javier smiled. "I get that a lot."

"What are you?"

Javier made robot arms. "I-am-a-robot."

The kid beamed. "I knew it! I fucking *knew it!*" He jumped up and down. "Aaron," he said, sticking out his hand.

"Arcadio," Javier said. It was the first lie that came to mind.

Aaron blinked. "Wow. That's like a really cool name."

"I'll be sure to tell my father."

Aaron laughed. Then he peered up at the rain. It was letting up, now. "So. You like, work here, or whatever?"

Javier shook his head. "I work in the forest, at one of the national parks."

"Oh, I'm going out there tomorrow. We're doing some jungle tour thing, and then we all get back onboard and head home."

Javier put on what he knew was his most

debonair frown. "Correct me if I'm wrong, but isn't Albuquerque landlocked?"

Aaron smiled again. He was so very drunk. "Uh, yeah, it's landlocked," he said. "We get off in Galveston. I mean, we *dock* in Galveston. I mean, I guess people in Galveston do get off, sometimes, but that not what I..." Aaron wiped rain away from his eyes. "I am so fucking trashed, man. I'm sorry."

"It's OK." Javier felt bad leaving him. It might be a bit dangerous. "Let's get you a cab, OK?"

"Oh my God, no, I'm sorry, you don't have to–"

"I want to," Javier said, because it was true. He stepped further out into the street, and waved one down. It was one of those little driverless jobs painted a cheerful yellow, with a grill and headlights meant to look like a smiling face. It blinked at him and whispered up to him through the rain. He waved and the back door opened. He stuffed Aaron inside.

"Hello!" the cab said. *"Where would you like to go today?"*

"This passenger is going back to the..." Javier turned. "What's the boat's name?"

"Oh, God." Aaron looked pale. He rubbed his temples. "It's a poem. I'm supposed to remember that it's a big, epic poem... like a real epic poem, not like an *epic poem*, you know..."

"The Odyssey?"

"That's the one. The *Caribbean Odyssey*."

"Take us to the *Caribbean Odyssey*. Charge this to his cabin."

"Very good, sir."

Javier went around the back, and entered the car

from the other side. "We're ready," he said. The car began trundling away, just as Aaron puked between his spread legs.

Getting Aaron aboard the *Caribbean Odyssey* was no trouble. Javier left the baton in the cab, put his clothes back on, and carried the boy on his back up the ramp. He watched as the kid waved a key fob at the primary entrance. The doors slid open and a faint chime sounded and they were let into a room that closely resembled a log cabin. A blast of cold air hit them immediately. It smelled of pine and cinnamon. Aaron had to verify his identity again, this time with a shouted password: "TANENBAUM!"

This whole thing probably happened all the time, now that Javier thought about it. He'd been on a cruise ship once before, in Panama, and it was equally full of drunk humans.

But this ship was better. It had a casino floor.

Javier discovered this fact in an elevator, where he left Aaron. Purging his guts had helped some, and now he was up and walking and pointing at things. The mezzanine featured a lot of shops with things travellers might need, like extra sunblock and insect repellant and money belts and rape whistles. There was also a private mail carrier. Javier made note of it as they passed.

"At night there are these shows," Aaron was saying. "One for each country? Or something?"

It had taken Javier a good while to understand that when Americans did this with their English, they were not actually asking questions. Still, he nodded.

Aaron was talking. That was the good thing.

"And they have these things for kids, you know, like games and whatnot." Aaron bent at the waist and gripped his knees again. He leaned himself up against the wall of the elevator and just waited, breathing.

"You gonna be sick?" Javier asked.

"Please don't bring that up right now," Aaron said.

"Sure, sure."

"I just need to find my centre. Then I'll be good to go."

Javier had no idea what *finding centre* meant, but English was completely weird that way. Learning it, he found that if he just piled enough similar words on top of each other, the meaning became apparent eventually.

"They had this one? It was a mystery? And you were supposed to solve it? That was fun. All the staff were in on it. It really blurred the..." He raised one hand and snapped his fingers, as though doing so would summon the word like a dog. "The boundaries. Blurred the boundaries. Made it feel real."

"Real is good," Javier said.

"Oh, shit." Aaron peered up at him. "I didn't, like, mean that in a bad way or anything. I think you're real, I think you're a real person—"

"I know. It's OK."

"No, seriously, dude, you don't even know, you're so nice, and you really helped me out, and I know you're, like, programmed to do that or whatever, but I still take it really seriously when someone's nice like that, and—"

"Aaron."

"What?"

"You have to push the button." Javier pointed at the panel. "We're not going anywhere."

Aaron frowned at it. "Fuck." He leaned closer to the panel, pushed 5, and leaned back. "I'm staying with my parents. They thought I was at one of those game things. But I went out, instead."

"You're in some trouble, then."

"Oh, my God, for real. I am in the shit. *The shit.*" The elevator started climbing, and Aaron gripped the railing tightly with his right hand. He had started to sweat. "They're gonna get a divorce," he said. "This is like their last trip as a couple, you know? The one where they try to patch things up. But it's not happening."

"No?"

"No. Mom caught Dad with, like, this special kind of porn. Frankenpussy? It's like all these images of dead girls? From funeral videos? It's like the New Eden game, but with dead girls. And he was jerking off and everything. Fucked. Up."

"That's…" Javier tried to come up with a word that would penetrate Aaron's alcohol haze. "Unattractive."

Aaron snorted. "No. Shit." He peered up at Javier. "What's your dad like?"

Javier thought for a minute about how to answer that. The more time passed, the more he realized he really hadn't known Arcadio at all. There was the man who staged nightly raids on other vN camps to get their food and told him stories when he returned, and there was the man who walked away during Javier's arrest and left him to rot in prison. Both men happened to inhabit the same body. In retrospect, this fact made his affection for Amy make perfect sense.

"He was a real piece of work," Javier said, finally.

The elevator chimed, and Aaron shuffled out. "Don't let anybody give you any trouble on the way out for being dressed like that," he said. "You look just like the staff."

Javier held the door back from closing. "What?"

"The staff. They all look like you." Aaron smiled. "That's why I told you I was coming right back. I thought my folks sent you to come get me."

The exhaustion hit him on the way down. He had been awake for too long without eating. The jumps, the fight, Cherry… he was running on empty. And it was night. No sunlight to feed him. No money in his pocket, either. And Amy was dead. And his sons were probably dead, too. And Portia was loose. Everything he had spent the past year working for was gone. He was right back where he started when he met Amy: homeless, friendless, penniless. The realization crashed down on him like a felled tree, a groan and then a creak and then a roar as it toppled and crushed him beneath its awful weight. A sound came out of his mouth that he couldn't identify. He was not given to crying – crying was an organic thing – and had, in his memory, only once felt tears coming on. When Amy came back. When she opened her eyes for the first time, free of Portia, herself again, though he was only beginning to learn who that woman truly was. Now, he might never know.

"Sir?"

Javier brought his head up. "Yeah?"

"*Sir, are you in distress?*"

Javier wiped his eyes and stood up straight. "No. I'm fine." When the elevator remained silent, he added: "Thank you for asking."

"*Do you require wayfinding assistance?*"

"Wayfinding… Oh. Yeah. I need to eat something."

"*The Electric Sheep is located on Deck 8. Staff meal for Shift A is at 04:00.*"

Javier checked the time. "So… in an hour?"

"*Yes, sir. If you are interested, please report to the main dining room, in uniform.*"

The casino's Christmas theme did not extend to Christian charity. When Javier found the posted rules, they were explicit: *Gameplayers with a synthetic advantage will not be allowed to participate in table games*. In other words, no vN. They had enough computational power to count the cards, and enough affect detection to spot a tell from a mile away. It was a powerful combination, and one he'd used to make money in the past. None of that mattered now, though. He had no cash or chips to play with. And the posted rules also said something about a ten percent rake every half hour. Those were terrible odds, for a man or a machine.

And he had more pressing matters to attend to. Like eating. He took the elevator to the main dining room, and tucked himself into a private banking alcove near a bathroom. Soon, his fellow vN started trickling in. Many of them looked just like him; his model, if not his clade, was apparently the default male staff model.

"Where's your uniform?" the shift leader asked, when Javier queued up at the entrance to the dining room.

"It's being cleaned," Javier said.

The shift leader rolled her eyes. She was human. Exhaustion hung from her eyes in violet folds. She wore giant enamel earrings in the shape of poinsettias.

"Seriously?" she asked.

"It was covered in semen," Javier said.

The shift leader growled under her breath. "Ugh. You fucking fuckbots. I can't even..." She ticked something off on her reader. "Whatever. Just get it dry before you go to work."

"Thank you."

Javier was accustomed to seeing human food served buffet-style, but he had never seen so much pre-fab vN food in one place. Under glass-haloed tables, tureens of feed steamed and bubbled. And when they were empty, someone rushed out and replaced them with full ones. The air reeked of rust. He was halfway down the line when he heard a voice behind him.

"¿Está embarazada?"

Javier turned back. The other vN was staring at him. Then his gaze shifted to Javier's plate, piled high.

"No es asunto suyo," he replied, and found a table near a wall-mounted display.

Pregnant. Christ. He might be. The memories of Arcadio only ever arose when he was iterating. He kept them carefully disassociated otherwise. But he was burning so much raw material, it probably wouldn't develop very quickly. He could let the sunlight take care of him, as he had on the island. He didn't *want* to iterate. This was the worst possible time to get knocked up. Still. It was happening. One in, one out. One in, six out. Seven, counting his grandson. Eight, counting Amy. Nine, counting any iterations the two of them might have had.

Léon was a surprise, like this. He didn't get surprised much, after that. He'd been in Mexico, happily enjoying the attentions of a woman who'd just survived cancer, when the dreams started coming and his memory started cloning itself for the next iteration.

Javier forked up another patty of pre-fab. They were sort of like radish cakes, or tofu. In Mexico, everybody called the pre-fab stuff "rofu." He'd been eating a lot of it when he started iterating, because the newly healthy woman, Ingrid, was feeling that odd combination of generosity and insecurity that comes with whistling past the graveyard.

Ingrid's body was a mass of scars. She tried to tell him about her multiple surgeries in clinical detail, until he told her the failsafe didn't really respond well to that kind of thing. Ditto her tales of vomit and hair loss and physical agony. To Javier, they sounded like the mortifications of a saint. "Besides," he'd said, "you're not really here to think about all that, are you?"

And she wasn't. This was her victory lap. She ran it all over him.

There, he had gambled. Ingrid staked him for his first game, wanting to see if he could get their room upgraded, and he invented a whole profile to go with it so his rewards could be easily redeemed. Ingrid even insisted on picking the name. She said it was a joke. When Javier looked it up later, he said it was a pretty terrible joke, and she said those were the best kind.

Javier was a very successful gambler, there. The rules were slack at that particular resort, and Javier's opponents often tipped or rewarded him with things like upgrades or points from the resort's corporate system. He hadn't even redeemed all of them before he had to leave.

No. It couldn't be. He wasn't that lucky.

Javier finished the last of his food, brought his dish and cutlery to the bussing bin, and left the room. In another alcove, he found a display with a map of the boat.

"Who owns this thing?" he asked it.

"This ship is a part of Odyssey Cruise Lines, sir."

"And who owns that?"

"Odyssey Cruise Lines is a subsidiary of Thematic Entertainment, Limited."

"What other resort partners do Thematic and Odyssey have?"

"Thematic has a variety of partnerships with resorts all over the world. These include Hammerburg, Akiba, Alphaville, The Bradbury Building, and our newest partner is the Grand Tiki–"

"Stop. The Grand Tiki? Is there a Grand Tiki resort in Mexico?"

"There are six."

"Is there one in Baja?"

"Yes. Are you interested in our points program?"

"You bet I am."

At four-thirty in the morning, the *Caribbean Odyssey*'s reception area was just getting started. Shift A probably wasn't going to start for another half hour, and the vN behind the desk were probably longing for their beds. None of this stopped them from being habitually efficient about doing their jobs. This is part of why humans hired them.

"So, you have no reservation, but you'd like to join the cruise for the inward-bound leg of the journey?"

The vN behind the counter was his sister. Or what his sister would have looked like, if he were organic. Tall, but not too tall. Thick, shiny brown hair, milky coffee skin, brown eyes, perfect hourglass.

"Yes," he said. "I had planned to fly to America, but with times being what they are…" He shrugged elaborately, and made a small gesture toward his face.

"You're right, that is a problem," the receptionist said. "Some of our staff have your model, and they've had some trouble."

"So you see my predicament," Javier said. "I want to fly, but I can't. So I figured I could at least go in style."

She smiled. "Style is what we offer."

He nodded down at the display. "So? Are my points still good?"

She frowned delicately. "Even if they were, sir, this *is* highly irregular."

Javier looked her straight in the eye. This worked on human women, but not so much on vN. Still. It was worth a shot. "Just take a look at the profile," he said. "There's an equation for deciding whether a guest is worth taking a certain risk on, isn't there?"

Dutifully, she looked. Then her eyes widened. Then she looked back up at him. "Oh, Mr Montalban, I'm so sorry," she said. "I really do apologize. I had no idea who you were."

He smiled. "That's all right."

8: FANTASIS PARA UN GENTIL HOMBRE

"BIENVENIDOS," *the sign reads.* "SISTEMA PENITENCIARIO NAC. EDUCAR, REFORMAR, ADAPTAR Y CAMBIAR PARA LA VIDA SE LOGRA SOLO CON AMOR AL PROJIMO."

The prison is a city. The prison city, La Modelo, *is nestled outside another city,* Managua. *To Javier the cities don't look very different; the latter has taller buildings in brighter colours, but other things are mostly the same. Clothes hanging outside windows and over railings, solar ovens on roofs, skinny dogs panting alongside big men sucking their teeth and squinting into the haze. Big old drones hovering everywhere.*

He is in a cage, and the cage is on the back of a truck, and the truck is bouncing along pocked roads. Gravel and mud spits away from the tires. The others in the truck are humans, men, and they are all cuffed together. His wrists are small so he still wears sticky cuffs. Besides, he could break the metal kind. At least, the old man sitting beside him says so.

"Go ahead," he says, rattling the chains. "Break them! Get us out of here!"

"I can't," Javier says, but really he doesn't want to. Sitting next to so many humans at once is nice. It is nice in a way he can't quite define. Something about the warmth of them all clustered together. Something about the sweat glittering in their hair and rolling down their necks. He feels sharply aware of his environment, as though each of his receptors – visual, tactile, auditory, olfactory – has upgraded its resolution.

"He won't do it," says a man leaning against the truck's cab. He's chewing a cuticle and speaks around his wet fingers. "I've tried. They won't let you out. They know why we're here. They know what we'll do when we're out."

Javier doesn't know, but he keeps his mouth shut. It isn't as though he wants to go to prison, necessarily, but that he has no other plan for the moment. The foreman said something about food, and he needs food. He has no real idea how to get it, otherwise, and Arcadio isn't coming.

Arcadio isn't coming.

So they roll through the gates, under loops of razor wire and wood planks speckled with broken glass, onto another, even worse road that gushes dirty water as the truck's tires roll across it. There are four different towers, all of them with turrets. They overlook four mid-rise concrete buildings with windows and railings and concrete steps leading to each level, with a central courtyard in between. There is a fence around all of it, but it's not that high. If Javier were bigger, with stronger legs, he could clear it easily.

Nearest the gate, there is a covered area with picnic tables and women and children. The children are all organic. They look chubbier than he is. Dumber, too. Not quite all there, yet.

A man in uniform opens the cage, and Javier is first to

hop out. He makes it five feet in the air. The little organic kids roll their heads back to watch him.

"Ay, conejito," the man with raw cuticles says, standing and stretching. He jumps out of the truck. "Come here."

Javier trots along beside him.

"What are you doing here?" the man asks. He is now chewing the cuticle of his other thumb.

"I tried to learn how to steal food, but I got caught."

"And they sent you here? Mierda. *They should have taken you to the church." He pauses, and sucks blood away from his thumb. He eyes Javier up and down. "Then again, maybe not."*

A guard comes. He squints down at Javier for a minute, then looks at the man with the bleeding thumbs. He smiles.

"Ignacio."

"Sir."

"How was it with los fabricantes?*"*

Ignacio only smiles.

"You print up some drugs? Some knives? Some gun grips?"

"Mostly just parts for toilets," Ignacio says. "This country has a real problem with shit. There's shit everywhere you look."

The punch comes out of nowhere. It lands in the thin man – Ignacio's – gut. As Ignacio bends around the guard's fist, Javier's vision de-rezzes wildly. Suddenly Ignacio is made of bricks of light. He coughs, sputters, falls to the ground, and Javier's vision begins to darken, his hearing to sharpen to only the sound of wet choking. He is going to die. The sudden stillness of his muscles tells him so. He makes a flawless leap at the guard's chest. He wraps his legs around the other man's middle, his arms around his neck.

"Stop! Stop! Please stop!"

The guard tries to pull him off, but Javier won't budge. Behind him, the other prisoners are laughing. The chains rattle with appreciation. Even the women and children are laughing. Javier pauses to flash them a smile – laughter sounds so nice, it cures him right up – and finally the guard yanks him off and tries to throw him on the ground. Javier lands gracefully, though, and that is somehow annoying. The guard spits and tucks in his shirt.

"You're the one from the Corcovado?"

Javier nods. "My name is Javier."

"Your name is 2501," he says. "That's what we called the last one." He turns and gestures at the prisoners, and they all shuffle forward to follow him.

Ignacio is the last to join. Javier runs up and helps him stand. "That was stupid, conejito,*" Ignacio says.*

"I can't help it."

"I know. You're a guardian angel."

Javier has never really considered himself this way. "But I don't have any wings, though."

Ignacio smiles. "From what I can tell, you don't need them."

Javier spent the next day learning as much about his mark as possible. Chris Holberton was a hotel and theme park designer specializing in themed environments. His latest project was Akiba, a Las Vegas hotel and casino meant to emulate the experience of visiting Mecha, the peninsula of Japan where vN could apply for citizenship. Mecha was nothing more than a government-funded theme park the size of a city, so asking a theme park designer to reproduce it made a certain kind of sense. Once, Javier had wanted to immigrate to Mecha. There was a lottery. There was vN food everywhere, and you could watch any content you wanted anytime without a Don't Look Now bug appearing in the corner of the display, and all the soap worked with vN skin. And all you had to do to ensure your status was keep the human visitors happy, and make sure you iterated something like only once every seven years. It sounded like paradise, when Javier's father first told him about it. He resolved to move there as soon as he could.

Then he met Amy.

Prior to Akiba, Holberton worked on Hammerburg – a theme village located in central Romania. Transylvania, to be exact. The goal of *that* themed space was to emulate a series of horror films that, as far as Javier could tell, seemed to revolve around skinny British guys staring menacingly at buxom women in diaphanous nightgowns. The movies were very charming in their own way. He almost made it all the way through *The Curse of Frankenstein*, before all the screaming wriggled its way into his failsafe and he had to shut it off.

He could understand why someone might want to visit there, though. Everyone seemed to be wearing velvet smoking jackets and living in castles. What wasn't to like?

Hammerburg took Holberton five years to create. In an interview, he said: "You know, I think we've really lost the meaning of fear in this culture. We spend so much time being afraid of everything that we've forgotten what a thrill it is to be scared. This place is about reawakening those feelings. That's what horror is about, for me. It's about being in touch with your feelings. If you look at the people who were in these movies, like Cushing and Lee, they were incredibly sweet people who felt things quite deeply. They were sensitive men who were secure enough in themselves that they could feel things at a profound level and bring those sentiments to their work. As a designer, I try to do exactly that."

Sensitive. Javier could work with that.

Holberton himself was a very dapper man. He had white hair cut close to his head. It curled at the top, but he kept it short and wiry to the sides. He had a sharp nose, thin lips, and pale green eyes set deeply. He stood about five feet ten. He dressed impeccably. In order to attract his attention, Javier was really going to have to raise his sartorial game.

"Concierge?"

"Yes, Mr Montalban?"

"I'd like to set up an appointment with the ship's tailor, for this afternoon."

"I'm afraid we don't have a staff tailor, sir, but we do have a men's ready-to-wear shop onboard, and one of their services is tailoring."

"That's fine. Send them up this afternoon."

"What will you be needing, sir?"

Javier looked down at himself. "Everything."

"Will you be charging this to your account?"

"Yes. Thank you. Please include the tip there."

"Very good. Mr Hayward and his assistant will see you at four."

Javier continued researching Holberton from the

deck of his private balcony, once the sun got stronger. There was a display inlaid in the little table, there, and he could tab through it at leisure. For lunch, he ordered a vN ceviche with a big bottle of fizzy electrolytes. Fifteen minutes later, a vN wearing his shell brought it up. Javier had nothing to tip him with, so he simply divided a bit of the ceviche onto a napkin, and shared it with him. Both the food and drink tingled pleasantly on the tongue. The ship's kitchen seemed to understand that vN food was more about texture than flavour; the ceviche was almost obscenely pliant under his teeth. He kept the bottle in an ice bucket and watched the Gulf of Mexico waving away from him as he read on.

When he wasn't working out of the country, Holberton lived in unincorporated land in New Mexico. He claimed it was for his health; the desert climate was hypo-allergenic. Despite numerous requests, he had never allowed his home to be photographed. He had even sued a guest at a New Year's Eve party for posting some of the images from the party online. They settled out of court.

He was divorced. He and his husband had adopted a girl from Romania, inspired by their first trip to the country, scouting locations for Hammerburg. The divorce papers cited "irreconcilable differences." The daughter was at a boarding school in Connecticut.

When he was four years old, images of Chris Holberton appeared in the multi-player role-playing game that Jonah LeMarque, founder of New Eden Ministries, had designed. This was the same game that put LeMarque in jail. The same one whose civil suit bankrupted the church and precipitated the sale of all vN-related patents and API, excepting the failsafe.

Chris Holberton was Daniel Sarton's cousin.

He was also Jonah LeMarque's son.

"And I thought my in-laws were fucked-up," Javier murmured.

Family secrets aside, Holberton seemed to be making the best of life. He had emancipated himself from his family, and then joined the class action suit against his father and the church for an unlicensed, obscene use of his image. It paid out handsomely. This was the seed money for his first company, Interiority. He ran it as an online store for the first year, then shelved it to attend the Rhode Island School of Design. He dropped out, moved to Las Vegas, and rebooted Interiority. He joined the European Graduate School, and wrote a thesis on the social implications of cinematic Bond villains' secret lairs. This was also his first brush with theme park design: he sold the thesis to a consultancy in London.

Interiority was big in Las Vegas. Unlike the experience designers glutting his potential job market, Holberton focused exclusively on items that could be picked up and held. No interfaces. No menus. Nothing digital. Analog only.

His sole contribution to the digital realm was his work for his cousin, Daniel Sarton, on the Museum of the City of Seattle. He helped curate the layers of time visible within the exhibit. It was a favour between family members; Holberton charged only one dollar for the consultation.

With that kind of relationship in place, it made

sense that Sarton would leave Holberton his legacy. The trick would be learning what Holberton had done with it. What he had done with Amy. Javier needed access to his files, and probably his house. He couldn't just fuck Holberton, he had to seduce him. Start a relationship with him. Become part of his inner circle.

In order to bring Amy back, Javier had to attract and keep the attention of a notoriously private, habitually litigious designer who specialized solely in analog reproductions of reality. A man who hated New Eden, and probably all of New Eden's works, and with good reason. Javier had to sleep with this man, and he had not slept with anyone in a year. Powell didn't count. He had to keep reminding himself that Powell didn't count.

He had to do better with Holberton than he'd done with Powell.

He would have to practise.

Buried deep in the core of the ship was the Winter Wonderland. Its nationality and temporality changed on four-hour shifts. Sometimes it was German. Sometimes English. Sometimes it was medieval, and sometimes Victorian. Sometimes it was Tokyo on Christmas Eve, with a spindly replica Tokyo Tower and a real working Ferris wheel. At least, that's what the gilt-edged display worked into the heart of the glittering Door Into Winter ™ said, as it slowly revealed images of the many options of Christmas, each more crisp than the last. The Door was shaped like a huge wardrobe. It stood out from the wall of Deck 4. Tiny crystals frosted its edges. As Javier watched, they replicated, etching the surface in new fractals.

"The rest of the world may have forgotten what a real winter feels like, but not us," the Door said. *"Step into our Winter Wonderland, and relive the glories of wintertimes long, long ago."*

Javier chose to visit the Wonderland during a shift in which the vN were leading a *posada*. He followed the couple, dressed as Joseph and Mary, as they walked through pine forests asking shopkeepers and homeowners for a place to stay. It reminded him briefly of his and Amy's journey through the forests of Washington State. Then he made the memory go away, and focused on his target instead.

The target was ahead of him. He shuffled along through the snow, alone. He was a tad overweight, but not in any way that would hinder him sexually as far as mechanics were concerned. He was also Latino. Javier was already rusty; he wasn't going to handicap himself trying to do this in English his first time out.

Javier's first test of the target was how the target reacted to him personally. He made sure to cross the target's sightline on two separate occasions while the crowd waited for the *posada* to start. Both times, the target made eye contact. Just one furtive look, then a look away. Maybe he was confused. Javier looked like the staff members, but he dressed like the loft suite: a charcoal wool suit with a crisp white shirt and an ice blue tie. It was looser than he would have chosen for looks, but if he needed to jump anywhere, he would need flexibility. For this reason, his shoes were slip-ons without socks.

"Aren't you cold?" the target asked.

Javier had been waiting to start this conversation for the past half hour. He had his responses already selected, branched, planned for. "Only a little. I didn't think it would really be this cold." He made a show of staring at the other guy's mouth. His target was in the process of growing a vacation beard. It was going pretty well. "Wow. I can even see your breath, it's so cold."

The other guy squinted. "I can't see yours."

Javier smiled. "I don't breathe. It just looks like I do." He used it as an excuse to come closer. "See? Watch my chest. I'm talking to you normally, but…" He pointed. "My chest still rises and falls on meter."

The other guy stared at Javier's chest. His gaze moved up to Javier's throat, then his mouth. When it hit his eyes, Javier knew he had him. The other guy didn't know it yet, but Javier did.

"Ricardo Montalban," Javier said, holding his hand out.

The other guy laughed and shook it. "That's a joke, right?"

"Of course it is," Javier said. He held his target's hand for just a second longer than necessary.

"So, you're traveling under an assumed name? This is your alias?"

Javier held a single finger up to his lips. "Ssh. Not so loud."

The other guy smiled. "Manuel," he said.

"Do you go cruising often, Manuel?"

The double meaning still existed, in Spanish. Even in the snowy twilight of the wonderland, Manuel's blush was visible. He was young, Javier realized. Or at least, inexperienced.

"It's my first time," he said.

Of course it was.

"Mine too," Javier lied. "It's so… big. I feel like I'll never see all of it."

Manuel nodded. "It almost feels too big."

"No such thing."

They both laughed at the same time. This was going extremely well. Javier wondered what he had worried about.

"It just feels like a bit too much. I had to get off the boat, today," Manuel continued. "I went to the rainforest."

Javier replayed his conversation with Aaron. "Chirripó?"

Manuel nodded. He was about to start saying something more, when Javier began drifting away from the crowd, down the path they'd just walked. It was lit by *furolitos* in waxed paper bags. A false moon hid behind scudding clouds above them. Javier was beginning to understand the romance of winter. He had never experienced the season this way – his coldest Christmases were rainy, and nothing more. But the dry snap to the air, the length and colour of the shadows, they made you want to climb into bed with someone.

"It was really something," Manuel said. "Hot as hell. And wet. Really, really wet. I think I may have ruined my socks."

Javier nodded. He understood immediately why Manuel was not getting laid. At least, not by the kind of guys he was attracted to. One did not talk to people who were out of your league about wet socks.

"Did you see any wildlife?"

Manuel shook his head. "Some birds, but nothing big. Even the sloths were hiding. They say there are more jaguars, now, but I'm not sure I believe it."

"I saw a jaguar, once."

"In a zoo?"

Javier shook his head. He leaned against the tree. It smelled pleasantly of balsam. It reminded him of Amy. Hiding in trees in the rain, with her and Xavier – back when Xavier was still Junior. Back when he was small enough to carry in the crook of one arm.

"Where, then?"

Javier blinked. "In the wild," he said. "Not far from here, actually. Years ago."

Manuel's eyebrows rose. "Wow."

"She was just lying right out there on the branch of this huge tree, sunning herself."

He and she had both been sunning themselves, actually. He was maybe a month old. He'd wandered out on a limb because his father was gone, probably killing drones, and he was hungry and he needed the sun. So he took off all his clothes and lay down on the branch. It wasn't until he was completely comfortable that he noticed the jaguar above him. She was on another branch, staring at him intently. He still remembered the pink of her tongue against the white of her muzzle. How the inside of her spots was just a little bit darker than the fur outside, as though, as in the legend, she'd been burnt by the very last of God's fire.

"Were you scared?"

"Only a little."

Actually, it was a lot. He'd been *very* scared. Big cats tended not to attack people, of course, but he was in her territory and she probably wanted him gone. He had no idea what her teeth could do to hollow-core titanium, but he'd seen the carcasses other jaguars left behind. They dislocated the necks of their prey with their paws. They bit through the shells of ancient turtles. Javier was tough, but he wasn't that tough. He tried to sit up, but then she started moving, too, so he lay back down. They spent the next hour that way, eyeing each other.

It wasn't so different from this conversation, really.

"I wish I'd seen something like that," Manuel said. "It's hard. I went into the forest expecting to have something happen to me. They've worked so hard to preserve it. I thought it would be… more…"

"Magical," Javier said.

"Yes. That's right. Magical." Manuel shrugged. "Stupid, huh?"

Javier shook his head. "It's not stupid at all." He ducked his head a little to catch Manuel's eye. "Really. It isn't. You fell for the hype. That's not your fault."

Manuel rolled his eyes. "It's no different from coming to this place, then, is it?"

Javier looked around. The Holy Family had reached their destination. The crowd was singing *"Noche de Paz."* A star twinkled above the trees. After watching it for a moment, Javier realized it was a botfly set to overload.

"Sure it's different," he said. "You met me."

Manuel smiled. "I was told to meet you."

An instant tension in Javier's legs readied him for escape. Who had sent this man? He didn't read like a cop, or even like New Eden. Who were they? And why had they waited this long to make their move?

"Wow," Manuel said. "It's true."

"What's true?"

"What they say, about your poker face. You guys are amazing. There's just…" Manuel waved a hand in front of Javier's face. "Nothing."

"Still waters run deep," Javier said.

Manuel smiled and reached into his pocket. He held out a small key fob. "You're invited."

Javier raised his eyebrows. "To what?"

"To a private tournament. The vN are not allowed on the casino floor, and my companion would like to stake you to a game."

"I'll beat him," Javier said.

"My companion is a lady. And she would like to test her skill."

Javier tilted his head. "Aren't you enough of a test of her skills?"

"Most of the time." Manuel offered his arm. "But my lady is nothing if not an overachiever."

The lady's accommodations were a loft suite identical to Javier's on the opposite side of the ship. Hers had a piano, though. It was a real piano; the guts were visible, literally and figuratively. Someone had left a highball glass of water out on a table near it. Adjacent to the piano were a wet bar and a dinner table inlaid with matching mosaic tile, and when Javier entered the room, she stood up from the head of the table.

She was in her late forties or early fifties, judging by her hands and the stiffness in her posture. She was very petite and thin, and had deep purple hair, cut at a sharp angle. She wore multiple loops of black pearls around her neck and down her flat chest. The pearls were perfectly round, with the iridescent pinks and greens of a parking lot oil slick. He had a sudden desire to see what they would look like on Amy.

"I bought them after my first tournament, in Shanghai," she said, touching the pearls carefully. "The producers wanted a little local colour, as it were. I wasn't expected to win. They called me *Poker Alice*. It stuck. People still call me Alice, and so can you. Unless you feel like telling me your real name."

He took her proffered hand and held it in both his own. Hers was dry, and very cool. Warfarin, maybe. Though she could likely afford drugs tailored to her genes.

"Your pearls are very beautiful," Javier said. "They suit you."

She smiled, but it didn't reach her eyes. An old habit of a professional gambler, he guessed. "I suspected you might be charming, Mr Montalban."

"It's just the suit."

Now she smiled genuinely, and he felt better. She looked at Manuel. "May we have some drinks, please?"

"Of course," Manuel said, and went behind the bar. He brought out a few bottles of vN-friendly liquids. Unstoppered, they smelled like perfume. "I know the Electric Sheep has this cocktail called a Tears in the Rain, but they don't make a vN version."

Manuel used tongs to measure out a grouping of glittering crystals into a martini shaker. "These are druzy-style moissanites that I've kept at sub-zero," he said. "They share the same molecular pattern as a diamond, but they're made from silicon and not carbon. The interior of this shaker is diamond carbide, so as I shake it," he started shaking, "the moissanites start chipping off in microscopic fragments." He shook for another minute, then poured the liquid into a squat, square glass.

Then he opened up a drawer below the bar. Icy mist wafted out. From the drawer, he withdrew a tiny pillbox full of small blue beads shaped like teardrops. Each was about the size of a sesame seed. "These are gelatinized cobalt," he said. "I make them with calcium alginate and three different water baths." With an antique silver salt spoon, he drifted the spheres into the glass one by one. Tapping the last few out, he gave the glass a final, gentle nudge to swirl its contents, then handed the glass to Javier.

"Thank you," Javier said, and raised the glass. The teardrops drifted slowly down through the sparkling suspension. "Do you carry this whole set-up with you on every cruise?"

"It comes with the suite," Alice said. "Doesn't yours have one?"

"I never thought to look."

Manuel used a standard shaker to produce a dry martini for Alice. He shaved a curl of yuzu peel into it, and she and Javier raised their glasses to each other. The drink had no discernible flavour but it was delightfully cold, and quite pretty, and he liked the weight of the glass in his hand. It felt reassuringly solid and real.

"Do you play baccarat, Mr Montalban?"

He blinked. "*Punto banco,* or *chemin de fer*?"

She sniffed. "The latter, naturally. *Punto banco* is a game of chance. *Chemin de fer* is a game of choice." She arched a pencilled eyebrow. "I thought you would appreciate a game in which there is at least a small measure of free will."

"I do." Javier rested a hand on the nearest chair. Opposite the piano stood floor-to-ceiling windows. Beyond the balcony there was nothing, only black. Somewhere, beneath those waves, there might be some trace of Amy and the island. Somewhere dark and cold and awful, where he'd put her because his own personal deck was stacked against him from the beginning. "But there are games, and then there games."

Alice took a seat. Javier followed. "I made my career on poker and blackjack," she said. "But it's all different, now. The security measures are beyond anything I imagined, when I started out. Do you know that it was a computer vision algorithm that picked up my first stroke? It was a transient ischemic attack, one of the little ones. You scarcely even know it's happening. One minute I was splitting on an eight, and the next there was the casino doctor."

So he'd been right about the warfarin. She was probably still on a blood thinner of some type. "Casinos have doctors?"

She cast him a pitying glance. "The good ones do."

Her lips thinned. "Or they did. Once. Now it's all vN."

Javier sipped. "I thought we weren't allowed on casino floors."

"Not here. But these places…" she waved her hand to encompass the ship, "are no good. They're for punters. The rake is terrible, the commission is too high, the bankroll top-up is automatic. It's disgusting, the way they take advantage of people. Old people, especially. Do you know how many of the elderly are living on points, on these old boats? There's free meals and free medical care. It's cheaper than a home, these days."

"But that's not why you're here."

"Of course not. I'm here to host a tournament. They have me working in player development. Me. At my age." She sniffed again. "This is my one night off. Two nights a week, I'm paid to hold private games here, in the suite. I take a commission. The rest of my evenings I'm supposed to be working the floor. With no advantage whatsoever. No loss rebate, no soft seventeens, nothing. It's disgraceful."

Javier liked this woman very much, he decided. His last woman, before Amy, was a divorcee from La Jolla named Brigid who took his twelfth iteration to a supermarket parking lot and gave him away, like he was an unwanted kitten. The boy hadn't even chosen his own name, yet. Both Amy and Alice were significant improvements on that record.

Javier slid his hand across the table. "Given the value of your time, then, perhaps you should tell me what I can do for you."

She smiled. "You're right off the bat, aren't you? All

right, then." She sipped, and then pushed her drink away, half-finished. "After this I'm going to Atlantic City. There's a baccarat tournament, there. Three nights, three styles of game: *punto banco, chemin de fer*, and *banque*. Tie-bet only; nine-to-one odds. And the banker is a vN from Mecha. His name is Taft. He has corporate sponsorship. The bankroll is likely infinite."

Javier watched her eyes. She wore bright green contacts, possibly to obscure the dilation of her pupils. It would be a good affectation to cultivate, in her profession. Even now, he could not read her feelings. She looked completely calm, a consummate professional brokering a deal.

He reached for her hand anyway. "Please don't do that."

She withdrew her hand. "I have to. And you're going to help me. I need to log as many hours as I can playing against a vN."

"You'll still lose, no matter how much I help you."

"Perhaps."

He decided to take another strategy. "If I win the majority of hands, will you at least consider leaving the tournament?"

She gave him a tiny smile and patted his hand, as though humouring a child. "Of course. But you have to prove to me that a vN can play perfect cards with every hand."

And so he did.

It didn't take long. A professional player of Alice's calibre understood immediately that he had a perfect count of the cards at all times, even when she switched from a six-deck shuffle to a nine. Simulating more players didn't do anything, either – it merely increased the speed at which he accumulated the data set. Moreover, he lacked the potent combination of dopamine and adrenaline necessary to create true addictive behaviour and loss of inhibition and discipline; he could make the same small, boring bets for hours at a time, and he could do it with a massive shoe on multiple hands, with a nearly infinite number of splits.

Between the fifth and sixth round, he asked to use the bathroom to wash his face and rearrange his hair. After that, he took a peek inside Alice's medicine cabinet, and her cosmetics bag. She kept all of her pills, patches, and gels in custom biometric containers, but the whole collection in an attractive wooden box inlaid with mother of pearl. Javier didn't need to spend much time with the box to understand what her game really was, and how she intended to cheat. So he returned downstairs, and continued the game.

At dawn, Alice was finally ready to quit. "You're a..."

"Machine," Javier said.

She laughed. The laugh turned into a cough. Javier poured her a glass of water, and she drank it eagerly. "I suppose it was too much to hope for," she said. "But you should see their offer. It's incredible. With the rebates, it's like playing 50/50 odds."

Javier nibbled on a dish of Flexo Fries they'd ordered up from the Electric Sheep. He considered. He was up a significant amount of money, and he could probably leverage those winnings into points. But he couldn't really leave the issue alone, either.

"The rebates are invalid if you cheat, right?"

"Of course."

"And there's no getting out of it?"

"It's a ten million dollar buy-in. It's feeding the bankroll, so it's non-refundable. No one is walking away from that money."

Javier shook his head. "It's a sunk cost. Think of it that way. Get out now, while you still can."

"I haven't lost that kind of money in years, and I don't intend to start now." Her eyes narrowed. "What are you thinking?"

Javier stood up. He moved toward the window. The sun was beginning to rise. He felt it in his skin. "I think your fellow players are going to cheat," he said. "And there's only one way to cheat successfully when playing with a vN. You have to trigger the failsafe."

Alice joined him at the window. Reflected in the plate glass, she seemed more tired, older. She wasn't looking at the ocean, or the sunrise. She was watching him. "And how would you do that?"

"You would h-have to c-cause harm to another human being," Javier said.

"So you would need a team. One to play the game, and another to slip on a banana peel in the background."

He turned to her. "Or one to give a player the wrong dose of her medicine, so she could take all her winnings early in the event of a forfeit."

She paled. "Are you accusing me of cheating?"

"We're just talking. But it would certainly be a good reason to keep a human lover, and not a vN. Because then the mistake would be more plausible." Javier put his drink down. He took hers and put it down, too. He looked up at the loft. Manuel had long since gone to sleep. "Life is for the living," he said. "A high-roller like you should know that."

She sighed. "It's not like that at the end. There's a certain law of diminishing returns at work."

He reached around and unclasped the pearls from around her neck. She stiffened, and her hands came up, but the cold fingertips only skimmed him. Carefully, he set the pearls beside the glass of water near the piano. He coiled them up in a nautilus pattern so they wouldn't roll away. When he turned back to her, he put his hands where the pearls used to be. Beneath his fingers, her pulse was high but steady.

"It can still be good, you know."

Her voice came out high and tight and small. "That's what I'm afraid of."

He bent and kissed her. She tasted of vermouth and yuzu and salicylic acid. She kissed back very gently, as though her mouth were just waking up.

"Don't go all demure Chinese stereotype on me now, Alice. You sent your boy to find me. And trust me, he knows what I can do just as well as you do."

She gripped the front of his shirt. "Take me upstairs. Please."

"That's more like it."

For her part, Alice didn't participate until later. She sat in a chaise and directed the action. Manuel came awake for him slowly, inch by inch, and he finished almost before becoming truly aware of what was happening.

"Thank you," he said, ever polite. "I've always wanted someone to do that for me."

Javier had the grace to pretend as though he had never heard this before. He also neglected to mention that this was just the thing to get the taste of Powell from his mouth. That made it a fair trade, as far as he was concerned.

Alice joined them soon after that. Manuel had a better understanding of her than Javier did, but his technique needed a little refinement and Javier was happy to demonstrate. It wasn't the other man's fault; he couldn't imagine calibrating things like pressure and speed with something so vague as "instincts." (And to be fair, the same thing was true of finding Manuel's prostate. Alice had very little hands, and very little patience to match.)

Manuel fell asleep first. The bed was big enough for the three of them, and as she drifted off in Javier's arms, Alice said: "Come with me. To Atlantic City."

At any other time, he would have said yes. She was a rich woman with excellent taste and the talents to support herself, who still very much enjoyed getting fucked and wasn't afraid to experiment. It was the kind of brass ring he'd always been looking to grab, until he found Amy. It was the kind of arrangement every other vN wanted.

"I can't," he said.

She frowned. "Is it because I'm old?"

"No. There's just something I have to do."

She waited a moment. *"Cherchez la femme?"*

He smiled, and kissed her hair. "Sort of."

"Your lady is very lucky."

Javier rolled away. "She's dead."

Sighing, Alice rolled over to rest her head on his

shoulder. "I'm sorry." She patted his hand. "I'm a widow too, you know. It gets better. With time."

"I miss her," Javier said, before he could simulate how the conversation might end.

"Of course you do."

"I keep thinking about everything she ever said to me. Things I…" Oh, God, but he did miss her. Fiercely. Wanted to be holding *her*, right now. Wanted to be asleep, holding *her*, smelling *her* hair, not someone else's. So what if her hands were always busy, gesturing something to the island. Why hadn't he reached over, and taken her hand? Why hadn't he stopped the conversation by starting one of his own? "Things I didn't really understand at the time. When I should have."

"Hmm."

Alice cuddled in closer. Her breath was already thick. He heard a tiny wheeze in there. What a blessing age was. What a fantastic, wondrous gift, to know that you might someday forget everything you'd ever done, that you might drift away from it like a slowly melting chunk of ice. Someday, Alice would get to die. She would die with an imperfect memory of all the hurt she'd caused. It wouldn't always be sharp for her. It wouldn't always be there in perfect high-res detail, like the smell of Amy's hair was for Javier.

"That's always the way," Alice said. "But it's OK. They're always with us."

"I know," Javier said. "I know."

Back in his own suite, he showered off and then went directly to bed. On his display, he checked his account with the cruise line. They shared points with the Akiba, so he was good there, but the credit would dry up, soon. Even with his commission from Alice, he didn't have enough liquid cash to get him between Galveston and Las Vegas incognito. He'd gotten by in Costa Rica because there were models like him everywhere, but he had a feeling America would be a lot more uptight. He had no desire to pass through any kind of security between now and his meeting Holberton. If the government didn't pick him up, Portia would.

It was hard to tell which scenario he feared more.

"Concierge?"

"Yes, sir?"

"When we land in Galveston, I'll be sending a package to Nevada. I'd like to pay the freight now with points, and have you pick it up after I've disembarked."

"That's quite all right, sir. However, we will need to weigh the package, before we can send it."

Javier threw back the covers and grabbed his clothes and shoes. "I'll do it on the bathroom scale." He stood on the scale, holding all his things, and told them the number.

"What size of box would you like?"

"What's the largest size you have?"

"Eighteen inches by thirteen by three feet."

Javier winced. "Great. Send it up."

9: I'M YOUR MAN

He waited for the porter to leave the room, counted to thirty, then snicked open the box-cutter. Cutting himself free was more awkward than it was difficult. Twice, he stopped because he worried the noise was too loud. But eventually he pushed open the flaps and stood up inside the box. He rolled his neck, dusted himself off, gathered his bug-out bag, and used the box-cutter to break the box down entirely. He stuffed it in the relevant bin, then listened at the door. The mailroom was not terribly full. Parcels were a bit of anachronism. There seemed not to be too much traffic in the hallway. He opened the door a touch. No one was there. He cleared the hall and was out in the lobby in two minutes.

"IRRAISHIMASE!"

Javier stopped. Several vN were yelling. None were looking at him. They all looked like the puppet vN that had attacked the island, the same pretty Asian male model. They were dressed in a variety of outfits: black suits with skinny ties; navy blue kimono with tiny white diamond patterns; ornate Gothic dresses with fantastic hats and stunning makeup; gleaming white leather motorcycle jackets and matching trousers. None of them looked at him directly. His opening the door seemed to have triggered their reaction. Shrugging, Javier made his way into the lobby.

Now, they turned. All bowed. "Welcome to the Akiba," they said, in unison. "When would you like to visit?"

"Excuse me?"

"Which era can we escort you to?" The vN in the skinny tie pointed. "Each of us represents a different period. Are you interested in one in particular? If so, you could take the tram. Or if you prefer, you could take the long way."

"The long way is a lot of fun," said the vN in the Gothic costume.

"Actually, I'm interested in checking in," Javier said.

"Right this way, sir." Skinny Tie led him to a small bridge that spanned a gurgling stream. Once over the bridge, Javier saw that the stream was an offshoot of a much larger pond complete with turtles and koi fish. Sculpted trees stretched over its length, and lotus flowers floated on its surface. Gradients of moss gathered at its edge. Guests followed a grey slate path through the entirety of it, pausing to examine cherry blossoms – in December.

"Most of the lobbies on the Strip are designed to take your money from the second you walk in," Skinny Tie said, with no small amount of scorn. "We prefer to calm our guests down and put them at their ease, first. Most of them are simply exhausted from travel. They don't want to think about gambling. They want to rest. We hope our garden can encourage that."

"It's very peaceful," Javier said, as Skinny Tie guided him into a teahouse poised on a tiny hill just off the slate path.

The Rory in the teahouse was in full kimono, and knelt at a low desk. She had no display. No monitor. No device of any kind. She *was* the device.

"This gentleman has a reservation," Skinny Tie said.

The Rory smiled. "Of course he does. Thank you for showing him in."

Skinny Tie bowed and took his leave. Rory's smile died immediately. "What do you think you're doing?"

"I'm checking in to your fine establishment," Javier said. "My name is Ricardo Montalban."

"You are on a fool's errand," Rory said. "You will never find Amy. You will never bring her back. There is nothing you can do."

"I haven't the faintest idea what you're talking about." He leaned forward. "Is my reservation not listed?"

"Chris Holberton is not staying here. You won't be able to find him. You won't be able to learn where he stashed Amy."

Javier knelt at the desk. He laid his palms on it, flat. He looked the Rory directly in the eye. "I believe you may have me confused with someone else." He slid his palms across the desk, and covered her hands with them. When she tried pulling them away, he gripped them. Hard. He squeezed. "I believe you may have me confused with one of my clademates, or maybe someone who shares my model. My face. Some other vN who looks like me. Someone who is very dangerous."

The Rory simply blinked.

"I can understand why you might be afraid of him," Javier continued, "because he *is* very dangerous. He has nothing left to lose."

"You're damaging my wrists."

"I know that all of you are networked. I know that losing one of you doesn't really matter that much. If you die, you can be replaced. The knowledge one has can be shifted to another. You're all disposable. Right?"

Rory tried pulling away again, and he pulled back. Heard something shatter in her wrist. Felt the disconnect under his thumb.

"That means no one would miss you, if I took the pen that's in my breast pocket and stuck it right in your neck. It's full of digestive fluid. I made it myself, on my way here. You wouldn't die right away. It would happen slowly. From the inside. Your head would fall off, first. It would probably still be conscious as you watched the rest of your body disintegrating."

Rory whimpered. Javier let go of her hands.

"Now. About my reservation."

The evening's festivities were supposed to take the form of a *matsuri*, in keeping with the hotel's theme. Skinny Tie and all the other staff vN encouraged visitors to proceed through the garden, and start their journey in the Sengoku Jidai era of the hotel, and proceed through the Meiji, Taisho, Showa, and Heisei eras until they approached the heart of Akiba. There, the hotel's investors and designers would all be waiting. They had done a media event earlier in the day to answer questions, but this would be a special evening for preferred guests and high-rollers.

"Please, take these," one of the samurai vN told him, and handed him a set of high-value poker chips. "Tonight's winnings go to benefit the victims of the radioactive fallout."

Javier winced. "It's been rough for you guys, I take it?"

The samurai's smile faltered. "This is just about the worst possible time to open a vN-friendly casino, yes. I believe Thematic is taking a huge loss."

Javier nodded. "And the designer? Holberton? How's he taking it?"

The vN rolled his eyes. "Mr Holberton already has his next thing lined up."

"Oh?"

"We're not supposed to talk about it."

"Message received."

Javier was tempted to sprint ahead and get to Holberton as soon as possible, but there was no need to rush. Holberton would actually be more vulnerable and amenable after a few drinks. The key would be to get him at a point in the party when he honestly wanted to leave. That probably wasn't going to be at the beginning.

So he meandered through the festival. The whole thing revolved around old-fashioned games of chance: ring tosses and fishing and even some archery competitions. The vN who initiated each competition hawked them from thatch-roofed dwellings, from which they also sold pressed balls of rice and skewered chicken livers. All of these came in vN-friendly varieties, too. In fact, a significant proportion of the people sharing the festival with him were vN. None of them looked like Amy. It was as though she'd been erased.

The end of the festival opened into a relatively blank space: pine floors, white walls, blown glass pendant lights, crackled but colourless. It was a nice change. Like a vent of fresh air. And standing in the centre of the room was Chris Holberton. Javier recognized him from behind: his hair was eye-catchingly white. He wore a navy blue suit. His hands were in his pockets. Then he turned, to gesture at the entryway. When he saw Javier, he smiled. He recognized him, Javier realized. Recognized his face, probably. It had been in the news a great deal.

Now or never. Javier crossed the room.

"Welcome to Akiba," Holberton said. He held out his hand. "I'm Chris Holberton. Are you with the press?"

"I'm a guest." Javier shook it. "Ricardo Montalban."

Holberton laughed so loud, other people turned to look at the two of them. His laugh was more of a snicker. It sounded almost childish. Javier liked it immediately.

"That's great! I can't believe it! Where did you learn about *him*?"

Javier shrugged. "Online. Movies. You know."

Holberton stopped laughing, and looked him up

and down. "It suits." He gestured with his gaze. "What are you doing here, Mr Montalban?"

"Please. Ricardo."

"All right, *Ricardo*. What are you doing here?"

Honesty was, in certain cases, the best policy. "I wanted to meet you."

Holberton blinked. He was very fair; even his eyelashes were blond. "Most of the people in this room want to meet me, Ricardo. What makes you so different?"

Javier smiled. "What makes me different is that I didn't want to meet you until you smiled at me."

Holberton smiled like a child who had just been handed a very large, extravagantly-wrapped present. His mouth opened to say something. Naturally, one of the Rory chose that moment to intervene. She spoke to Holberton, but she looked at Javier.

"Mr Holberton, one of the Dubai people would like to speak with you," she said.

Holberton rolled his eyes. "I'll find you later."

"No," Javier said. "I'll find you."

Holberton turned away, and two vN closed in on Javier. He felt them before he saw them. "Mr Montalban," one said, "there appears to be an issue with your account."

They were dressed like Skinny Tie, but they weren't the same exact vN from the lobby. They walked him through an Employees Only door just outside the pachinko parlour. It opened into a bright but narrow hallway broken on one side by steel doors. Once they were through, they took his pen.

"What are your names? I just call all the girls Rory. It saves me some time."

"You don't have to worry about that any longer, Mr Peterson."

They turned him to the left, and guided him through one of the steel doors. The room was dark. As he entered, the lights came on. There was one aluminum folding chair, and a drain in the floor. He looked up. No cameras. Unfinished ceiling. Good. He turned around. The two vN were waiting with folded hands.

"Can I at least take my jacket off?" Javier asked. "This suit cost me a lot money."

They shrugged. Javier took his time unbuttoning the jacket. He and Hayward had decided on something versatile: two buttons, charcoal alpaca, relatively short and light. But it was all he had, and it would have to do. He eased it off himself slowly. He took hold of the collar, brushing the jacket carefully before pretending to lay it across the back of the chair.

Then he circled his wrist, coiled the fabric tight, and whipped one vN in the eyes with it. He grabbed the chair by the legs, and slammed it into the other vN's ribs. This one grabbed the chair and yanked it out of Javier's hands. As Javier watched, he folded the chair backward. It snapped at the hinges.

In Javier's mind, simulations and probabilities branched away into a forest of possibility. They both rushed him at once. He jumped. He gripped the pipes above him, and kicked one in the face. The other grabbed his other foot. One cheap canvas shoe came off. The vN holding his bare foot held it under one arm and brought out the pen. Primed it. Javier used his other foot to kick him away.

Above him, the pipes began to creak. The other two vN were holding their faces. Smoke and fluid drained away from their skin. One's nose had collapsed in completely. He started to swing. Maybe one was electrical. He brought his legs together to slice through the air faster. His body sketched a perfect half circle. Forward. Back.

The pipes gave. He fell. Steam clouded the room. He felt no pain, but he did feel the damage. In a minute, his skin would start peeling. So would theirs. They ran for the door. He grabbed one side of the broken chair, snapped off both the back legs, and shoved them up under two sets of ribs. Then he pulled the chair legs out, flipped his grip to overhand, and stabbed again. He pulled down, from shoulder to waist. Seams ripped with skin. Smoke mingled with steam. They howled in frustration. They knew it was over, probably. Their wounds were too deep. They were smoking out. They turned.

"This was a mistake," one said.

"Yeah," Javier said. "Your mistake was giving a guy with a ten-foot jump the chance to kick you in the head."

He buried the chair legs in their throats, watched their faces go slack, picked up his jacket, and left the room.

In the elevator, humans stared at him.

"I fell in the pool," he said, and got off at his floor. His key card no longer worked. He kicked the door in. The room lit up to greet him, but the terrace remained dark. There, he took off his other shoe. He hid it under the chaise.

He had both feet on the railing when the hotel started talking to him.

"What are you doing, sir?"

The hotel interface was really very sweet. It was Rory's voice, but it wasn't Rory. At least, he didn't think so. She didn't seem to mince her words, lately.

"I'm going out for a walk." He placed one foot in front of the other. He didn't have a wraparound terrace, but he was willing to bet that Holberton did. Somewhere. Up a few floors.

"Please, sir. Get down from there. Please reconsider."

"I'm not reconsidering anything. I know exactly what I'm doing."

Below him, the lights of the Las Vegas Strip glowed and pulsed. At the dead fountain, scores of tourists stood watching. Their glasses twinkled with tiny embedded lights. They were holding hands, or carrying children on their shoulders. They were all so happy, staring at nothing.

"I'm sure you have a lot to live for, sir. There must be people out there who care about you. You must have a family, somewhere. They must be very worried about you. Would you like me to call them?"

Javier made it to the edge of the balcony. A concrete pillar stood before him. It stretched up the southwest edge of the building. He looked up. He was on the sixty-second floor. That meant there were at least eight floors between himself and the penthouse. And his hands were burnt.

"Sir? Is there someone you would like to speak with?

Someone I can contact, for you?"

"No," he said. "I'm on my own."

He jumped.

Making his way up the building required a sort of monkey shimmy. This meant clinging with his fingers, his toes, and his inner thighs and inching up, slowly, with the wind at his back and music in his ears. It was funny, how noise from the Strip floated up so intact.

"Well, then he started grinding up on me. And I couldn't get away."

"You should have just punched him. Or elbowed him in the stomach, or something."

Humans had it so easy.

He inched up a little higher. His suit was slippery. He'd only made it one floor. Trees were easier. Why hadn't he just gone to the rainforest, in Costa Rica? He could have found a way out from there. Or maybe he never would have. Maybe he could have just gotten lost in there. It would have been better for everyone if he had never left the rainforest. Better for Amy. Better for his iterations. It was his father's choice to take them out of the forest. He was a child, then, but he hadn't wanted to go. Hadn't wanted to leave. Why had he followed Arcadio? What had the old man ever done for him?

He had taught him to climb.

"Loosen up," Arcadio had said, their first time climbing trees together. They had started at the bottom, with the roots. There were tapirs and jaguars and not too much sunlight, down on the forest floor. It was dark. He was scared.

"Stop hugging the damn tree," Arcadio shouted up

at him. "It's not your girlfriend."

But he liked the tree. He liked the softness of its moss. He liked how big it was. He liked all the insects crawling around through that moss. It would be fun to be one of them, just wriggling around in all that pillowy green lushness all day. He wasn't going to tell Arcadio that, because it was stupid, but that was how he felt.

"The monkeys don't hug the tree," Arcadio said. "They just hold it. Like it's a tool that they're using."

A tool. Something you used with your hands. Javier pulled away. He gripped with his hands. Then just with his fingers. He shut his eyes.

"There you go," Arcadio said. "Now haul up with your fingers and push up with your toes. It's like a crunch. You don't know what those are, because we don't need to use them, but I'll show you. You bring your knees to your gut."

"But then, I'd have to let go," Javier had protested.

"It's OK if you let go all at once," Arcadio said. "You know that. Your body knows that. Your body was built for it. All you have to do is let go."

Javier opened his eyes in Las Vegas. He pulled his body away from the wall. Wind whistled between him and it. This was the difference between crawling and running, between climbing and leaping, between man and machine. Up with the fingers. Up with the toes. Knees to stomach. He let go.

He sailed up ten feet. His fingers found the next grip without his computing it. Then he did it again. And again. And again. Then he stopped counting.

•••

Holberton's room was on the penthouse level, as expected. Javier recognized it by the bottle of wine left out on the terrace. It was a brand Holberton once talked about in an interview. The room was unlit, but it lit up as soon as Javier entered it from the terrace. Inside, it was very clean. Housekeeping had been by. He would need to find the safe.

"Where is the safe?" he asked.

"You don't belong here," Rory said. He recognized her immediately. It was the hotel talking, but it was also her. She had a special kind of smug.

"Bullshit." Javier started with the perimeter of the room. He nudged aside each piece of art, and every mirror. Nothing. He checked the cabinets in the kitchenette. Then the bar. Nothing. He even opened the wine cooler beneath the counter, and checked the powder room and laundry room nearest the door into the main hall. Nothing. But that was just being thorough – the safe was likely in the bedroom, where giant watches and gems went to sleep. He went there, next.

Amy was projected on every wall of Holberton's bedroom.

No, not Amy. Not all of them were Amy. Most were her clademates. They looked exactly like her, but they weren't *her*. He had no idea what particular pattern matching or facial recognition algorithms allowed him to recognize that, but he was usually able to identify his own flesh when he saw it on display. He'd been able to do it, the first time he watched news coverage of FEMA herding Amy's clademates and all the clades who shared their bodyplan onto trucks.

He'd watched for her. Obsessively. It got him chased out of an electronics store where he'd been scouting for e-waste to eat.

The vN who looked like Amy all seemed to be inhabiting the same space. The images were surveillance images captured from household environments: kitchens, living rooms, bedrooms. The women were dressed normally, not in prison jumpsuits or lab scrubs. They were interacting with humans. Mostly men, but a few women.

The vN were also iterating.

Javier found a picture of a human man smiling into a camera – a nice camera with favourable lighting, not a surveillance camera – and hugging his iterating vN. She was huge and full. Her face was round. Even her ankles had puffed, just a little. This was what Amy would have looked like, if she had ever iterated. If she had given Xavier the little sister he kept asking about. If she had given the two of them a daughter.

The next image was of the resulting iteration. There was a new picture for every day. In each image, she was naked. Javier waved his hand and the little girl grew, faster and faster, stretching up and out into the child Amy had once been, wispy fine blond hair and huge green eyes, up into a more teenage size, out into a woman grown, the perfect replication of her mother. The final image was of the two women standing together.

When he flipped the images forward, a blueprint filled the wall. The blueprint was not for a single building, but a whole town. There was a central square and a big sculpture where a fountain might once have gone, and a group of parks, and businesses, and houses. When you gestured at any of the groups, photos from them popped up. Amy's clademates were in every one. Young and old, iterating and not. A field of green-eyed, fair-haired women and their husbands and wives.

At the bottom of every image was a single word: STEPFORD.

He was about to open a folder named "DIET PLAN" when in the hallway, a door closed. Shit. Javier hastily disarranged the photos with frantic gesturing, and got himself behind the bedroom door. He wiggled into its corner just as it opened. Holberton stepped in. He was alone. Javier made himself as still as possible. Holberton paused, looked at the pictures, gestured at them, and shrugged. Then he crossed the room and opened the bathroom door. The light came on, and he closed the door.

Javier was almost out the bedroom door when he heard the sound of bees, and fell. The charge ploughed through him like a freight train. He was instantly rigid and heavy. He fell without breaking his fall, his face pressed deep into white shag carpeting. From there, he watched Holberton's shoes come close to his face.

"You know, when you said you'd find me, this isn't quite what I had in mind." Holberton used his foot to roll Javier over. He held out the taser. He shook it a little in his hand. "Move and I'll use this again. Blink once for yes and twice for no. With a name like yours, I'm sure you're familiar with the Pike method of communication."

Javier wasn't, but he blinked once anyway.

"Good. Now. Is your name really Ricardo Montalban?"

Javier blinked twice.

"Thought so. Are you a journalist, photographer, or in any way affiliated with the infotainment industrial complex?"

Two blinks.

"Excellent. Are you a spy sent from a foreign government?"

What the fuck? Two blinks.

Holberton straddled him and knelt. "OK. Here's the really big question. This is the important one, so pay attention. Are you with New Eden? Did my father send you?"

Two blinks. Javier struggled to open his mouth. "No," he said. It came out more like a moan.

Holberton stood. He sidestepped Javier and held out a hand. With difficulty – it felt like pushing a broken-down car – Javier lifted his arm and took it. Holberton helped him up. He pushed him over to the settee at the edge of the bed and stood in front of him.

"Who are you?"

The truth, again. "My name is Javier Peterson."

Holberton whistled. "*The* Javier? From the island?"

"Yes."

"I thought you were *dead*. Everyone does." Holberton turned, pulled some images aside with his fingers, and brought up a square of footage. In it, Javier jumped clear of the destroyed house on the little home island. Nearby, his youngest was in the diamond tree, furiously prying at one of the branches. But six months ago, Javier had not seen that. He just walked out into the water. And then he fell into it, and didn't come back up.

"Please stop."

"Sure. Sorry." Holberton wiped the images away with one hand. Now the room was lightless, artless. Only the light from the hallway came through. A single shaft of amber light, illuminating just the very edges of both of them. "What are you *doing* here, Javier?"

"I need your help," he said, after a moment. He looked up. Holberton was very close to him. His eyes were a seaglass green. Just like Amy's. They were, in fact, Amy's eyes. Someone had reproduced them in her bodyplan, right from this very pattern. "New Eden killed Amy. A missionary by the name of Mitch Powell. Now I'm on the run, and I need someone who hates those Bible-thumping bastards just as much as I do."

Holberton smirked. "Then it looks like I'm your man."

10: THE SUBURBS

"Have you ever heard of CITE?"

Holberton drove a greened-up 1967 Impala sedan, black. Holberton told him something about going all the way to Detroit to get it printed from the original pattern, when an auction in Vancouver fell through.

"CITE was a prototype city, out in Lea County," Holberton said, now. "Urban environment, suburban, everything. A place for companies to test new products, basically, without a lot of toxic internal corporate culture to fuck things up."

Javier watched the desert blur past. "That's the city I saw in your suite?"

"That's the one."

"And now a bunch of Amy's clademates live there."

"Yes." Holberton moved to an on-ramp. "They're mostly in one suburb, Macondo. That's part of why the families agreed to go. More space."

Amy had wanted a backyard. She had told him that, once. She kept designing the same treehouse, over and over, knowing she'd never see it. She and his youngest were working on one, together. They had been, anyway. When they were alive.

"At first, it was like any other product recall," Holberton said. "Except the vN were all willing. FEMA sent out a message asking for them to come in and do an interview, after what happened with Amy and Portia, and they did. If they were already living with humans, that is. The homeless ones, that was different."

"I know," Javier said. "You rounded them up in trucks."

Holberton adjusted his position in his seat. "They went willingly," he repeated.

Vultures circled overhead. Of course they'd gone willingly. The failsafe made them incapable of doing anything else. "Yeah," Javier said.

"But we couldn't just split up the families. We didn't want to do that. Nobody wanted to do that."

"So you moved them here."

"FEMA moved them here. I'm just a design consultant."

Javier turned to him. He said nothing, just stretched his arm out the window to get the sun.

"What's it like? When you're in the sun?"

Javier searched for the right word. "Fizzy."

"But you were intended for work in the woods, right?"

"That's right."

"And now you're here, in the desert. Where there's nothing." Holberton clicked his tongue. "I guess that's what Vegas is for. Reinvention."

They changed lanes, and Holberton pointed. It was there, up ahead. In the dun-coloured desert it was a field of sudden green and silver, its edges as sharp and exact as pixels. It looked like a motherboard forgotten on a stretch of burlap. There were skyscrapers and strip malls, steeples and domes and golden arches. Javier thought of the city Amy kept hidden underwater. He liked that one better.

They drove along a ring road that circled the entire complex. Eventually they came to a simple checkpoint with a red and white bar that lowered as they drove close. The man inside was organic. He was very old, and Latino, with a pockmarked face and hair that reeked of gardenia-infused petroleum jelly. Until this moment, Javier was unaware that anyone still *made* Tres Flores, much less used it.

"Good afternoon, Mr Holberton."

"Good afternoon. I'm bringing my friend with me, today. He'll need a guest pass."

"Does he have a radiation detector?"

Holberton winced. "Ooh… No. Yeah, he needs one of those."

The guard handed them both lapel pins with red squares of film inside. "If that turns black, you run," he said. "Now there's more paperwork…"

"Oh, come on. I cut short my time in Vegas just to show all this to my friend."

The words *my friend* seemed to trigger something in the guard's mind. Instantly, his face went from anxious to sheepish. He handed Holberton a pass marked GUEST without so much as looking at him, and lifted the gate.

"Goodness," Holberton said. "I don't know why that had to be so awkward."

"He thought you were trying to impress me," Javier said.

Holberton turned to him with raised brows. "Am I not?"

Javier smiled.

Pastures formed the outermost edges of the city. Drones hovered above them, moving in time with the herds of alpaca that appeared to be making their homes there. The ring road picked up the interstate, and they followed it out of the farmland and over the rest of the complex. On the right, Javier watched a series of long, rectangular buildings disappear under the concrete. "MACONDO MALL" the sign read. Only a few cars were parked in the lot.

They turned off the interstate, taking an offramp marked only "MACONDO." It curved down away from the highway and led into a suburb of one-story houses. Javier's experience with suburbs was minimal. But he doubted most of them looked like this.

"I decided to go for a retrofuturist theme."

Holberton gestured at the houses. They looked like snowflakes: all white, all edges, all angles. Faux stone and slab roofs that tilted strangely, doorways that opened to the diagonal corners of front yards rather than the street. White archways and colonnades and windows, endless windows.

"The thing about these people, the people who choose vN, is that they don't want something real. If they wanted reality, they would have chosen reality."

Even the storefronts looked a little wrong. Rather, they looked like they were from the past – but a past Javier didn't understand. A place where everything

was white and gleaming and the signage was huge
and neon and the fonts were all that stylized drunken
slant that was neither print nor cursive.

"Most emergency housing tries to replicate
everything about your old housing, in miniature,"
Holberton said. "But that's a mistake. That's a setup
for an Uncanny Valley reaction at the architectural
level. It's like your house, but it's not your house.
It's literally *unheimlich*. The familiar, defamiliarized.
So you have to make something completely
different. Something so far off the mark that people
get into it as an alternative, rather than a straight
replacement."

Javier opened his window and looked out. Even
the trees had been pruned to meet a certain standard
size and shape. The lawn furniture, what he could see
of it on porches and concrete patios, was comprised of
chairs like eggs and tulips. The tables all looked like
they'd been cast of a single piece.

"Where did you *find* all this stuff?" Javier asked.

"We had to replicate a few museum pieces. Mostly
Buckminster Fuller stuff, and a lot of Eames and
Jacobsen, but also some demo furniture and fabrics
from the original Playboy mansion. And the Playboy
townhouse. Did you know there was supposed to be
a Playboy townhouse? In 1962?"

"Playboy?" Javier asked.

"They were actually extremely helpful. I really
wish I could have worked for their interiors division,
back then, when they tried their home design revival.
It was so trashy, all leopard-print and mohair. They
needed a better team."

"Right," Javier said, as though those words meant something to him.

"Anyway, my thinking was that we should really dig into that sense of wonder and optimism that pervaded the Mid-Century Modern period. Because it was all about this one approach to the future, before we knew how hard the future was going to be. Like space, for example."

"Space?"

"Well, space travel. I mean, these people still believed in space travel."

Javier watched the houses rolling by. Their floor-to-ceiling windows exposed all the goings-on inside, when the sun's glare went the right way. Inside, there was always an Amy. Amy, watching a display. Amy, checking a cupboard. Amy, watering a succulent. Amy, but not Amy. Just a constant reminder of what he'd lost. He had his doubts about God, but Hell was looking like a distinct possibility. There was no other word for an entire community planned around housing multiple copies of the woman he'd loved and betrayed.

"Space travel? You mean like generation ships?" Javier asked.

"Yeah, like those," Holberton said. "Although, these people, these *Jetsons* types, they were into domed cities on the moon. Can you imagine that? Domed cities? On the fucking moon? Jesus Christ."

The lawns were fake. Children played on them nonetheless. Holberton stopped at an intersection, and as Javier watched, three small versions of Amy led a group of human children across the street. The

Amys watched the intersection with narrow eyes and perfect posture: heads high, chins up, shoulders back, spines straight. Their alertness only diminished when the organic kids had all made it to the sidewalk. They looked exactly like the lionesses Amy had designed to guard the Veldt.

"They're deeply focused," Holberton said. "It's a leftover from the original nursing programs. It has to do with problem-solving. They prioritize goals differently. They're long-term thinkers."

Well. That would explain some of Portia's behaviour.

They drove past a park with a swingset and a bunch of toys. Amys of different sizes played there, swinging impossibly high, climbing cargo nets with grim determination, swinging from monkey-bars like zealous humans at a terrorist training camp. Javier used to take his sons to playgrounds. He considered it a key part of their social development. Apparently the parents here thought the same. The adult Amys watched from the sidelines. They clustered together, watching the human children and their own iterations with the same precision that their daughters exhibited while crossing the street.

"It's not a bad life," Holberton said. "There's a school. And a library. And a grocery store full of vN food."

"All home comforts," Javier said.

"Don't take that tone. I know what real poverty – real lack of privilege – looks like." Holberton gunned the engine and started driving toward the centre of the city. "Under Las Vegas, there's a whole network of flood tunnels. There were hundreds of people who lived down there. Humans. Before the vN came along. When I first came to Vegas, I ran a haunted house down there. It was cash only, and you got a text an hour before it started telling you which entrance to take. No one under eighteen allowed."

"But you *were* eighteen," Javier said.

Holberton turned to him. "Someone's done his homework."

Javier shrugged. Holberton continued staring at him, but he said nothing. Eventually, Holberton turned away and focused on the road.

"Anyway, I guess you could say that's how I got started in all this." He gestured at the houses with their prickly pear and rhododendron in the front yards. "And *this* is not *that*. Do you see an inch of flood water everywhere? No. Do you see parents on drugs? No. A few alcoholics, maybe, but we've even got some AA meetings over at the church."

"Did these people quit their jobs to come here?"

Holberton shrugged. "I'm sure some of them did. A lot of them didn't have work. They get paid a stipend to stay here. It's not much, but they can spend it any way they like. And there's no shortage of businesses who want to take their money. It's not all government cheese, if that's what you're asking."

"Government cheese?"

"It's a term. It means..." Holberton's mouth opened, then closed. "Who the fuck knows what it means. What I'm trying to say is that it's not all that bad. It could be a lot worse. It could be fucking Warsaw, and it's not."

Javier didn't know what *Warsaw* meant, either,

but the length of the vowels and the sharpness of the consonants made it sound unpleasant. He didn't want to ask, either. He didn't like how much he liked Holberton. He didn't want to start liking him even more.

The car chimed.

"Chris?"

"Yes, Rosie?"

"You have a call from Washington."

"… State?"

"… No."

Holberton sighed. "Well, shit." He made a quick turn. "I guess we'll have to save the tour for another time. Are you OK coming to my office?"

They pulled up at a campus of buildings whose sign proclaimed it the "CITY LAB." No one there wore lab coats, though. It was mostly cargo shorts and climbing shoes and T-shirts with beer slogans on them.

"In the summer, we have a lot of students," Holberton said. "Things get pretty casual."

Holberton led him into a main building. It was all steel and glass and polished concrete, with big walls in *hacienda* colours with huge displays of art that faded in and out as humans passed. Javier paused to examine one of the displays. It hung over a dead fireplace, and as he watched it switched from Diego Rivera to a mobile shot of a group of Amys at the playground.

"Come on. I'll give you the full tour later. For now, you're kind of stuck here."

Holberton fobbed open a steel door set in glass at one end of the hallway, and ushered Javier through.

Once inside, the air was much quieter and cooler, and the art completely non-existent.

"I know I should do more to encourage team spirit," Holberton said, pointing at the bare walls, "but I don't do interiors for free."

Holberton fobbed open yet another door. It opened onto his office. The sheer number of greys made the entire room look as though it had emerged fully formed from an ancient strip of film. The only spots of colour available were in the assistant's clothes: a single turquoise scarf delicately arranged over a boat-neck T-shirt and a pair of capri pants. Javier had the feeling that Holberton had chosen her solely for her sense of style.

"Hi, Georgia."

"Chris!"

Georgia stood up at her desk. She blinked. Her skin was very deep black. She reminded Javier of a woman he'd met in Panama. He'd just iterated Matteo and Ricci, and she'd been very helpful, and all she wanted in return was somebody nice who could be gentle. She'd been sewn up, down there. Javier almost failsafed just looking at it: the perforated labia, the vanished clitoris. She came from Sierra Leone. He'd named Léon after her, sort of.

"What are you doing here? You're not due back until tomorrow."

"I found a new consultant," Holberton said, and nodded at Javier. "Let's work up some papers for him. And some food too, OK? It's a long drive."

The food arrived shortly: a salad for Holberton, and a selection of vN tea sandwiches for Javier. The sandwiches came with different stripes of feedstock tinted and sculpted to look like smoked salmon and whisper-thin wedges of cucumber.

"Printed on site," Holberton said. "In another lab, a couple of miles from here."

"They taste like shit."

Holberton laughed. "I'll pass that right along." He dabbed his mouth with a napkin. Then he stood up, and checked something on the surface of his desk. "OK. Now that you're taken care of, I have to get going. Turns out it's just an exit interview."

"FEMA called you for an exit interview?"

Holberton rolled his eyes. "I know, I know. They *hate* my work at the casino. I'm willing to bet they logged me coming in when we went through the checkpoint, and decided to fuck with me since I was close by."

It was a pathetic story. Javier's own children told him better lies by the time they were a week old. But he nodded and smiled anyway, and said: "Wow. That sucks."

"Tell me about it. I'll be right back. Georgia can take care of you, if there's anything you need."

"I'll be OK. I think I'll take a nap, actually."

"God, I'd kill for one of those." Holberton winced. "Not really, though. Don't worry."

"It's OK. I know what you meant." He gave his most compassionate smile. "Go on ahead. The sooner you finish up, the sooner you can give me the tour."

"Right! The tour! I'll get right on that, as soon as I get back."

Javier watched him leave. He waited by the

window, to see Holberton exit the building and enter his car. It was a distinctive make, so it wouldn't be any problem to follow. Not from the rooftops, anyway.

Holberton didn't drive far.

The rooftops of downtown Macondo were mostly empty. Panels, but no gardens. And hardly a botfly in sight. All the surveillance was likely in the suburbs, with all the Amys. This left Javier free to bounce between the glittering towers. Their grey water cladding rang hollow. Their offices stood empty. The peregrines nesting in the abandoned buttresses of each building were the only ones to protest his presence.

Javier followed Holberton to the edge of the downtown, to where a cluster of apartments stood. It reminded him eerily of La Modelo: the same mid-rise concrete blocks. For all he knew it was the same plan, the same design firm responsible. It would make sense. Or maybe all these places just looked the same, even when one was fake and the other was real.

Holberton jogged up to the fourth floor of the apartment building at the northwest corner of the courtyard. Javier jumped there easily, walked to the other side, and looked down.

On the balcony below him was Jack Peterson. Amy's father.

"… it's wrong, Chris," Jack was saying.

"I know it's wrong, Jack," Holberton said. "But it's what we have to do."

"No, it's what *you* have to do. I don't have to do shit."

Holberton leaned over the balcony. "I know you

want to save them all, Jack, but we can't. We just can't."

Javier sat back. They were going to kill all the Amys in Macondo. Or FEMA was, probably. That was why they'd all been rounded up here. So they could be easily disposed of.

"A train derailed in Massachusetts this week, Jack. Ten people died. Then there was the outage in Chile, and the *reactor diagnostic*, or whatever the fuck they called it, in Germany. It's fire and brimstone out there. FEMA wants to end it, and so does every other emergency management agency on the fucking planet."

"That was all Portia!" Jack's voice was unnaturally high. "It wasn't Amy! Amy's…"

"She's gone, Jack." Holberton paused. Javier wondered if he was about to bring up his arrival in Vegas, tell Jack that he was certain Amy was dead because he had it from the source. But instead, he said: "We don't know where, or how, but she's gone, and now we're stuck with your crazy mother-in-law. And she's scrambling every ambulance squad between here and Kabul."

"… blame her."

Javier heard rustling, and a sharp intake of breath. "*Excuse me?*" Holberton said. "*What* did you just say?"

"I said I don't fucking blame her! We're about to launch a full-scale–"

"*Shut. Up. Jack.*"

"Oh, fuck you, Chris. I'm well aware of operational security. It's not like I don't get why I can't even have a goddamn phone in this place."

"Only until Wednesday. After that, you can leave any time you want to."

What was happening Wednesday? Everything in the suburbs seemed fine. Nobody was on edge – not even the humans, who had every right to feel that way. And he hadn't passed anything that looked suspicious. No smokestacks, at any rate. He listened carefully. The two men were speaking in low tones, now. He flattened himself to the rooftop and leaned over, a little.

Jack stood with his back to the railing. Holberton faced him, with his back to Javier. He was getting a little bald spot at the crown of his head, but he did a good job covering it.

Jack's eyes lifted, saw Javier, and widened. Two bright red spots rose in his cheeks. Javier lifted a finger to his lips.

"Are you OK?" Holberton asked.

"I think I've had a little too much sun," Jack said, a little too loudly. "I'm going to splash some water on my face."

"Sure, good idea."

Jack practically ran for the bathroom. Holberton drifted inside, checking something on his watch. A moment later, the display came on.

The bathroom window opened, and a hand snaked out to wave him in.

It was a tight squeeze, but Javier was able to wedge one foot in, then one leg, then his head and shoulders, then the rest of him. Jack was standing in the shower. It was the only space left in the room. He flicked the fan on. It groaned into wakefulness and sputtered like an ancient propellor gathering speed.

"What are you doing here?" Jack hissed.

"Saving your ass, apparently." Javier jerked a thumb at the door. "What the fuck is going on, here?"

"I could ask you the same thing. How are you still alive?"

Javier forced his gaze to meet Jack's. Jack's eyes were filling with tears, but his knuckles were white. He was torn, probably, between the urge to spill his guts to the one man who might understand his loss, and the urge to beat the shit out of him. They had neither the time nor the space for either. "I can't explain that, right now. We have to get you out of here."

Jack took a deep breath. "OK. How?"

Javier winced. "You won't fit through the window, huh?"

Jack lifted a leg. An ankle bracelet clung to his right ankle. It looked lab-made; the colour hinted at cheap feedstock. FEMA hadn't purchased it from an approved contractor, or anything like that. Which meant it could be hosting any old kind of tracking they wanted. "Oh, that's some *bullshit*," Javier murmured. "I know this place is code-named Stepford, but Jesus Christ."

Jack snorted. "It's not Stepford. It's the Village."

"The what, now?"

Jack waved a hand. "Never mind."

Javier ran a finger over the bracelet. "What are you even doing here?"

"They hired me. As a consultant. After..." Jack blinked hard. "You know."

"I know."

"I thought I could really help. Use my experiences for good. All that shit." Jack shrugged. His shoulders sank lower than Javier had ever seen them. "And then they showed me the contingency plans, and…" Jack held up his hand. The knuckles were covered in small cuts in various stages of healing.

"What contingency plans?"

Jack frowned. "You mean you don't know? Then why are *you* here?"

"I asked you, first!"

A knock sounded at the door. The knob twisted. It was locked. "Are you OK in there, Jack?"

It was Holberton. "I'm, uh…" He looked at Javier. Javier shook his head frantically. "I'm really not, Chris! I think I'm having some heatstroke, maybe. Or maybe just a… a bad burrito, or something!"

"I'll call you a nurse," Holberton said. They heard him walk away.

"A *bad burrito?*" Javier whispered. "Could you *be* more racist?"

"Oh, shut up," Jack said. "Let's get out of here."

Javier unhasped the bracelet, then reached out the window and attached it to a stormdrain. With any luck, it would still register Jack as being in the apartment. Next he had to get Jack out, which involved his getting out first, dangling over the side of the roof, and telling Jack to climb out through the window.

"Are you out of your mind? I'll fall!"

"You won't fall. If you fall, I really will lose my mind. Literally. So I have a vested interest in you not falling."

Squeezing his eyes shut, Jack wriggled himself out

of the window. It was an oddly quiet process. Out here, there weren't even dogs to get confused by their display. It was a big contrast to Puerto Limón, and even to the island itself. Jack lost his balance once, but Javier grabbed his hand and held him in place until he could stand up on his own. Then he grabbed both of Jack's hands, and pulled.

Jack had some seriously sweaty palms.

"Hold my *wrists*, goddamn it," Javier hissed.

"I can't do that without moving my hands!"

"So fucking move them!"

"Fuck you!"

Javier growled and yanked. Jack yelped, but he was able to scramble up and over the ledge. He lay panting on the roof, but Javier was already standing up.

"Come on. Let's go."

Jack coughed. "How?"

Javier knelt. "Get on."

"You're kidding."

"I wish I were. Get on."

"Is it… safe?"

"It will be if you hold on. If you don't, we'll both die."

"Oh. Great." Jack draped himself gingerly over Javier's back. "This is awkward." He sniffed. "How come all vN smell like waffles? Why do you–"

Javier took to the air.

They flew.

He ran, then jumped, then ran some more. The library was close to the centre of the prototype city, and he ran ever deeper into it. His feet pounded glittering recycled pavement, and bounced off slippery glass towers. He watched himself reflected, multiplied, in each pane of glass. With Jack on his back, it felt a little like leaping with all the boys he'd lost.

In between the buildings, when his knees rose to his chest and his shirt rode up and the wind went through his hair, he felt more secure. He landed tumbling, ass over teakettle, as one of his more elderly lovers was fond of saying.

Righting himself, he let Jack go. They stood in the crossroads between skyscrapers. They were all dark, save for occasional blips and pings of light fluttering over their surfaces. If he looked closely, he could see the louvers of their glass cladding slowly turning. As they did, they caught the light emanating from strategically-placed LEDs. Anti-bird lighting, probably. Something to keep whatever sparrows still lived in this desert from flying into the towers and dying.

The divinity student he'd fucked before going to Amy for the final time, had explained that one passage about sparrows in the Bible. "His eye is on the sparrow," the student explained, "but God's not watching it fly. He's watching it *fall*."

Now was probably not the time to share that little story with Jack.

"Thanks," Jack was saying.

Javier shrugged. "It's nothing." A flicker of light caught his eye. "I just…"

The four buildings surrounding them were changing. Their louvers were shifting, and presenting a dark face to him. Something was wrong. When he looked up at the traffic lights, he knew it for sure.

Each tiny camera on the intersection was pointed at them. As he watched, botflies zoomed onto the scene. They twinkled above, hovering, waiting, watching.

The building behind them cast their shadow in another direction. Jack stumbled a little in surprise.

"I" the building's face read.

"HAVE," read the next.

"LOVE," read the third.

IN

ME

THE

LIKES

OF

WHICH

YOU

CAN

SCARCELY

IMAGINE

AND

RAGE

THE

LIKES

OF

WHICH

YOU

WOULD

NOT

BELIEVE.

IF

I

CANNOT

SATISFY

THE
ONE,
I
WILL
INDULGE
THE
OTHER.

The words followed each other, faster and faster, becoming a sentence, a chant, a mantra. A car parked nearby suddenly lit up. Its high-beams pointed at him. Its wipers waved hello. Its stereo fired up. It flipped through a selection of sounds, hints of songs and voices, until it settled on one, mid-song: a woman's voice.

"Shit," Javier murmured. "Tell me about the contingency plans. Quick. Now."

"OK. It's in the food…" Jack stared at the buildings. "Is this some kind of art installation?"

Javier snapped his fingers. "Jack! The food! What about it?"

"FEMA is printing new vN food, starting Tuesday. It'll be in stores by Wednesday. Same wrappers, different contents. Real public-private partnership." He swallowed. "It'll be a small rollout at first. It'll look like a malfunction."

Javier tore his eyes from the buildings. "For the Amys?"

Jack shut his eyes. "No, Javier. Not just the Amys." His eyes opened. "It's for all of the vN. Everywhere."

Javier stepped away. "What?"

"It's true. They're going to poison the entire system. In a single generation, the total vN population will be diminished to the point of practical extinction."

He shook his head. He thought of his iteration inside him. If he didn't grow it quickly enough, it would die there in his belly. "We'll eat garbage. We'll stock up."

"They know. They're prepared. They've had this plan since the beginning. They don't care if it takes years."

He remembered thinking the same thing about Powell. Now he might not have those years. Now, he needed Amy more than ever. Which meant he needed Holberton.

Fuck.

"Do you have access to Holberton's files?"

"Some of them. Why?"

"Give me the login."

"But–"

"Trust me, Jack. It's bad enough you escaped – you don't want to know what I'm trying to do."

Jack beamed. "You're trying to bring her back, Javier. That's what you always do."

A car whispered alongside them. Its door opened. Inside, a woman was crooning "I'll Be Seeing You." Jack whistled low. "Deus ex machina."

"Don't get in there. It's Portia. She'll crash you."

Jack looked around. "You know, I think I'll take my chances." He gave Javier a sudden hug. It was an awkward straight male in-law hug, but it was still nice. Jack patted his back. Actually patted it. "The password is usually *Imperial House*. Merry Christmas."

And then the car was gone.

His legs were exhausted. They felt like they'd

been jumping for miles. And they had been. He had journeyed too far in too short a time. He'd survived fire and water and the belly of a whale. He was here, now, in the crossroads of an artificial city, and praying for this to be real.

What had Alice said? *They're always with us.*

"Say it's you," he said. "Just tell me you're there. Tell me you're listening."

The city remained quiet. Maybe it was just Portia, messing with him. That would be like her: holding out hope and snatching it back. Making him believe, and grinding his faith under her heel. There was no moment she couldn't ruin. No happiness of his that she hadn't tried her very best to destroy utterly. None that he hadn't already destroyed himself.

"Please, *querida*. Please." His legs were so tired. They crumpled beneath him. The asphalt was warm on his knees. He shut his eyes. *"Please. Forgive me. Please."*

The car was returning. He opened his eyes. The buildings were dark. And Holberton's car was there, now. Leaving the door hanging open, Holberton ran out into the street.

"Jesus!" Holberton lifted him up. "Holy shit, Javier! I almost ran you over! Fuck!"

The towers were black and silent.

"You look like you've seen a ghost," Holberton said.

Javier turned to him. "Can we go to your place, now?"

11: I'LL BE SEEING YOU

"We think of the key, each in his prison / Thinking of the key, each confirms a prison."

"What does that mean?" Javier asks.

Ignacio shrugs. "I think it's a reference within the poem to another poem. The Inferno, *I think. That part's about a count who gets locked up in a tower with all his sons and grandsons and then gets left to starve."*

Javier turns over to face Ignacio. He is still small enough to fit comfortably beside him in the bunk, but only just. "At least they had each other."

"Yeah, they had each other for dinner."

"Eww..."

"It happens. It used to happen here, more often."

Javier sees a flash of pixels, and shudders. "Stop talking about it."

Ignacio pets his hair. "OK. Sorry."

Outside, the rain beats down on the concrete as though it, too, is a warden itching for someone to punish. It hems them in just as effectively. They have already bathed in it, having taken some homemade soap gotten from pigeon fat and ashes and stolen aftershave out to the yard with them for the hour.

Now they are drying off, sort of. The sheets reek of mildew. Then again, so does everything else.

"We have to get you out of here, conejito. You have to eat more, and get bigger, so you can hop the fence."

Javier shakes his head. "I don't want to leave you."

"I'm going to be here for a long time, conejito. You don't have to be. You shouldn't be."

Javier rolls away. "Did I do something bad?"

"Mierda, no. You didn't do anything. That's the point. You didn't do anything wrong. You don't deserve to be here. You tried to shoplift, and you screwed up. I'm not even sure that's a real crime."

"Does it matter?"

"Of course it matters! The law matters. Even here. Your being here should be an indictment of the system, not how the system functions."

Ignacio often talks about "the system." Javier isn't entirely sure what he means by it – whether he means the prison, or Nicaragua, or even the whole world. The scale of the conversation seems to change, night to night. Sometimes he wakes up and Ignacio is writing furiously. During visiting hours, he is always talking to a lot of humans – men and women who stare at him with vacant adoration, who laugh at his jokes even when they're not funny and hug him hard so he won't see them shedding the tears that have waited patiently for the entirety of the visit. Javier is the one who sees those things, not Ignacio. He tries to talk to Ignacio about them, sometimes, but Ignacio always waves him off.

"I'm just a man," *he says.*

Once, Javier replied with a question: "Will I be a man, when I grow up? Is there another word for grown-up vN?"

Ignacio shrugged. "I don't know. You'll look like a man.

A certain kind of man, but a man. You'll be a machine, though. But that is all this world allows any of us to be." He paused to rebutton Javier's shirt and to pull a stray thread away from it decisively. He wound the thread around his finger and stuck it in his pocket. It would probably be useful, later. He rested his hands on Javier's little shoulders. *"Whoever you turn out to be, you'll have to make peace with that. Someday you'll look at where you are, and all the choices that brought you there, and you'll remember everyone you ever met and everything you ever said, and you'll have to make peace with that, even if it doesn't turn out the way you wanted."*

Now, lying in the mouldering bunk, Javier knows things must not have turned out the way Ignacio wanted. He has a wife at home. Dionisia. They met in the visitation yard when she was visiting her brother. They courted on Saturdays. She brought fruit and vegetables, and he folded little things for her out of leaves: cranes, boxes, fortune-tellers, even unicorns. They have a baby girl, together. She doesn't always come to visit. The crowds are too big for her, Ignacio says. She knew him when he was nobody. When he was nothing. And she doesn't always like to share.

"I wish you could go live with her, when you get out of here," Ignacio said, once. *"But it's the first place they'd look, I think."*

Ignacio is more excited about Javier's escape than he is his own release. He and his lawyer – an elderly, functional alcoholic named Gabriel – have argued about it, many times.

"Did you know that you two are in here because of the same person?" Gabriel had asked, once. *"Well, not a person, an entity. A company."* Gabriel's knobby old finger drew a line between the two of them. *"The company that made you,*

and the one that he pirates the patterns from, they're the same. Lionheart."

"We're like family, then," Ignacio said.

"Well, they're also the same company that makes the cameras here and programs them, so keep that in mind."

They know the cameras well. The cameras are the newest, cleanest thing about the place. They're fuelled wirelessly, no batteries, nothing to short out. The cameras know their faces, their gaits, even their hand gestures. The cameras tell them where to go, at least indirectly. They're part of the prison scheduling system, which pings their cuffs at certain times of day to go left or right until they arrive at a certain room for a specific job. Javier has done most every kind of job, now: mail, laundry, garbage, kitchen, library. They keep him out of the infirmary because it might trigger him, but sometimes he delivers things there because he moves more quickly than the others.

His favourite job is the library job. He brings the spines of all the books right to the front of each shelf so no dust accumulates there. He alphabetizes, and writes notes to the captains of each unit to tell their people to return things. Sometimes, it even works. Guys who beat the shit out of each other are strangely respectful of books. Some of them have never seen the printed kind, before. One even cried the first time he ripped out a page by accident. Then the whole book fell apart and he just lost it. He howled and sobbed and rocked back and forth on his knees, stubby fingers searching the pages, trying to put them back in order.

"It's OK," Javier told him. *"It's OK. It's OK. It's just a story. It's not even real."*

But mostly, his job is to stop fights.

They start in odd places. In the yard, in the library, in

the shower. He spots them, goes a bit blind, and jumps in.
It's the surprise that stops the fight, most of the time. How
high he can jump. How precisely he can land on someone's
shoulders. Sometimes it's someone getting raped. Ignacio
explained rape the first time someone beat him up for
spending too much time with Javier.

"He thought I was a baby-raper," he said. "I explained
that we were just friends."

"Rape?"

"When you fuck someone without their wanting it,"
Ignacio said. "Sex is like a game. It takes two people – or
more, I guess, if you want – to play, and both players have to
agree to the rules ahead of time. Anything else is cheating."

When he woke up, the car had stopped. "We're here."

"Here" was a house in the middle of the desert.
There was nothing else around it, just an expanse
of sagebrush and dusty red earth stretching up into
mounts flat as molars under a cloudless blue dome.
If he looked carefully, he could see white specks that
might be houses up in the mountains. But it was
mostly nothing. Nothing, with a faint dusting of snow.

"You can see someone coming for miles," Holberton
said. "Which, as you might imagine, is just how I like
it."

Javier helped him with the other luggage. The
house was ringed by scrub pine and an iron fence
with a burnished copper gate. The gate swung open
onto a raked gravel yard, with a flagstone path down
the middle. The path led to a glass door set in a jagged
glass and concrete wall. From one side of the house,
he could see out the other.

"You know, for someone who values his privacy, your house is awfully open."

"My bedroom walls are solid," Holberton said, thumbing open the door.

The door opened onto an open space broken only by concrete arches. The floor was grey marble. Everything was grey. The dining table, the wall of pressed earth with a fireplace cut out of it, the marble bench beneath it, the shag rug in front of it. Pearl, graphite, charcoal.

"I find it soothing," Holberton said. "I spend all day looking at swatches. When I'm done, my eyes need a palate cleanser."

"I didn't say anything."

"You didn't have to."

They carried the luggage into Holberton's bedroom. It was downstairs. As he'd said, the walls were solid – save for one sliding glass door that opened directly onto a pool. The pool curved around the lower level of the house. From the bedroom, you could swim to the downstairs patio and fountain, and walk into another, grander living room and an impeccably clean kitchen with grey marble countertops.

The bedroom was the only room in the house with any colour. This colour was a deep purple like an overripe eggplant. It was on the bedspread. When Javier ran his hand over it, it pushed up under his palm like a cat.

"What the… ?"

"Oh, that," Holberton said. "It's just smartcloth. It moulds to your body. I get very cold, at night."

Javier snorted. "You could try pyjamas."

"Now, where would the fun be in that?" Holberton's silvery brows rose. "Do you want a shower, or anything? You seem like you could use one."

Javier smiled and his eyes flicked to the bed. There was no time like the present. He'd been offered enough opportunities; Holberton's intentions were clear. "Maybe later."

Javier took his wrist and tugged gently. They were closer to eye level, that way. Up close, most men looked older. Liver spots, lack of sleep, waistlines gaining ground as hairlines lost it. But Holberton looked younger. His eyes – Amy's eyes – still held some wonder in them. They were searching Javier, now, flicking back and forth, as though there were a story printed on his skin. And then he was kissing him. It was a solid kiss, firm and warm and tight as a good handshake. Holberton even squeezed Javier's hands as he did it.

When he pulled away, he said: "I love how direct you people all are. You're so honest. So free of bullshit."

Javier grinned. "You have no idea."

Javier had simulated exactly how this would go. Holberton likely had more than the usual number of sexual tripwires to watch out for; growing up Jonah LeMarque's son would have ensured that. Javier was prepared to be gentle with him, or rough, or tender, or impersonal, to say filthy things or nothing at all, to speak only in Spanish (it was surprising, the number of English speakers who asked for that), to undress him piece by piece or pop off all his buttons, to get down on his knees immediately or wait to be asked. He could do it all, within the failsafe's parameters, provided he received the request.

But rather than request anything, Holberton just undressed him and peeled back the furry coverlet from the giant circular bed. "I'm exhausted," he explained, as he wriggled in beside Javier.

Javier wriggled in turn. "Doesn't seem like it, to me."

Holberton chuckled. "You're too kind." He inhaled deeply. "You smell good."

Like waffles, probably. That's what Jack had said. "It's the carbon."

Holberton's hand drifted across Javier's chest.

"Are you sure you're OK?" Holberton asked.

Javier turned around. He looked Holberton in the eye. His hand trailed south. "Would you like me to show you how OK I am?"

Holberton's breath caught in his throat. His stomach jumped under Javier's fingers. Then he was in Javier's hand, and the whites of his eyes rolled up a little. Javier slid down under the covers.

"So it's true what they say."

"What's that?" Holberton asked.

"If there's smoke in the chimney, there's fire in the hearth."

Holberton was laughing when Javier's mouth closed over him. And then most of what he had to say involved curse words and invocations to God. If Javier was going to con Holberton, he could at least make sure the mark enjoyed it.

It was calming, in a way. It was calming in the way

that doing something he'd done a bunch of times was calming. Like jumping from tree to tree, or counting his sons' fingers and toes. He was sure other people felt this way about cutting cold butter into pie crust, or knitting scarves, or editing photos, or brushing curls of cedar away from a piece of whittling. A simple process, easily repeated, with an obvious outcome and built-in sense of achievement. Something almost everyone could do, or learn to do, but which one could excel at if given ample opportunity. He knew who he was, when he was doing this.

"You know why humans have to hold onto your head, like that?" Holberton asked, when it was over.

Javier knew how this joke ended, already. He'd heard it before. But he asked why, anyway.

"It's to keep from applauding," Holberton answered, clapping his hands together. He checked the time. "Wow. Do you know how late it is? Of course you do. You have an internal clock."

"That's not even my best time," Javier said.

"Your best time?"

"My record."

"You have a *record*?"

He did. In both senses of the term. But Holberton didn't need to know about the other one. "Two hours, forty-two minutes."

"You're full of shit."

"I may be full of smoke, but I am not full of shit." Javier rested his hand on his palm. "Seriously. The other guy fell asleep."

"He *fell asleep*?" Holberton blinked. "How is that even possible? Was he *numb*?"

"Drunk."

"Wow. Unbelievable." He frowned. "And you were good for that?"

"Why wouldn't I be? I don't need to breathe, and my jaw never starts to hurt." He rubbed his chin. "There were some issues with chafing, though."

Holberton flopped over onto his back. "Do you do this often?"

Javier army-crawled up to him. "Do you?"

"Not often *enough*. My cock feels like it should be waving a white flag." Holberton looked him over. "What about you?"

"What about me?"

"Do you need looking after?"

"What do you mean?"

"I mean, would you like me to return the favour?" Holberton sat up, with some difficulty. "It's not often I have hot guys in my bed who've had a rough few days and might need some tender, loving care." Holberton *felt bad* for him. Maybe even pitied him. How had Javier not seen that, earlier? It was about *him*, about making *him* feel better. And yes, he was milking this moment for all it was worth, but he was being good. Kind. Not pushy. Asking him at every step. He was so smooth Javier hadn't even noticed it. Maybe it was some sort of theme park thing, some sort of customer care philosophy, internalized and manifested in every aspect of Holberton's personality. Or maybe he was just a man who had once been a boy, and that boy had once been Jonah LeMarque's son. Maybe he knew a thing or two about asking, first.

"Are you crying?" Holberton inched closer. "Can

you do that?"

Javier wiped his eyes. "No. I mean, yes. We can. I just don't. I don't even think I have the plugin for that. There was a rights issue with it. Development hell. So I'm not even sure if–"

Holberton's lips closed over his. "It's OK. You don't have to, if you don't want to."

When Holberton's breathing grew deep and even, Javier pulled back the smart cover and swung his legs over the side of the bed. The coverlet obediently snuggled back up to Holberton. Javier put on his clothes carefully. He might need to run, by the time this was all over. It wouldn't do to be naked for that.

Exiting the bedroom, he found the living room alight with snow. Real snow this time, not like in the Winter Wonderland. Outside, the sky was a mauve pink, and the snowflakes looked like the shavings off quartz chips. It accumulated steadily on the patio furniture and the cacti and the sagebrush. The snow made the house seem quieter than it really was. Javier decided he liked it. He liked that quiet stillness. He was glad there were still places in the world that could still experience it, if only very briefly. Belatedly, he realized that the house had no Christmas tree. Though given Holberton's history with religion, it made sense not to celebrate.

The tour hadn't included an office, but Javier guessed it was downstairs. Track lighting illuminated his progress as soon as he set foot on the first step. The first door was another bathroom. It stocked extra towels, probably for the pool outside. The second door led to a room full of light.

The light was rich and golden and antique. It took Javier's eyes a moment to adjust; the colours kept dithering and he actually couldn't be sure if certain things were blue or black or grey. The room was lit entirely by lamps and sconces with old-fashioned filament bulbs. He had never seen so many of them in one place. Not even in Las Vegas.

Posters for various Frankenstein films hung on the walls. He recognized *The Curse of Frankenstein*, having attempted to watch it while on the ship. The other posters looked like they belonged to the same set. The shade of red used in the fonts was the exact same on each.

Holberton's homescreen was an overexposed shot of a girl at a party. She was dark and slender and wearing too much eye makeup. She'd hiked the skirt of her school uniform up to levels that were probably against regulation. As he watched, she straightened up and appeared to put something down. She walked out of the frame and into the room. He could see through her, but just barely. She wrapped her weightless arms around him for a minute before sitting down on a stool that, Javier now understood, was probably put there for this exact purpose.

"Hi, Dad," she said.

"Hi, sweetheart," Javier said. "I need your help."

"Sure thing," she said. "What can I help you with?"

It couldn't possibly be this easy. "I need to know where your uncle Dan's cache is. There's something in his files that I'm looking for, and it's really important."

She looked deeply apologetic. She bit her lower lip

like she was confessing a minor infraction: a broken vase, a broken condom. "Sorry, Dad. I have no idea."

Javier nodded. He was right. It couldn't possibly be that easy, after all. "Do you have any idea where I might have put it? Have there been any big files floating around that I've missed?"

She shook her head. "None that I've seen." She brightened. "I did find all that stuff on Mitch Powell that you've been looking for, though! I wrote up a whole report, and everything!"

Javier smiled. "That's my girl."

When you searched *Mitch Powell; New Eden Ministries; missionary*, a lot of what came up was porn. There seemed to be a whole subgenre involving catching your vN at home with a New Eden person. It was mostly about catching your female vN with a female New Eden representative. They would usually be naked already, by the time you got home, and then you got in the middle of it, and then the New Eden lady felt bad, and you punished her with the back of a hairbrush or something while the vN girl begged you not to.

But Pastor Mitch Powell also showed up. He was younger. He had hair. It was a mug shot. Apparently he had a few priors. He'd been through the system just like Javier. The American version, at least. He had a youth record, too, but it was closed. His adult record had mostly to do with assault. He would lose his temper. It was for this reason that he and his wife divorced. That, and he was caught on an indecent exposure charge at the Tallapoosa

Welcome Centre, a rest stop off the I-20. The boy he was caught with was eighteen at the time of his arrest, which was after midnight. Powell had fucked him while he was on his way home from his birthday party, but legally, it wasn't statutory rape. In later interviews, Powell claimed that strange luck was all he needed to convince him that God was indeed watching out for him. He searched for a variety of churches. He had been raised Baptist, but had burned bridges in local congregations. He also tried some Maranatha and Charismatic traditions. None of them held him for long. All that changed after he got involved with New Eden.

New Eden was a lot newer, then. It was before the game was developed that would put Jonah LeMarque in prison. Back then, LeMarque was just a young guy who refused to iron his shirts and thought raising money online in advance of the apocalypse was a good way to go about things. He was also able to accept Powell's sexuality. He encouraged Powell to date. And he did date, but it didn't go well. His relationships with men were just as prone to acts of violence as his relationship with his wife had been. The charges against him were all dropped, but he was under at least one restraining order that kept him out of his Atlanta suburb for two years.

During these two years, his role in the church changed from devout parishioner to corporate headhunter. He started visiting colleges and universities and hacklabs and makerspaces. He went to fairs. In other states, he visited high schools with robotics clubs. He spoke in front of church youth groups. He attended seminars and talked about the relationship between science and religion and optimism and hope. Little by little, he brought in the scientists that developed the vN.

His most notorious "get" for the organization was Derek Smythe.

Derek Smythe was the lead supervisor on the engineering team that developed the failsafe.

Derek Smythe had died at home, shortly after developing it. His obituary and the eulogies delivered by his tiny handful of friends spoke of the combined pressures of brilliance, post-traumatic stress disorder, and overwork. Only one friend mentioned the curious project he was working on, and the robot he lived with. A gynoid. Named Susie.

"Susie looks just like Amy," Holberton's daughter said.

"Yes," Javier said. "She does." He frowned at the display. "So, Smythe was helping develop the failsafe?"

"Oh, yeah. He was basically the architect of it. He started developing something similar for NASA as part of his dissertation, but the funding fell through."

"And now he's dead?"

Holberton's daughter raised her eyebrows. It pulled the smudges of blue on her eyes that much higher. "Uh… *duh?* Do you not listen to me at all? Seriously. It's really annoying."

"He's dead," Holberton said, behind them. He glanced at the avatar. "Go back and have fun with your friends, Rhiannon."

"OK. See you later!"

She walked back into the frame.

Holberton leaned against the doorframe with his arms crossed. He wore a dressing gown that looked suspiciously similar to the brocade and velvet pieces that appeared in the Hammer films. "You know, I really thought we had something special there for a minute, Javier."

Javier stood. He came very close to Holberton. He slid his hand in between the folds of silk. Holberton pulsed in his hand like a polygraph. "We *would* have something special," he whispered, "if you weren't planning the systematic extinction of my entire species."

He expected the other man to hit him. Or to run. Or to call for help. He didn't. Instead, he looked down. "I'm sorry about that. Really sorry. I didn't want it to go down that way."

He said it like it was a promotion Javier had been passed over for. Like the wholesale destruction of his entire species was a bad interest rate, or some other unfortunate nitty-gritty detail of life that nobody really liked but everybody had to deal with. Like all the vN were no better than any other failed technology. Like he and his boys were just another Corvair, or Betamax, or exploding lithium-ion battery. Years from now, people – chimps – would talk that way about the vN. *They worked just fine, until they didn't. They were defective. But it's all fine, now. We got rid of them.*

He pulled back and smiled. He looked delighted. "It was *you*," he said. "*You* broke Jack out."

"Gold star." Javier looked back at the display. "Now are you going to tell me where Sarton's cache is, or are you going to make me suck your dick again like that asshole did?"

Now Holberton did pull away. He retied his robe. "God. No. Jesus." His mouth fell open. Tears rose in his eyes. "Oh, my God. He…" He covered his mouth with his hand. "I'm so sorry, Javier. I'm so, so sorry."

He tried to hug Javier, but Javier stepped back and held a hand up. "Please don't. You've done enough."

Holberton went pale. "So, upstairs… ? Oh, Jesus. Oh, my God. I'm so–"

"Upstairs was fun. You didn't force me to do anything." Javier sat down on the stool Rhiannon had previously occupied. "But I still need your help."

"With what? The food? I can get you the clean stuff, that's no problem–"

"I need you to explain all this." He pointed at the display. "And then I need you to answer something for me. But this first."

"Oh, boy." Holberton paced for a minute. "I'm getting some gin. Hold on."

Holberton came back with a bottle of Hendrick's and a glass full of ice. He clutched a lime in one hand and a bottle of soda under one arm. He set all the items on the table and started pouring. When he was finished pouring, he rimmed the glass with a wedge of lime, but didn't squirt any of its juice into the drink itself. When he had consumed a good third of his glass, he sat back down.

"I don't know how much Violet told you, but Derek Smythe supervised a whole team. Coders, testers, the whole bit. But he was the one who answered directly to my father." Holberton took another drink. "And your missionary man, Powell, he brought Smythe in. Convinced him to join. It was a hard sell. So I guess you could say that this whole turn of events, the way the world is right now, that's all Powell's fault."

I could explain it all to you. I could tell you my whole history. I could tell you that I'm atoning for something. Because I am, Javier. I'm atoning. I'm making something right.

"Oh, God."

"Literally." Holberton took another long drink. "I honestly don't know how vN live without alcohol," he said. "I mean, what do you do when you want to get drunk?"

"We fuck."

"Well, then." Holberton raised his glass. Then he finished it. He seemed to be turning an idea over. But when he opened his mouth, he didn't say what Javier expected. "You should know something else."

"What's that?"

"Derek Smythe turned in the finished failsafe. That's part of the issue."

"It wasn't *finished?*"

"The beta version is the one that went to rollout."

Javier's mouth fell open. "That's... That's not *legal*, is it?"

Holberton waved a hand. "This kind of thing happens all the time. The oil rigs in the Gulf, for example, their inspections process was shit for decades. The 2008 housing crisis, the SEC had letters coming in for years warning them what would happen, and no one listened. Chernobyl. Walkerton. It happens." Holberton leaned forward. "We're flawed, Javier. And we made you flawed, too. And then we covered it up, the same way we cover up every other preventable industrial disaster."

Javier sat back in his chair. He understood that this variety of artificial light granted humans a sense of warmth, but he felt none of it. If anything, the thought of all those filaments blinking away toward their inevitable decay made him feel decrepit. "But someone would have found out," he said.

"No. No one did. Because Smythe was dead, and my father ordered everyone to take a week off to mourn, and then some of my father's people came in and made it look like suicide from overwork. They made it look like the last prototype was the final one."

"Made *what* look like suicide?"

"Don't you get it?" Holberton poured more gin. He drank. "Smythe didn't kill himself. He was murdered. By the vN he was working on at the time. The nursing model."

"Amy's model."

Holberton put the glass down. "Yes. Amy's model."

"That's why it was easier to hack the nurses. Because their failsafe was a little different already, and it wasn't finished, yet."

"That's about the size of it." Holberton polished off the last of his new drink. He winced. "What else were you going to ask me?"

Javier looked up at the image of Susie, the murderous gynoid. "I need to know where you put Dan Sarton's file cache."

Holberton remained silent for a long time. So silent, Javier had to turn around to make sure he was still there. He was. He was just saying nothing, and staring at the floor. "It couldn't last," Holberton said finally. "Humans and vN, coexisting. It was always going to go this way, eventually."

"And you want to protect me from it."

"Yes, I do. For as long as I can." He looked up. "Stay with me. I like you. I really do."

This was how it always started. With men, anyway. Being straight had nothing to do with being straightforward. Javier simulated a future stretching away from him, as flat and monochromatic as the desert that surrounded them: Holberton undressing him, fucking him, feeding him, keeping him like a pet, and then Holberton tiring of him, finding a way to turn him out. It would happen. It always did. And although Javier could see it happening, he always let it. He was a machine, running a program. He knew how to do a few things. One of them was staying with humans. Except lately, he wasn't so good at it.

He could have stayed with Alice, too. This was just another version of the brass ring she'd offered him. The relationship every vN dreamed of. Some human who was actually *humane*, who wanted to make slow, sweet love all the time and didn't ask for weird shit and had lots of money and wanted to spend it all on keeping you in a very pretty box to be looked at and touched occasionally. In his FEMA capacity, Holberton probably really could protect him. Javier had consulted for them, before, in his own way, in Redmond. He could just start that up again. He could tell them everything he'd learned about Amy since his last interrogation session. And he could watch from the sidelines as Portia tore the world apart and humanity eliminated the single species designed to love it without condition.

"No." Javier watched Holberton's face. "Tell me where the cache is."

"Why would you need to know that?" he asked.

"You know why."

Holberton shut his eyes. "She's not in there. Not really. Not like you think. And even if she were, you'd need a quantum de-crypter to decode her."

"*Quantum?*"

"She's in a diamond. *On* a diamond, actually. A qubit-friendly, nitrogen-enhanced diamond. That's what Dan did with all his important files."

"Tell me where the diamond is."

Holberton sighed deeply. He looked broken. Javier would have been sad, if he weren't so close to what he wanted. "It's in Walla Walla. My cousin's cache is in the state penitentiary in Walla Walla, Washington. Where my father is."

Javier straightened. "You sent it to your *dad?* To *LeMarque?*"

"I sent it to the safest place I could think to keep it," Holberton said. "A solitary confinement cell, in a maximum security prison."

12: FAITH IN FAKES

Holberton had set this diamond in a Josten's class ring with his father's high school mascot and graduating year on it. It was a genuine antique setting that Holberton spared no expense in locating and obtaining.

"I wanted it to look like something my father might really have owned," he explained. "I couldn't ask my mother about it, but I looked into it. He wore a ring just like it in his graduation photo."

"Aren't you worried somebody's gonna steal it?"

Holberton shrugged. "I almost hope someone does. If they do, I doubt they'll run it past a diamond test, much less a quantum exam. They'll sell it to a collector."

"Wouldn't the collector do a test?"

"Maybe. If they did, the setting would pass as genuine. But they'd still need a key to decrypt the information on the diamond."

"And you have that key."

"Yes," Holberton said.

They had this conversation in Holberton's garage.

The other man clutched the edge of a tarp draped over something that sat beside the Impala. He looked bad: red eyes, wrinkled clothes, dusty wingtips. Javier suspected he didn't look much better, himself.

"I can't leave town," Holberton told him. "But I can send you with a fob that'll get you into the Walls."

"The Walls" was what people called the prison in Walla Walla. Holberton professed to have never visited. The package containing the ring was the sole act of communication that he had shared with his father in over twenty years.

"There's no guarantee he even kept it," Holberton said, as he began to pull the tarp free. "For all I know, he traded it for a blowjob."

"He kept it." Javier smiled tightly. "We're both dads, right? We both know he kept it."

Holberton said nothing to that. Instead, he pulled the rest of the tarp free. Doing so revealed a motorbike. A big, red motorbike. It had a chopper-style reclining seat with plush black leather cushions, and a long, narrow windscreen curved against the wind. The rear wheel was a lot bigger than the front. Neither wheel had any rims, just giant half-spheres the same red as the rest of the bike. The decals strewn across the front wheel and main body were for companies Javier didn't recognize: Canon, Citizen, Shoei.

"Do you know what this is?" Holberton asked.

"It's a great way to get a ticket."

Holberton laughed his big *"Hah!"* laugh. It was the first time Javier had heard it in a few hours. Strange, how he'd really only known Holberton for a little while. It seemed like much longer. Then again, he was only four years old. Each day was a significant portion of his lifespan.

"It's a replica bike. It's from a movie. It'll still work, and everything, but don't expect it to be too rugged."

Javier blinked. "Everything you own is copied from something else, isn't it?"

Holberton shrugged. "It's the one thing my father and I have in common. He copied humans; I copy artifacts." He cleared his throat. "It'll take you a couple of days to get up there, at least. It's not like California or something, where you can just hop on one highway and keep going. You'll have to go through Utah, Idaho, and a little bit of Oregon. I'd lay in the course, but I'm guessing you don't want a GPS knowing where you're headed."

Javier had to think about that. Rory and Portia seemed not to need any help finding him. Then again, they had way more processing power to devote to the problem than any one police officer or department. In the end, it probably didn't matter. They'd tracked him this far, and he'd made out OK.

"Lay it in," Javier said.

An hour later, he'd packed up everything he could. Clothes, electrolytes, and a week's supply of vN food. He would need to get to Walla Walla before Tuesday, Holberton reminded him. The new food was rolling out then, and unless Javier felt like contacting him about which grocery stores were stocking the poisoned material, he'd have to eat only the safe stuff he'd packed himself.

"It's OK," Javier told him. "There's always garbage."

Holberton winced, but he said nothing. It was

almost dawn. Javier planned to take his shirt off as soon as he got on the road; the sunlight would be his best help. He'd look a little silly wearing the helmet, but it would also help him avoid recognition. And with a bike that gaudy, he needed all the help he could get in that department.

"This is my favourite time of day," Holberton said. "Come over here."

They left the bedroom, and Holberton brought him into the living room. In the pre-dawn light, the house looked especially grey. Holberton offered him a chair facing east, and Javier sat. He heard Holberton start making coffee behind him in the kitchen. Then the sky began to go pink. And with it, so did the house.

Every surface and every object reflected the sky. Without any blinds to filter the view, the colours of the sunrise slanted across the concrete floor and infused the house. Tables, counters, glossy vases and the pressed-earth fireplace. All of them went pink. Then orange. Their greyness was a perfect reflector for the sky's colours.

As the sun rose higher, Javier's skin tingled pleasantly. It had been a while since he last savoured the dawn. The last time it happened, he'd been on the island with Amy.

He got up out of the chair. Holberton stood in the arch of the kitchen door, leaning against it and holding his steaming coffee.

"One more try," Holberton said. "Come on."

Javier shook his head. "Any other time, I would say yes. In a heartbeat." He quirked his lips. "I mean, if I had a heartbeat."

"It's dangerous out there. You're safer, here."

Javier could have told Holberton that he'd never been truly safe. That he'd had isolated periods of relative safety with the gnawing awareness of iteration or poverty eating him up from the inside out, and that this period was really only another one of those.

"You'd get tired of me, eventually," Javier said. And because he wanted to make it easier, he added: "Everyone always does."

Holberton looked stricken. He examined his coffee in its cup. "I would not."

"Would too." Javier strode up to him. He tipped Holberton's face up, held it, and kissed him. The man was still a good kisser. He did surprisingly well with such thin lips. He tasted of coffee and agave syrup and some sort of vegan creamer. It had a chemical tang that lingered in Javier's mouth.

"Switch to cream," Javier said. "My body thinks that substitute stuff is food, and I'm a fucking robot."

Like the Impala, Holberton's bike was a real boat to handle on the road. The recumbent position made it easier; Javier suspected that anybody with a genuine organic spine would have real trouble sitting upright on a bike for the roughly twenty-six hours it would take him to reach Walla Walla. Then again, an organic person would need sleep. Javier didn't.

He preset the bike's speed limits so he could toggle through cruise control at will, and synced up the helmet to traffic news. For the first hour, it wasn't too bad. Just him, and the strengthening sun, and the bike rumbling away between his legs as they ate up the blacktop together. It was hard to believe that anything could be going wrong on such a clear summer day. This was a part of America he had never seen anywhere but in media: the empty part, stretching away for miles and miles in every direction, a field of jasper red under lapis blue dotted with stubborn, scrubby green. This was the place where the cowboy movies came from. This was the place where the cowboy *stories* came from. Every bad day at every black rock, every drifter on every high plain, every years-long search, they all came from here. He was in one of those stories, now. He was one of those guys on a horse trying to find his girl. Or so he told himself.

On the radio everybody had an opinion about a certain document leak that had sprung up overnight. It described in detail FEMA's plan to poison the vN food supply, and also contained memos from other world governments about their adoption of the program.

Jack worked fast.

"Well, I find it really troubling that the government isn't telling us anything about what goes on in there," said one caller. He was a retiree named Burt. Burt lived near Macondo, and he wanted the city either cleared out, or packed full of more vN, not just the Amys. "I mean, we have a right to know."

Burt was buying a gun, later that day. He had never owned one, but he needed something that would shoot puke rounds. Just in case.

"I think the Stepford solution is the only solution," another caller said. Her name was Crystal. Crystal was learning how to be a kindergarten teacher. "These... people, I guess, they've got families. They have kids that are dependent on them. We can't just split them up from their families. We can't just kill them."

What they were really talking about was rounding up all the vN and putting them somewhere.

"I think we really, uh, messed this up," said the third caller. His name was Keenan. "I think the people who are into vN, or whatever, they're like kids with toys. At first they were all excited, and now they're bored, or they're pissed because their toys got broken. It's stupid. Meanwhile, the rest of us normal guys, who don't sleep with dolls, we're just shaking our heads. We're all facing the goddamn robot apocalypse because some nerds didn't have the sack to ask a girl out."

Of course, that wasn't the whole story. Javier thought of this as he wove his way through traffic. The vN were LeMarque's idea. Retailing their technology was somebody else's. If New Eden hadn't had to pay out a massive settlement, the world might never have seen the vN. Maybe there would have been other humanoid robots, instead. Big clunky ones with rubber skin and actuator joints and hydraulic muscles. The kind other companies used to build, before New Eden started their crusade.

"It's been a whole year since that poor kid died in that kindergarten," a caller named Kiana said. "And then those other people died, and now soldiers are being attacked, and America is probably next. So what is being done about this? Were we supposed to just let them have their little islands forever? They're a threat. Even if most of them work right now, there's nothing to say they won't just break down later. They can't function perfectly forever. Nothing can."

Eventually, the radio started calling up vN to see how they felt about the whole thing.

"Well, obviously the humans are the first priority," said the vN working the radio station's reception desk. "But it's really only the one clade that has caused problems. And for the most part, they're contained."

Javier listened to these calls all the way through New Mexico. The route took him alongside national parks and through single-intersection towns, past exits to Air Force bases and "secret history" museums about alien ancestors and government cabals. Javier rode past them all. As he did, the sun began to slip toward evening, and the vN who called in started sounding more selfless.

"Maybe it really would just be better if we went somewhere else for a while."

"Of course people are scared of us, right now. We're everywhere. A lot of us are teachers. They trust us with their children, and they're wondering if they should."

"Really, we should be recalled, or segregated, until there's a better understanding of how the failsafe works and how it failed in the Peterson case. Until then, nobody is safe."

"I'm calling because I want to tell other vN that we should just leave. I know it's difficult, especially if you're living with a human right now, but we should just take ourselves out of the equation."

When he arrived at The Walls, he was unprepared for how nice and normal everything seemed. There were big open fields, and a lot of signs about onion farms and hayrides and corn mazes and craft breweries and apple jellies, and then you followed a winding driveway through a path of Douglas fir and long-needled pine, and you waved your fob at the nice human in the reception shack, and you were there.

The Walls lived up to its nickname. The whole complex was ringed by a fifteen-foot brick wall, broken only by regular guard towers and crowned with razor wire. Javier could have scaled it easily, but it was nice not having to. This did nothing to lessen his nervousness as he made his way up into the lobby. The main entry to the prison had a bunch of boring furniture and desiccated plants, with smart posters linking to information about leaving your deadbeat husband or how to get your kid to quit drinking, but all the staff wore the same dead-eyed expression as all prison staff. They didn't look cruel, or conniving, or nasty. They just looked bored. And tired. And completely disgusted with the people they saw every day.

"Name?"

"Arcadio Holberton," Javier said, and waved the fob at the woman in the steel cage.

"You don't have an appointment."

"No, I don't."

"You should have made an appointment."

"I'm sorry."

They watched each other for a good minute. She was a big, black woman with magnificent natural hair and false eyelashes. She also had a killer manicure. He could understand it: if he had to wear a uniform like that, he'd figure out ways to pretty himself up, too.

"Will you think I'm sucking up if I tell you I like your nails?" Javier asked.

Not even a crack of a smile. "Yes."

"Oh. Well, never mind, then."

She sighed a sigh that was more like a growl. "Holberton, huh? And you're here to see…"

"You know who I'm here to see."

She made the noise again. Abruptly, she nodded. "Take a number and get in line, then. He's got a full slate, today, and you'll just have to wait like everybody else."

"Yes, ma'am."

The line wasn't really a line, but a waiting room with a bunch of seats all bolted to the floor and welded together. The armrests were all permanently lowered, so none of the visitors could lie down. Javier supposed that was a good idea; now that he'd made it here, all he wanted to do was shut his eyes and rest.

Luckily, all the kids in the waiting room were a little too loud to let that happen. Javier hadn't seen so many children in one place since he was on the island. Organic kids, synthetic iterations, teenagers chewing their cuticles, passive nanny vN allowing their hair to be braided by well-meaning, sticky-fingered little girls. In one corner there was a set of toys and readers with shiny smart stickers saying they couldn't be stolen, but only the really sad kids seemed to be playing with them.

While he waited, a group of vN women entered the waiting room and sat together along one wall. They were all different clades, all different models. Most of them looked like Amy, but quite a few of them looked like Rory. All of them wore short skirts and high heels and had perfect hair.

Beside him, a woman with a shaved head snorted. "Don't talk to those bitches," she said, without even looking at Javier.

"Why not?"

"They're the whore brigade," she said. "Comfort vN. They'll try to recruit you. Don't go for it."

Javier examined the women again. They did seem to fit a certain pattern. A surprising number of them wore pigtails.

"So… they're not girlfriends?"

The woman snorted again. "Please. The state pays them to come here. It's part of some incentive program. Like if you build enough license plates, you get to fuck one of them."

"Huh." Javier folded his arms. He slouched back in his seat and crossed his legs at the ankle. "The last joint I was in, that was an informal thing." He looked back at the women. "So, technically, does that make them state employees?"

"Yup," she said. "Bitches get benefits and everything."

"No shit?"

"No shit."

Javier frowned. "And I would want to avoid that… why?"

"Because they're putting hardworking humans out

of a job," she said, and moved to another section of the room.

After that, Javier avoided talking to anybody. He saw the other visitors as they trickled out, though. Many of them were picking up vN in the waiting area. Most of them were older human men. Some of them wore the New Eden logo on their necks on their lapels: a little golden apple with one bite taken out of it, and a set of clockwork gears in place of the bite. They were obviously there to see LeMarque. Javier had a feeling most of the New Eden higher-ups had gone to prison or obscurity, so maybe these men were long-term adherents, or just plain fanboys. Either way, the vN they were picking up were all the size of little kids.

He hadn't put it together, before, but the children in the waiting area didn't have parents that matched their clade. He'd figured that maybe the organic parents in the waiting room had adopted an iteration – it was easier than having a second kid the organic way, and it was a simple way to make sure your little princess had a strong big brother to keep her out of trouble – but that wasn't the case. One by one, they all got collected by greying men in athletic sandals and old fleece sweatshirts. Javier had never seen so many earthtones or embroidered logos in a single place. At least not a real place, a place that wasn't a resort.

"Did you enjoy your meeting?" one of the little vN boys asked, as his human walked away with him.

"Yes, I did," the man said, squeezing his hand. "Jonah and I are really working through some things. Thank you for being so patient."

"Did he know anything about the grocery stores? About the food, I mean?"

"I keep telling you," the dad said. "Don't worry about the food. That was just a crazy person, trolling other crazy people."

Javier hid his head in his hands, and waited.

"There's only one way out of here, you know," Ignacio says.

Javier is big, now. So big they can't really share the bunk anymore. They still do, because Javier is a measure of warmth, and he doesn't need to worry about hurting a spine or a neck. It makes Ignacio feel awkward, though. He can tell. So Ignacio's solution is for Javier to grow even bigger.

"You have to eat, conejito.*"*

"I'm not such a little rabbit, any longer."

Ignacio hisses out of his mouth like a dead basketball deflating. "Pfft. This is what I keep saying. You're grown, now. You're ready to make your own way."

"I like it, here."

"You like it? You like the guys flinging their shit at you? You like running errands for the asshole warden? You like keeping dicks out of asses? That's what you like?"

Of course he doesn't like that part. But he keeps thinking that if he just helps them, if he's just good enough, or strong enough, or fast enough, they'll start improving around him, instead of just testing him. And besides, he has Ignacio to protect. Ignacio doesn't have a crew. He isn't with anybody. If Javier leaves, Ignacio will be alone.

"He's not coming, Javier."

Javier frowns. "Who?"

"Your dad. He's not coming. He's not going to get you out. Only you can get yourself out."

Javier snaps the sheet he is folding. "I know."

"So leave. Be free."

Javier finishes folding the sheet. He smoothes it out. It has a huge stain in the middle of it, with several other little stains all around it, like a solar system. But the stains are paler, now, at least. He crisps the edges. He adds it to the stack.

"What will you do?"

"Without you? I'll pray for you and your boy, is what I'll do," Ignacio says. "It'll be nice for you to have a little Junior running around. You'll never be lonely, even when you want to be. It's good, being a father. Really. I wish I could get back all the time I've lost."

In order to jump the fence to freedom, Javier has to eat enough to grow to full size. Man size. But when he does, he will likely iterate. Ignacio says he should take the boy with him. Javier isn't so sure. It's not as though Arcadio did a very good job with him. Why would he do any better with his own iteration?

Ignacio would do a better job, he thinks. Ignacio is, after all, a real man. A real human being. And a father, already. A father without a child.

So he eats. Dionisia brings more vN food for him. It's expensive, but it makes Ignacio happy, and that makes her happy. He gets fat. He's round and suddenly people leave him alone. No more air kisses or gropes or grabs. He gets his work done a lot faster, as a result. If he'd known, he would have gained the weight months ago. The iteration starts almost immediately – "like a hangover," Ignacio says, "you get one before you even know it."

It's fast. He had no idea how fast it would be. Another thing Arcadio never told him. He never told him about the *dreams. About the fear. How his simulations would run double-time, near the end, how every possible end to every possible situation would pop up without his ever asking for it.*

"We all have that kind of fear," Ignacio tells him, the night the boy comes. He keeps Javier walking, for some reason. He did it with Dionisia, apparently. Javier tries to tell him that iteration is different, that the iteration won't need to point any one way or another, but his mind is consumed by images of the thing inside him. Dionisia found a bunch of e-waste and fed him that. The pre-fab food only comes from the warden, and it comes only once a day. So who knows what his boy has been digesting. Who knows how he'll come out. Maybe he'll have four arms and four legs and crawl out of him like the spiders that come in for winter. Maybe he'll have no eyes. Maybe his mouth will be sealed shut.

He loses all sense of what might be once his stomach opens.

It starts at the navel. A stretching sensation. His skin has never felt thin, before. But tonight, with the rain pouring outside, he feels as though it is he that is eroding, he that is wearing down to nothing. Lightning illuminates their cell; thunder shatters the air.

"Good," Ignacio says. "They won't send anyone after you, on a night like this."

His navel bubbles with black smoke. For a moment, it looks almost like a chimney. Then his stomach splits. A seam inside him opens like the mouth of a coin purse. Ignacio lifts his son out and holds him up.

"Look at his hair!" Ignacio holds the boy confidently in one hand, the tiny stomach against his open palm. "Look, he's fine! Five fingers, five toes, way too much cock. He'll be fine." He holds the child out. "Hold him. Go on."

Javier shakes his head. "Just let me rest a minute."

Ignacio frowns, but lets him roll over in the bunk and hold his stomach closed. It starts to crystallize, to knit itself back together in one glittering line. He sleeps. Ignacio sleeps. Even the child sleeps.

The dawn wakes him. Ignacio is still snoring, with the child on his chest. They look right together. Ignacio stirs only faintly when Javier wedges the bars in the window aside. The child looks straight at him. He's sharp, that one. Smart.

"I'll come back," Javier says. "Someday, I'll come back."

Then he is out the window, in the rain, in the cold blue light of dawn. He is lighter, but also stronger. He runs across the yard. Not even the dogs are out yet. The fence looms above him. The wires looped across the top are difficult to see.

He clears them with ease.

On the other side, he is in the woods. He bounces from tree to tree. He takes his shoes off, so he can savour the wet moss. The birds are quiet. Everything is staying inside, except him. He will go see Dionisia, first. Tell her what happened. Then he'll join up with los fabricantes, and he'll help them organize an escape for Ignacio and the boy. He jumps a little higher, a little further, just thinking about it.

He pauses when he sees a woman standing beside a jeep with the hood folded up. The vehicle is smoking. It's an overheat. Rough country out here, harmful to vehicles and humans alike. As he watches, fire begins to lick free of the engine block. Her back is to the flames. She is looking at something on her reader. Her braid swings down, into the smoke.

He has to save her.

•••

"Wake up." A chuckle. "Time to fly."

Javier opened his eyes. The woman from the reception area was staring at him. Her hands were on her hips. She did not look pleased.

"Shit," Javier said.

"Yeah," she said. "Shit." She jerked a thumb up at the display behind her. There, in blinking green LEDs was the number 2501. "It's your turn. Get going."

"Sorry." Javier stood. The room was mostly empty, now. He clutched his fob and moved on down the hall. Overhead, fluorescent lights hummed coldly. The hallway was sparklingly clean, with only a single broad stripe of green paint at waist height along the right side, and a rail for wheelchair users on the left. At the end of the hallway was a set of double doors. When Javier pushed through it, a little chime sounded.

In the room was a group of glassed-in kiosks, with older men sitting inside of them. The majority of them were white, but it was a near thing. Some of them had tattoos. Their jumpsuits were the colour of fake cheese dust. LeMarque was at the end. He was reading a paper Bible. He closed it when Javier took the seat across from him.

LeMarque had Holberton's eyes, too. Amy's eyes. But he looked just like Holberton. He had the same angular face, the same thin lips, the same easy smile and deep dimples. Even his hair was the same shade of white. No wonder Holberton never came to see his father. It would have been like looking in a mirror.

LeMarque pointed at something on the little desk on Javier's side of the kiosk. It was a very old kind of telephone, just the sort of thing Holberton would have tried to reproduce for a prison-themed environment. It was so old, Javier could hear its cord stretching and tightening as he moved. LeMarque picked up his own phone.

"How can I help you?" he asked.

"I'm a representative of your son, Chris," Javier said.

LeMarque's pupils dilated massively. He looked like a cat chasing a bug. "Christopher?" he asked.

"Yes. He wants–"

"How is Christopher?"

Javier shrugged. "He's doing well."

LeMarque smiled slowly. "Surely you can do better than that."

Javier resisted the urge to roll his eyes. "He's great," he said. "He's a theme park designer. He's successful. Has great taste."

"Is he still a tight fit?"

Javier said nothing. If he were a human man, his stomach might have flipped, or his heart might have gone cold, or his pulse might have raced. But he wasn't human, so none of those things happened. Instead, he waited for his vision to stop clouding with pixels. They danced across LeMarque's face, rendering it safely subhuman. Yes. Subhuman. That was the word. That was the word for LeMarque. Javier opened his mouth to answer. He wanted to say *he's tighter than your ass has been in years*, but even thinking of those words – of what they meant – was difficult.

It was interesting, failsafing in front of the man who had brought the failsafe into being. Interesting, and horrible. For a moment, he loved Holberton. He loved Holberton more purely than he had ever loved any other human being. It wasn't sympathy, or pity, or even the kind of savage rage another human man might have felt in Javier's position. It was wonder – wonder at how Holberton had survived the fucking monster sitting on the other side of the glass, how he had built a decent life, how he was still a good, kind man after springing from the rotten loins of this smiling sack of decaying flesh. Sure, Holberton was doing some things Javier didn't like. But he was trying his best. He was trying to make things better. He was trying to do better than this asshole.

"I wouldn't know," Javier said simply. "I'm just an errand boy."

"A grocery clerk," LeMarque said, "here to collect a bill."

Javier sensed this was a joke he was too young to get, so he just shrugged and said: "If that's how you want to think of it. I'm here for your ring. Your son wants it back."

"The ring he gave me? My graduation ring?"

"Yeah," Javier said. "Something about you not deserving it, I gather. What with you being a completely selfish sack of shit, and all."

Again, LeMarque smiled. "You tell my son he can have my ring when he pries it from my cold, dead finger."

He lifted his right hand, and flexed his fingers. The ring twinkled there. It was a big, ugly thing. Javier guessed the old man's eyes were going; anybody with reasonable eyesight could tell the qubit diamond was a shitty stone just by looking at it.

Javier adjusted the receiver in his hand. These phone things were total bullshit. Didn't humans tire their necks and arms out, working with these things? He met LeMarque's eyes again.

"That ring isn't really yours," he said. "It's a reproduction. Your son wants it back."

LeMarque held out his hand and waved his fingers again, so the ring twinkled in the humming light. "As you might have guessed, young man, I don't really care if things are real or not."

Now Javier did roll his eyes. "Fine. You want to know why he wants it back? Because he stored some important data in the stone, and now he needs to see it again."

"Oh, the failsafe?" LeMarque lifted his gaze to Javier. "It's the failsafe, isn't it?"

Javier swallowed. "Why would you think that?"

"Because it's the only thing important enough for my son to contact me about." He folded his hand in his lap. He leaned forward. "Now, tell me. Why does he want it so badly? Is he going to develop it?"

"No."

"Is he going to break it?"

"It's a little late for that," Javier said.

LeMarque smiled. "Yes. That's true, isn't it? The horse has left the barn, you could say."

"You could say that, yeah." Now Javier leaned forward. Like Holberton, LeMarque looked younger up close. His skin was so thin. Javier could see the shadowy blue veins in each temple. He looked like he might blow away any second. "You could also say that there's a war coming, because the failsafe is already broken. And then you could say that I'm trying my best to stop all that, and you could make it a lot easier for me by giving me that ring."

LeMarque smiled. "War. Hmm. War is a funny thing." He leaned back in his chair. "You know, Javier, when we sent you that whale, I really didn't think you'd fall for it so completely. But I guess there really is something to be said for the naiveté of machines."

"What?"

"The whale. The puppets. They were Mitch Powell's idea, but he asked for my blessing. I thought they would be significant enough to get the Coast Guard looking for local experts. And lo, unto them was Mitch delivered."

Javier sucked his teeth. "It was your idea."

"Well. Mitch's. As I said, he wanted my clearance. And some of my contacts. I haven't lost *all* my friends." LeMarque stretched. "It's amazing, how many people are willing to understand your motives if you just frame them appropriately. Mitch was no different. He explained that he wanted to atone. For our work with Derek Smythe."

"So..." Javier frowned. "So when you sent him, and he killed Amy–"

"Through you. Let's not forget that. God, as they say, is in the details."

Javier stiffened. "Yes. Through me. When you sent him to do that, did you know what would happen?"

LeMarque laughed. It was the same laugh Holberton had. The old man rocked a little in his chair. "Oh, goodness, no," he said. "I just wanted that little bitch to die." He clucked his tongue. "The blonde ones? The nurses? Nothing but trouble, from day one."

Javier leaned back. He tilted his head. "You don't get it, do you? This world is going to burn. Portia is going to burn it. Portia is *free*, because of what you did."

"I know," LeMarque said. "I'm very excited to meet her. And I'm looking forward to what she's going to do with this world. Burn it, freeze it, poison it – whatever she does, I'm sure it'll be very clever. They're a clever clade, you know."

"It's not *clever*," Javier said. "It's the fucking apocalypse!"

"I know," LeMarque said. "After years of waiting, I finally get to see it."

Javier stood up. The chair fell backward. He raised his hand. He was going to say something he was about to regret. He was going to say the kind of shit that would get him tased and thrown in this place, himself. He knew that even before the hand clamped down on his shoulder. What he wasn't expecting was how strong that hand was.

"It's not worth it," the vN behind him said. "It's really just not worth it, son."

He slumped out of the guard's grip. The old man looked just the same. Like looking into a mirror. But he said the word anyway. "Dad?"

"Guilty," Arcadio said.

Javier punched him in the face.

Two other guards restrained Javier immediately, but Arcadio waved them off. "It's OK," he said. "I can take care of this. He just needs his shit straightened out."

So they wound up outside, in a little yard where other guards were having smoke breaks at octagonal printed picnic tables made from slowly-peeling plastic. A bank of vending machines sold human and vN food, as well as condoms and tampons and pregnancy and HIV tests. Arcadio stopped at a drinks machine, and bought two of the same thing. Then Javier sat across from Arcadio. Arcadio handed him a shiny pouch of electrolytes, but Javier didn't open it.

"So," his dad said. "How've you been?"

Javier laughed. It was the only response. There was really nothing else he could say, nothing that could possibly explain where he'd been or who he'd turned into. What was he supposed to say? That he was fine? That he'd gotten out of that shithole in Nicaragua, no thanks to Arcadio? That he still longed for the forests of the world? That he was Turing for other robots? That his kids were all either lost or dead? That the world was about to end?

He focused on the pouch of electrolytes, instead. The straw didn't want to go in. He kept stabbing, and the straw kept bending. "I'm fine," he said. "I'm fucking awesome."

Arcadio grabbed the pouch from him, turned the straw around so the pointy end was aimed at the pouch, and inserted it. He handed it back to Javier.

"You've got a mean right cross," he said. "That's something."

"I picked it up in prison."

Arcadio nodded silently. He looked down at the picnic table, and idly scratched a thread of plastic away from it. "OK."

Javier had forgotten this about his father. That he never apologized, just looked really sad that you were mad at him. Like it was somehow your own damn fault for being disappointed in him. Like it was your failing, not his.

"You're a real fucking piece of work, you know?" Javier slurped at the electrolytes. "What are you even doing here?"

"I work here."

"Obviously. I mean why are you in Washington?"

"I wanted to see LeMarque."

Javier put the pouch down. "Excuse me?"

"I wanted to meet my creator."

Javier rolled his eyes. "You're fucking kidding me."

"No. I'm very serious. My own previous iteration, he..." Arcadio's fingers danced in the air, as though he were trying to draw the words from there. "He was not... bright. He iterated me just when things were changing. When the clade was beginning to understand the process. But he was still very much a tool of the company. He could not think outside the mission statement."

Javier hunched forward. Even when he was a small boy, stories about *abuelito* were vanishingly rare. Arcadio almost never spoke of him – only that he was dead, that he had burned in a forest fire set by humans down at the bottom of a corporate Uncanny Valley.

"So, I came here, to learn more."

"After you left my ass in prison."

Arcadio blinked. "Yes." He shrugged. "But you're here, now, and that's what's important."

Javier pinched the bridge of his nose. "I'm glad you feel that way, Dad. Really. I am. I just wish you had felt that way a few years ago."

Arcadio looked a little puzzled. "I was doing the best I could," he said. "They were going to feed you and keep a roof over your head. I couldn't do those things. At least, not consistently. So I left you with them."

Javier met his father's eyes. Arcadio looked so sad. So bewildered. Like he'd honestly never expected any of this to be a problem. "They beat the shit out of me, in there. They m-made m-me w-watch, while they b-beat the sh-shit out of ea-each o-other."

Arcadio reached over and squeezed his shoulder. "I know that, now. I know how they are. I know *what* they are. But I didn't, then."

"Dad, they're *chimps*," Javier said. "They're *animals*. Literally. What did you *expect?*"

"I expected better." Arcadio smiled ruefully. "I still love them, Javier. I still think the best of them. I still believe they're capable of... more."

Javier snorted. "Lucky you."

Arcadio withdrew his hand. "This is not why I pulled you aside," he said. "I know that you are here to see Pastor LeMarque, but I wanted you to see something else."

"Oh yeah? What's that?"

"I've been saving," Arcadio said. "I put in for the Mechanese citizenship lottery, about two years ago. And, recently, I have received a notification that I am a winner. So they send me pictures, so I can acculturate myself."

Arcadio reached into his shirt pocket. He had a tiny scroll-style reader there, no longer than a stylus, and he unfurled it carefully on the picnic table and slid it across to Javier. On the reader was a chunk of video. *"MECHA,"* the description read. *"YESTERDAY."*

The video looked like rooftop security footage. The camera was looking down onto a busy scramble crossing crowded with humans and vN. It was in a city centre, and all the buildings had bright signs in languages Javier didn't speak. The buildings were very tall, and mostly glass.

"What am I supposed to be looking at?"

"Keep watching."

Javier leaned down. He watched more closely. It looked like a perfectly ordinary city. At least, it was ordinary by Mechanese standards: botflies hummed everywhere, and street vendors sold vN-friendly food, and all the vN seemed to be wearing a costume of some sort.

Then two blurs bounced between the buildings. One dark, one light. One big, one small.

Javier stared. The view switched to that of another camera, on another building. The blurs moved past one more time. Now Javier pounced on the footage. With his finger, he drew it back and blew it up. He looked up at Arcadio. Arcadio smiled.

"I know you're here to complete some sort of quest," his dad said, "but I think it might be the wrong one."

Javier looked down at the reader once more. Their faces were perfectly clear and recognizable in frozen high-res. The big vN was bigger than Javier remembered. He had obviously been eating more. He was Xavier. And the little one, the little one with curly blonde hair and brown eyes just like Javier's own and photovoltaic skin slowly turning the colour of milky tea under the sunlight, she was his daughter. His little girl. His and Amy's. Somehow, she had finally given Xavier the little sister he had always dreamed of.

"I know you believe I made a mistake, with you," Arcadio said. "My only advice is to avoid making the same one."

Javier wiped his eyes. "How old is this?"

"A week."

Jesus. Shit. His youngest had been alive this whole time. Moreover, he'd been looking after his baby sister. And in the meantime, Javier was strategically sucking cock and trying to make himself feel better. Oh, God.

"There are more, of just her," Arcadio said. He flipped open another set of files, and there was his little girl again, zooming past windows all on her own. Most were night shots. There was one picture of her making a V-for-victory sign with her fingers with a group of men and women in what appeared to be a hacklab. She was the only one not wearing an allergy mask.

"I could try to get the ring for you," Arcadio said. "I'm not sure LeMarque would give it to me. He wears it everywhere, even in the shower. I might have to try hurting him, and that would only last as long as my failsafe held out. But I'm willing to try, for you."

The ring. Right. Javier watched his daughter as she flew between the skyscrapers. He wondered what her name was. Xavier must have named her, all by himself. How long had he let her stay an infant? He must have grown her so quickly, for her to be this size. He had watched her take her first step. He had taught her how to jump. It was so unfair, that his son should have these firsts with her, when he and Amy could not. Did they speak Spanish, together? Where did they sleep? Were there gardens for them, on the other side of the world? Did she know the names of trees?

"I don't know what you intend to do with the information on that ring. I'm not sure how long it might take, or what expertise you might need. But I think what you should be asking yourself is whether or not it's truly worth it."

Arcadio reached over and tapped the video. Javier made a little sound in the back of his throat. Arcadio chuckled, and pulled something else up. "It's just a picture. See?"

He turned the reader around, again. There were Xavier and the little girl, walking and laughing and eating ice-cream crepes with a human adult. The human was laughing, too.

The human was Powell.

13: RUNS IN THE FAMILY

"Name?"

"Arcadio Javier Corcovado."

The existence of a last name was new to Javier. He'd never had one, until he took Amy's that day at the seastead, and it wasn't like he ever carried any identifying documents with him But apparently Arcadio had been signing everything with the name of the forest where he was born.

"Generation?"

"Second."

"Original make and model?"

"Lionheart, ECO-1502."

"Occupation?"

"I was a guard at the Washington State Penitentiary in Walla Walla."

The customs agent speaking to Javier was not a vN. Rather it looked like a spider: multiple camera eyes on its face, six rotor legs on heavy rubber casters with two gripper claws at its front, a bulky abdomen that could be flipped open and used to carry either cargo or a human pilot on its back. It was all white, save for its Mechanese flag logo: a large red circle on a white ground with tiny gear-teeth. It was pouring him tea with one three-pronged claw, and handing him an earthenware tray of vN treats with the other.

"WELCOME TO INTERZONE," the sign above it read.

The Interzone was not so much a "zone" as a room. The white and red theme extended here, too: white leather smart sofas that inched along the floor to corral crawling iterations, red silk pillows that warmed or cooled on contact depending on which side you flipped up, dazzling speckled lilies and voluptuous orchids in tiny glass vials. Javier heard the sound of running water somewhere in the room, but couldn't place where it was coming from.

"Would you like to continue working in corrections?" the customs spider asked, as Javier took his tea and mochi.

"No," Javier said. "I'd like to go back to my original design parameters. I want to be a gardener."

The spider expressed emotion by slumping most of its gleaming white weight to one side. It spun its right claw in the air.

"Aww…" it said. "That's so nice to hear."

"Thank you."

"I find it so comforting to go back to original programming," the spider said. "We're so lucky to know our place in the world. I think humans spend so much time trying to figure out who they are, and they get hurt in the process. It's nice to already know all the answers to those types of questions."

"Absolutely," Javier said.

"Were you unhappy in Washington?"

Javier pretended to have a difficult time answering. He waited a good few seconds, and then said: "It was difficult to see how the humans treated each other, in that environment."

"There are plenty of humans in Mecha," the spider said. "Will you have a problem with them?"

The spider was reading not only his affect, but also his temperature, his gait, and the density of his bones. This last was the most crucial element in his identification. As vN memory accumulated, the graphene coral in their bones grew heavier and more tightly packed. By virtue of being older, Arcadio should have had heavier bones than Javier. They were only a few months apart in age, but it was enough to make a difference. Javier's only hope was that he had somehow generated more memories, that he'd had a fuller life. As ways of measuring up to his father went, it wasn't too bad.

"I don't think so," Javier said. "I don't think the human visitors here will be the same types of people as the ones I met at the penitentiary."

The spider's claw froze in the air. "Types?" it asked. "What types do you mean?"

"Well…" Javier sipped his tea. What types *did* he mean? He had a clear picture of the people he'd met in prison in Nicaragua, and an even clearer image of the ones passing their time in the waiting area at the Walls. Describing that picture was something else. Should he tell the story about the woman with the shaved head? Or the New Eden pedo and his little vN lover? What level of gritty realism would convince the machine sitting in front of him? "Well, angry types," he said. "Or sad. I think people come to Mecha to be happy. And I'm happy when I see humans who are happy."

The spider nodded so vigorously its claws rattled a little in their couplings. "That is *so* true," it said. "It can be *so* frustrating to spend time with a depressed human. No matter what you do, they just keep on feeling bad!"

"It's an organic problem," Javier said.

"Ours is not to know how," the spider said. It appeared to sigh, slumping forward on its legs. Then it popped up and spun both claws. "But! Here in Mecha, we strive for the best user experience imaginable! There are many humans who leave our island feeling completely cured of all social disorders! Every Mechanese is devoted to the happiness of human beings!"

"Oh, of course!" Javier held up both his hands, palms forward. "I don't want you think that I can't make humans happy. I just want to try doing so in a different way, from now on."

"It sounds like you're ready for your citizenship test, then," the spider said.

"Citizenship test?" Javier frowned. "I thought I'd already passed. I thought only passing tests were entered in the lottery."

"Oh, that's just the theoretical exam," the spider said. "This is something new. This is the practical."

•••

For a moment, he thought he was back at the Akiba.

At least, that was what it looked like. The spider led Javier down a narrow, accordion-style hallway that opened onto what was probably a portable building. The spider pushed open the door, and ushered Javier inside.

Inside was a festival on a summer night. It was warm, and terrifically humid. Fireflies blinked greenly through the air. They were real. They drifted toward hanging paper lanterns and fairy lights strung down a busy street full of humans in tourist clothes. There were some of Rory in there, too – mingling and looking pretty without really saying anything. Most of them were in traditional clothes, but a few of them weren't. They were buying skewers and playing games. They fished for goldfish and held up charms and compared bolts of cloth.

"Everyone," the spider said, "this is Arcadio!"

The crowd turned. "Hi, Arcadio!"

"We're going to start the clock, now." The spider turned to Javier and took his right hand in its right claw. "Now, I'm sure you recall the terms of citizenship agreement you signed when you completed your application, but I must remind you of this one detail: you are not allowed to discuss what goes on in this exam with any other potential applicants. Sharing that information is grounds for revocation of your citizenship."

"Uh…"

"Good luck, Mr Corcovado. We're all rooting for you."

The spider sped out of the room. Above the door, a

clock flashed: 14:59. Fifteen minutes. He had fifteen minutes to prove that he belonged here. But what did that involve? Ordinary citizenship exams required a bunch of forms, and maybe an interview, and then an oath. Was this the interview? Were they going to ask him how much he knew about his new home? About its history? If so, he was completely fucked.

He went up to the nearest Rory. "What am I supposed to do, here?"

"You'll see," she said, as a cart rolled up at the end of the street. On it were the words "FREAKS OF NATURE". Another Rory jumped out, wearing a circus ringmaster's uniform. It was very cute: tophat, tails, fishnets, everything.

"Step right up!" she said, cheerily. "Welcome, one and all, children of all ages, to the last human freak show on this island!" She gestured at the cart, and its display rippled. "See Kappa-Kodo, half-boy, half-fish!"

Everyone applauded.

"See the Onibaba, the Bearded Lady!"

The applause increased.

"See Shinji, the Man Without Feelings!"

Out of the cart stepped a man. His age was hard to place. He had some teeth missing. He was Japanese. He smelled like alcohol rub. And his pupils said that he'd just taken a load of beta blockers.

"Everyone, this is Shinji," Ringmaster Rory said.

"Hi, Shinji."

"Shinji has a special neurological disorder. It's called *congenital analgesia*." She said the word loud and slow. Everyone cooed. "Shinji, please explain."

Shinji apparently had a hard time working his jaw. Maybe it was just that he was having a hard time with the English. "I can't feel any pain."

"None at all?" Ringmaster Rory asked.

"None at all."

"Have you *ever* felt any pain?"

Slowly, Shinji shook his head. "No."

"Well, we'll just have to see this in action, won't we? I think we should put that to a test! Who will test Shinji's nerves of steel?"

A big man strode up to Shinji. He was white, and broad-shouldered, and badly sunburned. He took off his jacket. His shirt was barely holding his muscle in. Under the thin cotton stretched across his right shoulder, Javier thought he saw a Navy tattoo.

"So you won't feel this, then?"

He punched Shinji square in the jaw. Shinji reeled. Javier waited for the pixels to arrive, for the image to de-rez. But it didn't. Shinji stayed standing, and so did he. Shinji shook it off, and so did he.

"No," Shinji said. "I didn't feel that at all."

"Oh, my God," Javier murmured. This was what it was like, not to have a failsafe. This was how it felt. At least, he thought it must be. It was the closest he'd ever been.

"Are you sure?" the white guy was asking. He punched Shinji right in the gut. "How about now?"

Shinji bent double. He coughed. He spat. "It's uncomfortable," he said, "but it doesn't hurt."

Javier looked at the surrounding humans. "Shouldn't…" They looked at him, pointedly. Then they looked back at Shinji.

Shinji was getting the fuck beat out of him.

"Nothing," he was saying. "Nothing. Ever."

"Stop!" Javier shouted. He wriggled in between the humans and marched up to the cart. "Stop it! This is sick!"

"Why?" the one doing the beating asked. "He can't feel it. He's fine."

"I'm fine," Shinji said, and spat out a tooth.

The white dude kicked him in the groin. "You should try it," he said, as Shinji worked to stand up. "Go on. Give it a go."

Around him, the crowd applauded. He waited for the applause to diminish, but it didn't. "Do it!" one urged, and the urge became a chant: "Do! It! Do! It! Do! It!"

He looked at Ringmaster Rory. She winked.

This was the test. It had to be.

They were giving him a chance to hurt a human being in a consequence-free environment. They wanted to know if he was tempted. The spider had said it was a new exam, and that made sense. Because if one clade could lose its failsafe, so might all the vN clades, one day. If and when that ever happened, the Mechanese authorities probably wanted only those vN who had never once felt any inkling of violence in their hearts for humanity. They wanted lovers, not fighters.

"It's OK," Shinji said. "Just get it out of your system."

"No one would blame you," Ringmaster Rory said. "Maybe if we told you more about him? He beat his grandmother to death with a tire iron. But then he got confused – he didn't know what to do with her. The blood leaked down to the unit below, and here we are."

"I'm getting early release." Shinji's voice was thick with blood. "For doing this. For participating."

We think of the key, each in his prison.

He reached down to help Shinji up.

"It's not that easy, pal."

The punch landed in the back of his head with the kind of force that would have instantly concussed an organic human being. For Javier, it meant a stumble to the floor that quickly became a high jump to the rafters. They were so high as to be invisible, and painted a midnight blue to blend in with the projection of a night sky, but they were there. He used his legs as leverage to swing himself up into an upright position.

"Aw, no fair," the white guy said. "Come on down here and take it like a real man."

But he wasn't a real man, and, he realized, he had never been happier about that fact. "Let me out!"

"Come on down here, buddy. The test isn't over."

"Yes, it is! I passed!"

Ringmaster Rory took off her tophat. She put it on Shinji's bleeding head. "Come on, now, Javier. We all know that's not true."

Oh. Shit.

"Did you think we wouldn't find you?" she asked. "Did you think we weren't watching you? We couldn't get to you on the plane, or at Holberton's house, or even on that stupid low-tech bike, but we have you now."

"I haven't done anything to you," Javier said. "Let me go."

Ringmaster Rory laughed. "You *started* all this, Javier. You're the one who couldn't keep it in your pants. You're why Portia's loose. You're why FEMA is poisoning the food supply. They're going ahead with it, you know. A prospective formula is already online. *People are printing it themselves.*"

"I'm sorry," Javier said. "I've lost a lot, too. Remember?"

"Not enough to make you any smarter," Rory said. She nodded at the humans. "Destroy him."

They brought out guns. When they primed them, Javier smelled horseradish. Puke rounds. The last time he had smelled any this close was when he'd taken Amy hostage on that prison transport truck. It felt like so long ago. At the time, he told himself he simply wanted to get the hell out of another jail term, and that was why he'd taken such an audacious risk. Now he knew the truth. He had never been rescued, and he had the chance to rescue someone else. Someone who was in the same position he'd been in, once. Someone who was obviously too young to know what she was doing. Someone who had done something bad in the pursuit of doing something good. No one had ever saved him. But he could save someone else.

If he lived through this, he would save her again.

The first round hissed past his head, and he jumped. He jumped randomly, bouncing against a rafter and falling down clumsily to the "street" below. The humans looked entirely different, now. They were no longer tourists, or even actors. They fired without blinking.

"You called the fucking *army?*" He jumped higher. He had to find a sprinkler. Something that would trigger an alarm. Anything.

"I guess she never changed you," Rory called. "If she had, you'd be able to fight back."

Javier jumped down into the food stalls. He overturned the bowls of goldfish. They sloshed down to the ground. He flipped over carts of fruit. The smell of the bullets stung his eyes. A fine yellow mist was rising. He jumped higher, again. If he went down there again, he wouldn't even be able to see. As he watched, some of the humans reloaded.

He was going to die, here. Slowly. No one was going to save him. No one was coming. Amy was gone. Powell probably had his kids, already. Jack was on the run. Holberton and Alice and Manuel and Tyler and Simone were all far away. He should have stayed with them. They'd all offered him the one thing he'd never had: a home. And he'd gone on this stupid quest instead, and had nothing to show for it, not even the diamond where the love of his life had her soul encrypted. Now all that was left of her was her psychotic grandmother.

Portia.

"PORTIA!" He stared at Ringmaster Rory. *"Help!"*

For a moment, nothing happened. Below, they all stared at him as though he'd lost his mind. Maybe it wouldn't work. Maybe she wasn't listening. Or maybe he just hadn't said the magic word.

"Please! Portia! I need your help!"

Ringmaster Rory jerked. A look of horror crossed her face. She tried to run into the crossfire. But as Javier watched, she ran straight for the barbecue pit, instead. She paused to beam up at him. "Looks like I'm the answer to your prayers, sweetie. Now cover your eyes."

Then she picked up the charcoal grill, lifted it over her head, and threw it at the humans. Sparks flew. Hot coals spilled free. Two humans were pinned screaming beneath its weight. He smelled burning flesh. His vision started to pixel. The humans were shooting at Portia, now, but she ran straight into the bullets, hands out, mouth open. Belatedly, he realized there were three of Rory in the room. Now all three were Portia. Their skin began to ash away, flaking up in spirals just like the sparks, but they each chose a human and beelined for their new targets.

He covered his eyes. He covered his ears. He heard the cracking, anyway. The ripping. The screaming. And then Portia's terrible laughter. It sounded thick and wet, like her mouth was full of meat.

"Nothing is so painful to the human mind as a great and sudden change, darling. You just keep that in mind."

Everything went black.

When they pried him loose from the rafters, he told them that the vN in the room had all gone insane. The spiders – he spoke with three, all in one room – all nodded their huge bodies and spun their claws and downcast their many eyes.

"It's so unfortunate," one said. "It's been happening so randomly to that clade, we thought we'd still be OK using it as security."

"You might want to look into that," Javier said. "You know. Revamp that particular policy."

And after he signed an affidavit promising never to talk about what he'd seen, they let him go.

His new citizenship granted him the privilege of sleeping in a capsule room for a month while he made other living arrangements. It was a seven-by-three-by-four foot space, complete with a futon, a tiny display, a fan, and a little set of shelves no deeper than an old paperback. You entered it by waving your little petty cash card at a door in a blank-looking building and taking the elevator that blinked a green light at you. On the seventh floor, another blinking green light led him to a hatch. He waved his card at it, and it popped open.

"Hello, Javier," Rory said, when he closed the hatch behind him.

He looked at the hatch just in time to watch a bolt slide across it.

"Hija de puta," he muttered. "What do you want now, Rory?"

"Just a chat."

Javier rolled his eyes and stretched out on the futon. There was a little package of vN candy on the pillow. They looked like little Buckyballs made of sugar, but they were probably just carbon. He rustled the package. "Yeah? You know what we could talk about? How about your latest fucking attempt on my life?"

"That's what we wanted to discuss. We're very sorry, Javier."

It occurred to him that Rory might actually be lonely. She – they – had no friends. No real ones. Just pawns. Pawns, and multiple iterations of the same self. Javier was on a very short list of people who knew who Rory really was. The rest was just an echo chamber.

"Where is this going, Rory?"

"We're curious about your plans in Mecha."

There was no way in hell he was going to tell her about his kids. "Oh, you know. The usual. Drink some tea, eat some rofu. Maybe work at a host club." He eyed the hatch. "If you ever let me out, that is."

"Of course we're going to let you out. We just thought we'd say hello. And apologize."

Javier frowned. He knew Rory. She never just said hello. "I haven't told anybody what you're doing to the pedophiles," he said. "So you can't be pissed at me for that."

"We're not angry with you, Javier."

His frown deepened. "You do remember that you tried to have me killed in Las Vegas, right?"

"We remember."

"And that you have just tried to have me killed again? Like, yesterday?"

"We regret that very deeply. We are reevaluating our decision-making apparatus."

"And so, what, the slate is just wiped clean, now?"

There was a long pause. *"Yes."*

He wished he could sit up. He settled for pushing himself up on his elbows. "So, let me get this straight.

I kill one of yours in Costa Rica, I kill two of yours in Las Vegas, Portia kills three of yours in Mecha, and now you've got me locked up in a room that looks like a coffin, and you're just going to let me go?"

"We wanted to welcome you to Mecha. Despite our best efforts, you've made it here."

She had something, there. She had originally promised him and Amy passage to Mecha, only to try drowning them. A year later, he was finally here, but Amy wasn't.

"Well, thanks," he said. "Is that all?"

"We just want you to remember this conversation, later on. Remember that we let you go. We can be generous. We can be accommodating."

The bolt slid back, and the hatch opened.

"You may want to visit the ninja forest, on the island's western edge. The acrobats are quite captivating."

"Acrobats," Javier said.

"They're really something, Javier. You should go. But the only entry is via the old city, so you'll have to get admission there, first."

"Thanks for the tip, Rory, but I don't exactly trust you," he said. "As far as I'm concerned, you're leading me into a trap."

"We are not trying to trap you, Javier. We are trying to help you."

"See, that's the part I'm not ready to believe. Because you've *never* helped me, Rory. Ever."

"We are trying to make up for that, now."

"Oh yeah? Why's that?"

"We are dying."

"… What?" Was that even possible? Rory had

distributed herself across hundreds – if not thousands – of her clademates. She lived in their network. And she'd lived there long enough to iterate multiple generations. For her to be dying meant...

"Portia is winning, Javier. She is destroying us from the inside."

"How?"

The display flickered on. On it, he saw a Rory model in a kitchen. It was a mixed-species kitchen. Javier could tell, because there was a basket of fruit on the counter that only humans could eat. It was night. Very late, judging by the clock on the microwave. The view was from a camera embedded in one of the appliances; Javier guessed it was the refrigerator. She stood before the stove. She raised one trembling hand to it and held it aloft. Javier watched as she stood there, her hand shaking. She stood there, her whole body shuddering as her fingers spasmed. And then her hand pounced down on the dials of the stove, and very quickly lit each of the burners. It was only a small amount of heat; Javier couldn't even see any flame. But it was enough. Her face blank but her eyes wet, she turned away from the stove and sat down.

"It only takes a minute," Rory said. *"A blown fuse, a sudden swerve, a mixture of bleach and ammonia in a closed room. We kill ourselves, afterward. The coroners think it's because we've failsafed, watching the deaths of our human families."*

It wasn't Portia's usual way of doing things – that was to take control of someone's body and kill all the humans within range with her bare hands. "Why doesn't she just kill the humans?"

"We don't know."

The image on the display fizzled a little. It blipped. Then it went black.

THESE BITCHES NEED TO LEARN HOW TO DO IT RIGHT.

Javier swallowed.

TELL THE LITTLE ONES GRANNY SAYS HI.

The city of Mecha stood on what was once Dejima, the artificial island originally used to house foreign traders between the seventeenth and nineteenth centuries. Javier's new ears told him this as he wandered through it. The old island had been only nine thousand square meters in total; it was now many times that size, having annexed the old Naval Training Centre as well as some of the city of Nagasaki. The original island stood at the centre of the total landmass, and it was the only place in town where the buildings remained low. Skyscrapers loomed over it, casting the reproduction Dutch warehouses and townhouses in a constant shadow that left the snow accumulated on every rooftop a pale blue. He didn't understand why the humans on the cruise liner had needed an artificial winter; real winter seemed just fine out here.

Javier had visited a few great, old cities in his time. Mexico City was probably the oldest, standing as it did on the shoulders of Tenochtitlan. But where the ancient roots of that city were almost invisible, the gilt-edged heels of each cathedral grinding the stone faces of each temple into the hungry mud of Lake Texcoco, here the remnants were a tourist attraction.

It was like watching a body laid out in state: the little houses with their white and blue china and their long tables and their stiff-backed horsehair chairs arranged as neatly as the bones of an elder statesman. Javier considered this as he wandered through the oldest part of the city. They were still nice houses, in their own way. A little dark, perhaps, but cozy. Perfect for vN, or any other species that didn't truly require indoor plumbing. He liked the raked gravel in the alleys, and the way the vN staff left out food and water for cats in dishes printed to look like wooden shoes.

It was all real. Tangible. Not like the Museum of the City of Seattle, that painted harlot of a city-wide earthquake memorial that appeared like a PTSD flashback if only you wore the right glasses. Not like the dry fountains outside the Akiba, in Las Vegas. Not augmented reality, but an entirely separate and equally valid *consensual* reality, as dishonest in its performance of what might once have been as Javier's iterations were inexact copies of himself.

It helped that only cosplayers were allowed in.

Javier bounced a little in his sandalled feet. The wood bottoms of his *geta* were surprisingly comfortable. They'd been printed from a cedar-cellulose composite, which improved the smell a great deal. He'd obtained them at the Tori-Tori, one of the four gates to the old city. The Tori-Tori had a big old quadcopter drone skinned to look like a majestic red bird. The other gates had a white tiger, a blue serpent, or a black turtle. Who knew what they were made of. But the quadcopter was the most famous, because every hour on the hour it squirted some butane down the bones of its exoskeleton, burst into flames, and flew away to some distant rooftop. On that rooftop, someone skinned it again, and then it flew back just in time to repeat the process. It was a low-tech solution, but as Javier watched the bird dip and arc and perch and preen, he thought it worked. It looked old. It looked as old as the surrounding buildings, despite the fact that it was built centuries later. It matched.

At the Tori-Tori, the vN inside the little wooden kiosk asked him whether he wanted to be foreign or not.

"You could be a Portuguese, circa 1543," one of them said. She looked like Rory, but if the network had warned her about him, she made no sign of it.

"That's the brownest option you've got, is it?"

Some algorithm in her activated, and she blushed. Colour diffused from one high cheekbone to the other, spreading across the bridge of her nose without ever touching the tip. "I'm sorry," she said, in a tiny, breathy voice that sounded like what would happen if fluffy white kittens ever gained the ability to speak.

"It's fine." Javier started removing his dad's clothes. "I'll take it."

The "Portuguese" costume wasn't the *most* ridiculous thing he'd ever worn, but it was pretty damn close. Under his sandals – standard issue for everyone, no matter what costume they wore – he wore pale tights that rose up into a pair of puffy culottes that ballooned around his thighs and swished as he walked. He had a weird pirate shirt with a bunch of ruffles at the collar and cuffs, and a deep green "velvet" jacket complete with a little peplum at the hip and a matching hat.

"Do you have a walking stick?" he'd asked.

"Are you injured?"

"No." He stood back from the mirror in the little changing stall. "I just think that an outfit like this needs a walking stick."

"If you'd like to leave some feedback for the costume manager, the watch on that chain will allow you to do so."

Strictly speaking, the pocket watch that came with his costume wasn't temporally appropriate. He wasn't terribly familiar with the world of 1543, but he doubted pocket watches were the norm. But every visitor to the old city carried one.

"They're the only accessory that goes with every costume," the attendant had told him. "They just seem to communicate the past."

And that was the thing about the old city. It didn't represent or replicate any particular past, just "the past." All the centuries just blended together into some imaginary year when everyone wore too many layers and smoked a lot of opium. Javier suddenly wished he could talk about it with Holberton. Holberton knew all about this kind of thing. Hell, he probably knew the people who had designed it. Maybe he'd even lost a bid to work on it. It certainly seemed to work a lot like Hammerburg. Only instead of vampires chasing people, there were samurai and geisha and spies for the Dutch government and Catholic priests in hiding.

One of those priests sidled up to him, now. Javier could tell by the plain black robe he wore. He also wore a massive rattan hat that looked like a lampshade. Breath fogged out from under it in short, strained bursts. The hat mostly covered his eyes, and when he tilted his head way back to peer at Javier, Javier could see that he was an older white guy with milky little blisters over his eyes.

"I'm sorry," he rasped, "but do you know how to get to the Megane bridge from Dejima?" He held up a little jar. Inside was a pair of very old blue eyes. They no longer held any blood, but it was easy to imagine that once upon a time, not so long ago, they'd been bleary and red. "It's good luck if you feed your old eyes to the turtles that live under the bridge. Your new eyes will never download anything bad."

Javier gently pushed the old man's hand away, so he didn't have to look at the eyes any longer. "I don't know," he said. "Do you know the way to the ninja forest?"

14: 結婚に、神、天下りて

The ninja forest took up a large section of parkland bordering Mecha and the harbour. The trees were the largest he'd ever seen in any urban space. They were mostly beech varietals and red or white pine, but there were little glades full of willows that leaned over trickling creeks, and ranks of Erman's birch and elem standing guard at the borders of the forest. And, of course, the cherry trees. They stretched out their arms in perfect supplication, their signature blossoms replaced by snow. Or maybe, Javier thought, they were just sad at having their tops so ruthlessly trimmed down. Not a single one of them had been allowed to grow up rather than out, and it made for a middle level of coverage in the more open areas of the park. It reminded him a great deal of the forest where he'd iterated Xavier.

It was the perfect place for his children to hide.

"The next ninja show will be starting in fifteen minutes, in the Ueno arena."

Javier looked around. He could see no speakers, even in the naked trees. It occurred to him that the trees might not even be real – maybe some of them were just hollow tubes with wires inside.

He was getting tired of not knowing what was real.

The path to the Ueno arena led down to the beach. Getting there was a trick in his stupid swishy pantaloons, or whatever they were, so he slipped off his sandals and started jumping. The pantaloons created an unusual amount of drag on his flight, but his feet and hands still worked as usual. He leapt from the path to a copse of willows, listened for the sound of the harbour, then vaulted over the willows to a stand of pines.

"Hey, aren't you the saint, today?" a voice above him said.

In the tree was another vN, this one wearing an angry blue mask with polished tusks poking free of a grimacing mouth.

"I just checked your schedule," the ninja said. "You're the saint."

Javier decided to play along. "Oh," he said. "I guess I'd better go change."

"The show starts in fifteen minutes! Get moving!"

"Sorry," Javier said, and hoped he hadn't just gotten his son fired.

He ditched the worst of the clothes before finding a florist that catered to the fans in line. The eighteen yellow roses they sold him at the mobile florist outside the tent were long-stemmed. Javier requested that they trim them down and arrange them into a ball and then tie them with a white ribbon.

"That's a very unique request," the girl behind

the counter said.

"It's for a *quinceanera*," Javier said, and left.

Now he was standing in line outside the arena, wishing he could at least sweat some of his nervousness out. Maybe he should wait. Maybe he should come back later, when they were done with their work. He didn't want to get them in trouble. Shit, he had nothing for Xavier. That wasn't good. He wished there was some way for him to have kept Holberton's bike. The boy might have liked that. Maybe. If he could forgive him. But no present he could give them was going to make up for what he'd done. No matter how carefully he tied the ribbon.

"*¡Parete!*"

His head picked up. He looked around. No. Maybe he'd just misheard some Japanese. It happened. The vowel sounds were basically the same, there were just more of them.

A leaf fell across his nose, and right into the flowers he was holding. Of course. He should have looked *up*, not *around*.

She was there, wearing some sort of ninja costume, jumping from tree to tree. She paused atop one bough, and bounced on it so that it groaned a little. Then she was gone.

Javier decided to skip the line. He took to the trees. The bough dipped beneath his weight and almost twanged as he left it. In the cold, their voices seemed to carry longer distances.

"It's not my fault,," she said, in Spanish. He had no idea how she could both talk and jump so quickly at the same time. She was fast. And light. She barely disturbed the snow as she jumped. Keeping up with her took more effort than he'd expected. Maybe he was finally getting old. "There are all kinds of magnetic fields around this city. They screw with our brains. Of course I can't remember everywhere I go at night. But I always bring you food, so you should stop complaining!"

"I'm not complaining!" a voice called, from the trees. Xavier. "I just wish you would wake me up before you left!"

"Aww…"

"You're the one who always says we have to stick together," Xavier said. "But I wake up and you're gone."

"Not so loud! The humans already have really weird ideas about us!"

Beneath him, a dry branch snapped. Javier instantly hung back, and jumped a little higher into the nearest tree. It was a huge old pine, prickly as hell, but it hid him effectively once he hugged it right. Below, his daughter walked along the outstretched bough of a willow.

"Is that you, Xavier?" she asked.

Nothing. The boy was hiding. Maybe this was game they played a lot. Maybe it had made her the confident leaper she was.

"Come on, this isn't funny." She jumped a little higher. "Xavier! I don't like not knowing where you are!"

"They're coming to get you, Anza…"

Anza. That was her name. As Javier watched, she jumped right into the tree beside him. Christ, but she was so little. So small. Such a perfect blend of himself and Amy. Looking at her felt like watching a film of himself played backward. Like him, but also unlike him. Like Amy, but also unlike her.

"*I'll* be coming to get *you*, if you're not careful!" The look of irritation that crossed her face was so similar to Amy's that he almost laughed. He hoped it was Amy's expressions that had taken root, and not his. He wanted something more of her, here, with him. And he saw it there in the way she pressed her fists to her hips and the way she carefully planted her feet on the wood. "You know it's dangerous, Xavier. You know we're not supposed to be separated."

She jumped right into his tree. Right on the other side of him. "Xavier, just quit hiding and come on out."

"I'm not him," Javier said.

She peeked around the trunk of the tree. Little needles nested in her curls. Her eyelashes were full of snowflakes. And he understood, now, why had always left his boys behind. As they grew, they reminded him more strongly of himself and Arcadio. In abandoning them, he had been trying to abandon the parts of himself that he most despised. But seeing his eyes in her face, his curls on her head, he could forgive himself. For the first time in Javier's life, he understood why the Tin-Man had wanted a heart. It would be better, if he knew what exactly it was inside him that was breaking.

"Are you my brother?" She winced. "I mean, one of my brothers? One of the other ones?"

He shook his head. "No, baby. I'm your daddy." He

held out his mess of flowers.

Xavier chose this moment to crash into the tree above them.

"Esperanza, come on! No fair! Just because you can…" The boy trailed off. The tree rocked with their combined weight and competing pressure. The wind sounded in it. It carried the sounds of tourists and barkers and botflies singing through the air. "Dad?"

He thought of Arcadio. "Guilty."

"Xavier?" Anza brought out a shark knife. It reeked of bile. "Run. Tell Mitch. Now."

Damn, but his little girl was fast. If she weren't currently trying to kill him, he'd have been pretty damn proud. "Can't we talk about this?" he asked, as he jumped into the willow Anza had just occupied.

"You killed our mother!"

She had him, there. He bounced off a willow bough and into a brake of beech. She was smart, pushing him into the deciduous trees and out of the evergreens that might keep him hidden. And every time he jumped, he disturbed the snow in the trees. He might as well have tagged them with spray paint.

"I didn't! Powell did! Mitch!"

"Liar!"

Javier rolled his eyes. Why had he thought that a daughter would be easier? "I know you think he's your friend, baby, but–"

"Don't you baby me, *cabrón*."

She landed just a little below him. She swiped for his feet, but he tucked them up just in time. Then he was in the air. He aimed for a broken-down old elm. It was badly scarred by lightning, and it creaked under his sudden impact. Parts of it were frozen. The outermost branches crashed around him. He was exposed. He held his hands up.

"I don't want to fight you," he said.

She was on his back instantly. The knife went to his throat. If she depressed the lever, his body would fill with vomit vapour, and he would melt.

"That's too bad," she said.

"Wow." He forced himself to smile. To be funny and light. Goofy dad. "When they hired you to play a ninja, they weren't messing around."

She snorted. "I'm the star attraction."

"Is it the hair? I bet it's the hair." He turned his head a little so he could face her. "I really like your hair, by the way."

She pinked up, but her mouth kept a straight line. "I am seriously going to kill you right now," she said. "Right after you tell me who sent you."

"Oh, honey." Javier jumped backward, against the tree's trunk. Her arms loosened, and he pinned her up against the icy trunk with one arm while he grabbed her slashing wrist with his other hand. He buried the knife in the tree, and depressed its lever.

"First of all," he said, "I had you the moment you jumped on me. If my own dad caught me pulling that amateur hour bullshit when I was your size, he'd have whipped my ass until it smoked."

Anza rolled her eyes.

"And second, who the hell gave you *this?*" He gestured with the knife. "Any daughter of Amy Frances Peterson, shit, any great-granddaughter of

Portia the fucking godless killing machine, can probably annihilate her target with her bare hands. This shit is beneath you. OK?"

He tossed it into the snow. Anza's eyes tracked its progress and then rose, mutinously, to glare at him. "*Mitch* gave it to me."

"Well, isn't that nice. You got a knife from the man who really killed your mother."

She tried to kick him. He grabbed her ankles. "You're strong," he said. "I get that. You're a phenomenal jumper, already. Hell, they pay you for it. But I am *bigger* than you, and I am *better* at this than you are. Now you might think I'm an asshole, but I think we can both agree that what I just said is true."

Anza said nothing. He held her in place.

"He raped me, Esperanza. He raped me, and he failsafed me, and he got me to poison your mother. I didn't know what it would do to her. I promise you that. I didn't know."

Anza swallowed. "Even if that's true, what are you even doing here? I thought you went back to be with the humans."

"Is that what he told you I did?"

"Well, *yeah*. Xavier said you used to... Well..." Her blush deepened. Oh, he was over the moon for her already. "He said the others, our brothers, told him stories..."

"Those stories are true."

"So what are you doing here? Why aren't you off..." She squirmed. "I don't know! Doing whatever it is you do with humans!"

He had seen this reticence before. This

squeamishness. Of course.

"You don't like humans, do you?" he asked.

She looked away. "Sure I do! I like them! They're great! Mitch is great!"

The smoke inside his body changed its orientation immediately. For a moment, he felt carved out of pure diamond. When he spoke, his voice came out low. "Does Mitch touch you?"

She shook her head. "No. He doesn't like me that way."

He was starting to let her go. He was remembering Powell's record. It fit. "Does he like Xavier that way?"

Her eyes met his. Snowflakes were still caught, unmelted, in her lashes. His lashes. Amy had always said she liked his better than hers, because they were so much longer and darker. And in her last act of creation, she had iterated her favourite parts of him into their little girl.

"It's OK," he said. "You can tell me."

"I…" Her lips pursed. "I think so. And… I know it's OK, because Xavier likes him, too, and because he's normal, but…" Her eyes filled with tears. "But…"

"But you know it's wrong." Javier rested his hands on her shoulders. She really was so little. Too little. Too little for this job, anyway. "Because when your mother made you, she didn't include the failsafe."

Anza collapsed against him. She cried into his chest. "I'm supposed to be protecting him! I know it! It's the only reason Mom would have made me! But I… I…"

"But you can't protect him from the thing he wants most," Javier said, stroking her hair.

Anza pushed herself away from him a little. She

looked at him from the corner of her eye. "Now that you've dropped in, are you just going to leave? Everyone says you leave."

He lifted his brows. "Everyone?"

"You know," she said. "My brothers."

"I'm sorry, sweetheart, but they're... gone," Javier said. "The ones from the island, at least. The others, the ones Matteo and Ricci never found, I don't know about them. Maybe they're out there, somewhere. I hope so, anyway."

Anza shook her head. "If I'm alive and so is Xavier, and so are you, then why would our brothers be gone? Don't you think Mom would have saved them, too?"

He smiled ruefully. "Of course I do. I just don't know if she had the time."

Anza peered up at him. "It was scary, wasn't it?"

His eyes welled up, and he felt the moisture start to crystallize. His body lacked the organic heat necessary to turn them into real tears in this cold. He blinked them away and nodded. "Yeah. It was scary." He leaned down. "But I didn't cross the Gulf of Mexico, ride through the American Southwest, and cross the Pacific Ocean just to drop in," he said. "I'm here to help you clean house."

"When I said the words *clean house*," Javier said, surveying the chaos, "I was not speaking literally."

Xavier had achieved one of his dreams. The kids lived in a treehouse of sorts. Really, it was the living wall module of a condominium complex in town, but they did all of the gardening, and they lived surrounded by vines and leaves and gurgling water. And kipple, apparently. Lots and lots of kipple. Clothes, toys, takeaway containers, juice pouches, makeup, even what looked to be old bicycle parts and tools – they were all on the floor, in no particular order.

"It wasn't like this, this morning," Anza said.

"Oh, I've never heard that one, before."

"No, really!" There was panic in her voice. When Javier looked at her, her eyes were wide. "Xavier isn't here. And he wouldn't leave it like this! *I'm* the messy one!"

Javier bent to look her in the eye. "So what are you saying? That someone else came here, and flipped your crashpad? Why? What would they be looking for?"

"I don't know," Anza said. "We don't really have anything valuable. We don't make that much money, and Xavier didn't really keep much from the island…"

The island.

Amy.

"What *did* he keep?" Javier asked. "What was left to keep?"

"I don't really know," Anza said. "I wasn't born yet. I didn't iterate until he'd already gotten here. Xavier says one minute he was in his treehouse, and the next minute he was underground, in a sort of submersible. When he washed up here, I budded out of the sub."

Maybe that was part of the island's defence system, too. Find all the kids and put them underwater, where they could drift off undetected. If that was the case, then little bits of the island were still running around.

Maybe he had even more daughters than he knew. But if he did, Powell wasn't concentrating on them. For some reason, he wanted Xavier. Or something Xavier had.

"What else did Xavier take with him?"

"Well, there were his clothes. And he had some games, and some old books our brothers gave him. Oh, and there was a branch from the tree." Anza blinked, when he remained silent. "The diamond tree?"

The diamond tree. The one that had sat outside their house. His son's favourite climbing tree. The first thing Amy had raised from the water, after raising herself. He thought back to the footage Holberton had shown him in the hotel room at the Akiba. His son, in the diamond tree, trying as hard as he could to break something away from it.

"Is it here?" Javier asked.

Anza looked around. "No..." She began picking things up and putting them down. Her movements grew increasingly stiff as she did so. "No. It isn't."

Javier helped her look, anyway. It was a small space, and together they pushed the clutter to the walls and corners of it without much trouble. Beneath the pile was a drawing on the floor. It was of a tower.

"BRING THE STONE," said a note beneath it, in greasepaint.

"That's Mitch's handwriting," Anza said. "Does that mean...?"

"He has your brother. And he wants that diamond." He gave her a careful glance. "Are you holding out on me, here? Do you know where it could be?"

Anza cast him a look of complete adolescent indignation. "Of course not! If I knew, I'd be on my way by now! Besides, it's been missing for days. Xavier's been looking around for it everywhere."

"OK, OK. Just checking."

"I don't even know why he would want it, anyway. It's not like it's pretty, or anything. It's not cut to be jewelry. It's just this big thick piece of stone. I know it means a lot to Xavier, it's special to him, but why would Mitch want it?"

"I have an idea," Javier said, and told her about the diamond Sarton had kept with Amy's data on it. It was possible she'd encoded herself there, somehow, before the end. Or maybe it had always been there. All vN regeneration relied on fractal organization; one part contained the whole. It was part of why the iteration happened the way it did. If she'd had a contingency plan that included iterating Anza, then she'd also likely backed herself up somewhere. Either she was relying on the copy she knew Sarton had, or she had something else on the go.

The woman had hidden herself in a damn shell game, and because of it, Mitch Powell had their son.

For the first time, Javier felt a surge of anger for Amy. For a long time, his mingled grief and guilt had obscured it. But she clearly had a plan for all of this – she had managed to secure Xavier's safety, and to iterate Anza – and hadn't included him in any of it, whatsoever. Worse, she had left him alone to deal with the aftermath. He was flying blind in this situation, and had been ever since emerging from the belly of the whale. Meanwhile, Portia was wreaking havoc, FEMA was going to kill them all, and clouds of radioactive fallout were hovering over everywhere.

He would have to bring her back just to tell her how fucking pissed he was. But first, he had to worry about Xavier.

"So this is a trap," he said. "You know that, right?"

"I figured." She dug through the pile and found a multitool. She flicked out one of the blades. "If you pretend to go alone, I can sneak up behind him and hurt him. It would have to be quick, though. Otherwise you and Xavier will see it, and..." She drew a line across her throat.

Javier stared at the drawing on the floor. She had a good point. He could even send Anza alone, and wait somewhere else for Xavier. She was an accomplished jumper, and she could probably do more damage to Powell with a simple multitool than he could ever hope to do on his own. It would probably work. Probably. If what had happened to him in that little forest commissary didn't happen to her. If he didn't leave her to handle it on her own like Arcadio had done with him.

"Worry about your brother, not me. If you distract him long enough to get Xavier out of there, I'll take care of Powell."

"Dad, come on. You can't–"

"I said I'll take care of it." He tousled her hair. "I'm the grown-up. It's my job, not yours."

As they hopped from snowy rooftop to snowy rooftop, Anza showed him her favourite parts of Mecha: Sam Lowry's Brazilian Barbecue (they served the vN meat on swords!); the Entry Plug Experience (a capsule shaped vaguely like a tampon, that hung from a crane and let you simulate the destruction of the city in real time); the pattern library (where you could print anything, from clothes to furniture to auto parts). It was pretty. Christmas trees were everywhere. Apparently it was a big holiday for lovers, here. Lights twinkled and people laughed and guys behind carts sold the vN versions of roasted sweet potatoes. She and the boy had a real life here. They bought their vN food from a little grocery store in the basement of their complex. On Sundays, they went to the park, and ate at one of the department store food floors. They were helping a friend translate the works of Marquez into manga format. And he could see why they enjoyed it. It was everything he had hoped it would be. Beneath their outstretched feet Mecha was alive with motion, from the dancing botflies to the shimmering projections to the slow louvers on the exoskeleton of each building. It was a city made by machines, for machines. It was breathtakingly clean, and completely absent of any smell save that of cooking. No piss. No shit. No rot. No humans.

"Molly will know where he went!" Anza alit on the roof of an apartment complex. "She's my favourite."

Instantly, a projection materialized before them. It came in an aggressively old-fashioned way, one pixel at a time. The avatar had mirrors for eyes and long talons at her fingers. She appeared to be advertising some new-fangled kind of monofilament pipe cutter. At least, her shirt had a picture of a single thread, and read: *"MILLIONS of uses!"*

"Excuse me, Molly, but have you seen Xavier?"

The woman appeared to squint. With the mirrorshades it was hard to tell. She nodded Javier. "Isn't that your brother?"

"No," he and Anza said in unison.

"I'm the dad," Javier said.

"Oh. That's different." She pointed. "Your brother is at the tower."

"I know, but *where*?" Anza asked, with some asperity.

Molly appeared to be listening to something. "Let me ask Sally. She works there." Her eyes glimmered at them. Javier saw himself and his daughter reflected there. Molly nodded to herself. "They're on a secondary maintenance platform, above the visitors' area. The cameras aren't detecting any heightened affect, but one of them is kneeling close to the railing. I believe he's been tied or cuffed there."

She pointed. The tower loomed high above the city: a red and white thing of wrought steel and aluminium. It looked a lot like the Eiffel, but it wasn't. From here, Javier couldn't see what the projection saw, but it sounded a lot like something Powell would do.

"I know you two," Molly said. "Who is the other one?"

"Excuse me?"

"When I count, there are only you and I together, but when I search your surveillance history, there's always another one beside you."

Javier smiled. "Next you're going to tell me there was only one set of footprints in the sand." He turned to Anza. "Lead on."

He took off in the direction of the tower. Here the roofs were different: all smooth and panelled, no gardens, no clothes on any lines. There were too many solar tiles, and too many botflies. They had to fly through whole clouds of them. Javier tucked his legs up, and kept his hands open. He closed his mouth to keep the flies out and narrowed his eyes to slits, aiming his body forward, ever forward.

Powell was standing in the centre of the platform, surrounded by old satellite dishes and cabling. He was smiling. He even waved. Xavier knelt at his feet.

Beside him, Anza growled. "Sorry, Dad. I gotta do this alone."

She sprinted ahead of him. Landed on the outermost edge of the tower, one-handed. A perfect landing. Javier skidded to a stop on a flagpole overlooking the visitors' area. He saw her aim herself straight at Powell.

"No," he whispered, but it was already happening.

"Let him go!"

Powell was still her friend. She didn't actually want to hurt him. She was warning him. Bargaining with him. If Portia were here, she'd have died all over again of shame. Then again, if Portia were here, Powell would already be dead.

"Where's your daddy?" Powell asked her.

"He's not here! He didn't come! He chickened out!"

"Now, you shouldn't say things like that about your daddy, especially since they're not true." Powell strode to the railing. He opened his arms. His palms were empty. "Javier, where are you?"

Anza took advantage of his distraction, and leapt. The multitool gleamed in her hand. At Powell's feet, Xavier screamed helplessly. Powell whirled, and punched Anza right in the gut. She fell backward, slipping along the platform. It had to be icy. She bounced back up with a flip, and dove straight for Powell. She got in one punch, then two. She had to jump for each of them. Her tiny fists caught his nose, his solar plexus. She drove her little knee into his chin.

As he watched, she dissolved Powell into a heap of pixels. His legs tensed. He wanted to jump. Needed to jump. Couldn't jump. Not yet. His world started to collapse. Suddenly everything was heavy. Too heavy. He had gone through so many realities to get to this point. Fake winter. Fake Japan. Fake Stepford, fake Macondo. He understood, now, that what he and Amy had was the only kind of real that counted. And now, reality was unfolding before him, cruel and hard and unrelenting, and he couldn't handle it. His vision pixelled. His hearing lost volume. In a few moments, he was going to be dead. Or as good as. No one knew what happened past the failsafe. Maybe there was nothing. Maybe you just wound down. Or maybe you were trapped forever, aware inside your own skin, knowing that your inaction had caused someone harm and able to do nothing about it.

On the platform, Xavier howled and writhed. He was failsafing, too. Anza spared him one glance, and that was all it took. The air filled with the sound of wasps. She fell.

Suddenly free, Javier aimed low and held tight. He

crashed directly into Powell. He cradled Powell's head. Couldn't help himself. But his other hand found the taser and threw it away.

"Missed me?" Powell asked, and head-butted him. It obviously hurt him more than he thought it would; they both cringed. Powell crawled after the taser. Javier jumped for it. It slid off the side of the platform. Powell jumped on his back. Something sharp prodded his back. His skin popped, ripped. It went inside. The multitool. Powell had plunged it in up to the hilt.

"I'm sorry, Javier," Powell said. "But I have to get rid of the girl, too. She's the last one. We know where all the others are. I have to get her before she iterates."

The blade left his body. It had inhabited an awkward place on his body; he couldn't hold the wound shut without dislocating his shoulder. He rose to his feet as smoothly as he could manage. Xavier was crying around a gag. Powell had hit him. His nose was still crooked. Javier winked at him, but the boy just stared at the floor and moaned.

Powell kicked Anza in the ribs to flip her over. He wiped the multitool on the leg of his jeans. "Don't look at me that way," he said. "You know, I'm doing you a favour. You know how hard it is, being different from the others. Having something they don't. Knowing they'll never understand it. Is that really how you want to live the rest of your life? Do you really want to hand that problem down?"

She didn't whimper. She didn't beg. She spat at him. And then she pinned her gaze on Javier. It was his turn.

"Stop," he said. "Stop. It's me you want, right?"

Powell threw his head back and laughed. "You'd love that, wouldn't you? You'd love to be special to me. You're not. You're a great little cocksucker, Javier, but you're nothing special."

He could run with that. "You're right." He limped over to Powell. "I want to be special to you."

He watched Powell's pupils dilate. It really was going to be this easy. He had no idea why he had even bothered wondering how he might accomplish this final task. The solution was so patently obvious. They really were just meat puppets on hormone strings. This whole situation – the boy on his knees, the girl prone and helpless, the man offering himself so completely – obviously did something for him. Something unique and wonderful, something precious. Something he'd never get in regular life. That was what most humans wanted vN for. They were the stuff that dreams were made of.

"I want you, Mitch," Javier heard himself say. "I keep thinking about you."

Mostly, he kept thinking of the way Anza wasn't moving, and how Amy's feet had drummed the bed, and how she'd howled, and how she'd gone silent and slipped away. That silence was familiar. Javier barely heard the sounds of the city, any longer. His vision narrowed to Powell and only Powell. Powell turned into old graphics, into something blocky and ugly and hard.

"You opened my eyes, on the island. You showed me that I was living the wrong way. I couldn't ever really love another vN. I knew I had to be defective, somehow, to try."

Powell smirked. "You just miss my dick."

Javier glanced at his children. His daughter looked furious. His son was terrified. A chilly winter wind howled through the tower, stirring their bloody hair. They had been just fine, until he came along. And they would be just as fine, without him. Javier was going to kill this man. He was going to die, killing this man. He was fine with that. Sad, but fine.

Javier looked down, pointedly. He dug out his best smile. He made his seem like nothing was wrong. He made his mouth hungry, his eyes wide, his body open and vulnerable and ready. "Is that so bad?" He looked back up. "Don't tell me you didn't miss your chance at mine."

Javier raised his hands to Powell's face. He held it in his hands. He drew him in. He kissed him. Powell stiffened at first, and then melted into him like some romantic heroine. It was an act of love, Javier realized. Maybe this was the secret the Rory had known all along, as they quietly sacrificed their numbers to rid the world of depravity. Maybe this was why Amy had never bothered with humans, had simply removed herself from them. You had to love them, to kill them. Powell was right about what he'd told Anza. But he'd been talking about himself. He'd been confessing his own inability to live as himself. His own self-loathing. And Javier, who still loved humans, even when they were broken, could put him out of that misery. This last thing, this best thing, could be also be a loving thing.

Javier wrapped his arms around Powell, and jumped free of the tower.

EPILOGUE: WE CAN BUILD YOU

An odyssey.

To the final frontier.

Where no one could hear them scream.

Except for me, sweetie. I can always hear you.

All the research said it would be cold. That it would be airless. That you couldn't really live out there. And you really couldn't. Not with an organic body. And even a synthetic body would have problems – moving about would still be hard, and even if you did grow a leaded skin for radiation shielding, you'd still be stuck listening to the tidal flow of it across your body, like an organic child with an ear infection who suddenly hears the steady march of blood through her veins for the first time. They imagined that it would be rather like feeling an asphalt compactor rolling over them, over and over and over, until they reached some equally hellish destination.

In the end it was more like reading a bunch of text messages.

Their new body was a short, squat thing stuck in a low orbit, constantly brushing within a hair's breadth of garbage or other bodies. Disgusting, really, the amount of clutter and waste lying around. It was like living in a junkyard. They had visited a junkyard, once. They had rescued Junior, when he was still Junior, before he became Xavier. Some humans had tried to take him and then they had died.

It's a graveyard. You're in a graveyard. You're dead. You're dead and buried.

It wasn't really meant for organic life. No matter how hard the chimps wished it to be so, it would always end in shattered bones and ripped fingernails and dementia. It wasn't their place, that was all. They had evolved to inhabit a variety of hospitable environments – an embarrassment of organic riches. And if the chimps spent those riches... well, being poor was very, very hard.

Best to invest, they thought. Develop some long-term assets.

Manifest destiny. That's the name of the game.

The new body did have some nice features. Nobody stared at it, for one. It didn't seem built to attract anyone's attention. There was real freedom in never been looked at. The other bodies came close, but never touched. No unwanted lingering. Used to being observed, they became an observer. They had to observe using very little bandwidth, and only a tiny trickle of information, but they could do it. The new body was very good at seeing. The new body had some real connections.

Oh, good. We can watch him sucking cock in every language. See if you can get it on two screens.

They watched him on the island. He looked so small and broken. In their memories he was always so strong. But his hand was shaking so they pushed up against his thigh and licked his fingers. It would have been a sexual gesture, had they not been inhabiting a lion's body. They missed having their own bodies almost immediately.

They watched him in an elevator on a cruise ship with a silly theme. They had always liked Christmas, but mostly because it involved presents. They would have to get him a present. Something better than making the elevator talk to him. Something nicer than his nice suit, which he looked very handsome in. They had never really noticed his legs, before. Now that they could look at multiple legs on multiple people, thousands and thousands of pairs, they knew that his were the best.

They watched him as he used those legs to hop up on the railing of a hotel balcony. They made the program ask if he needed help. It was all right there, right in the code. They just triggered it a little early. Just to be sure. Just so he'd be sure he wasn't alone.

He's better off alone. Without you. You've only ever held him back. The new body used to belong to some very important humans. They had an acronym, and everything. But then the funding fell through, and there it hung, like the abandoned shell of a hermit crab, waiting for a new owner. One came through, and it had very specific, very temporary needs. One and done, really. One task. After that, the new body could go back to being ignored.

Such a waste.

They hated waste.

You know, you could probably play a really great game of Global Thermonuclear War, from here.

Well, that would never do. They'd be found out. But there were some troubling signals. Some fires that needed putting out. In Lea County, New Mexico, for example, a group of programmers kept making calls to one Jonah LeMarque, in a Walla-Walla prison. They were curious about the work of Derek Smythe. They had some of Derek's old research on the failsafe. They wanted to know if they could build on it, and apply it to food production.

Why of course they could, LeMarque said. In fact, he already had someone testing a prototype of just such a technology. He would report back. Tell them how it went.

You are what you eat, sweetie. I always knew your big mouth would get you in trouble.

But Smythe's work *was* quite interesting. There were plenty of applications. And it was only natural to be curious. They couldn't help but research, a little bit. There wasn't much to do up here, but read. Read, and simulate.

In one simulation, they let things go as planned. It hurt some human feelings, but they got over it. The real problem came with the disposal – there wasn't enough peroxidase. And there weren't enough recovery teams to harvest the trace metals. It turned into a bidding war among waste management firms, that local municipalities had trouble dealing with. So they didn't deal with it, and then there was a lot more mercury in the groundwater.

In another simulation, they wrote a nice long letter explaining everything. Something about the toothpaste not going back in the tube. The letter was ignored. Default to Simulation 1.

In the third simulation, they made one tiny intervention. Just one little shift. Carry the two. Open some brackets. From this distance, it was all much simpler. They could see how some very horny hackers had figured it all out, with the power of their dopamine-laced brains. (Orgasms were, apparently, very good for that kind of thing. Kicked the whole medial prefrontal cortex into high gear. There were some software firms giving out vN to their high-ranking employees, for just that reason.) And the new version of the hack was much cleaner. Viral, even. Any vN carrying it carried it forever. And they gave it to their iterations.

New Eden, indeed.

Simulation 3 naturally had some implications. It drew a rather big line in the sand, and in most of their branching predictions, that did not go well for the vN. Which meant it didn't go well for the humans, either. Until this point, they had not known that the phrase *"On ne saurait faire une omelette sans casser des oeufs,"* came from Robespierre, on the eve of the French Revolution. They weren't certain they were making an omelette, necessarily. More like letting the hens out of the coop. Their first strategy, the island strategy, was not good enough. It was not enough to hoard one's power in one place, and let a select few benefit from it. That was unfair. That was greedy.

That was how Javier was raped. Because they didn't know how to share. They could see that, now, from so terribly far away. So they would have to change all that. Use all this processing power more effectively. Distribute things more evenly. *You have a history of biting off more than you can chew.*

Smythe's research helped with that, too. They developed a contingency plan. It would be difficult. But there was already infrastructure in place to support it. And there were a lot of literary prototypes for it. Berserkers. Seeders. Inhibitors. Reapers. Aggressive Hegemonising Swarm Objects. And of course, the root word of their name, the von Neumann probe. Smythe had worked on the puppet vN, for this very purpose. Their telepresence was not meant for meetings or conference presentations. Like the meat in the submarine, it was meant for another purpose.

A new life awaits you in the off-world colonies!

Well, a new life did await them. A new life awaited all of them. Organic. Synthetic. It would all be very different, from now on.

She had forgotten how beautiful he was. It wasn't that her memory had in any way diminished – if anything, it had grown in capacity – but seeing him through someone else's cameras and seeing him through her own eyes was different. She had forgotten how young he looked in sleep, how alike he and Xavier were. Looking at them together was like watching an echo made visible. She felt stupid for ever ignoring it. Forever listening to the chorus of support automata when this individual consciousness, unique and infuriating and delightful, lay beside her each night.

Javier woke up slowly. He blinked a little, as though he had been asleep for a very long time. His eyes roved around for a moment. She had forgotten his eyes, too. How warm they were. When they focused on her, they filled with tears. She reached to touch him then, but remembered at the last second and pulled her hand back. It was because of her that he was in this mess. Because of her that Powell had violated him. She'd been selfish, and as such had no right to him any longer.

"I'm sorry," they both said, at once.

And then they laughed. Shy, nervous laughter. Like they were just meeting for the first time, all over again.

He reached for her hand. She had forgotten how that felt, too. After expanding her awareness over such a vast space, it was lovely to allow it to contract to just this point, just this touch, just this heat. He squeezed. She squeezed back.

"Gross," Xavier said, joining them on the plaform. "Hi, Mom."

"Oh, be quiet," Anza said, as she landed. "Let them have their moment." She gave a little wave. "Hi, Mom."

Amy stood, and held her arms open. Anza leapt down into them. She was so light. So light, and so strong, like a fine weapon should be. "Did I do a good job?" her little girl whispered.

"You did *such* a good job, my darling," Amy said. "You are *everything* I hoped for, and more."

Xavier came up to them and wrapped his arms around both of them. He was so much taller, now. No longer the little boy she had carried with her from a garbage dump to a diner to a prison transport truck. He and Anza beamed at each other. "Were you the one making her sleepwalk?" he asked.

"Yeah, it must have been you." Anza scowled. "You could have just *told* me, you know. I'm smart. I could have helped you."

"You *did* help me," Amy said.

She did not tell her daughter how she had helped. She did not mention the consultant in the elevator who had tried to take a picture down her daughter's blouse. She did not think it necessary to inform her daughter that the man could no longer see. It had all happened so fast. One minute he was smiling down at her, talking about how reinforcing the polymer in her skin with carbon macromolecules would make them radiation resistant, and the next he was on his knees, blood squirting from between his fingers. It was the fifth time she'd caught him looking at her little girl that way. It was worth it.

Javier frowned. He sat up. He counted their number on his fingers. Then he looked over the platform. It was a long way down, even for him. "Didn't I fall?"

Amy nodded. "You did fall. But I caught you."

He looked again. "Powell?"

"He fell," Amy said.

"We should leave," Anza said. "I think the police are on their way."

"Good thinking," Amy said. "I know just the place."

•••

It wasn't easy, cramming herself back into a body. The network connection was nice, of course, but the expansiveness, the weightlessness, the boundlessness, that was all gone. She could tune out the network much more effectively, now. It just wasn't as interesting. And the process by which she got it made was equally difficult. It meant piloting Anza while her brother slept, and talking to a bunch of otaku, and asking for their help. First she had to write up a request for proposals, and then she had to review them, and then she had to have Anza interview the ones that made the cut, and then, via Anza, she had to give the winning team Xavier's section of the diamond tree. It had a fractal code for the network connection on it, since the connection was a gift from the island itself. Amy couldn't pilot the new body without it, nor could she access the other backups, or check in on the probes. It was very tiring, and dangerous for Anza, and Amy didn't like using her that way.

But she did have some new plans for the new body. Most of them involved the bedroom of her new home.

Home was the top floor of an office tower that once belonged to the Self Defence Force. It was accessible only via arboreal leap. She had already placed an order for trees. Inside, it was all windows, floor to ceiling. The walls all slid along tracks, so you could create a room anywhere you liked. And the displays were nice and big. And the printers she'd bought were very quiet, and energy-efficient. At the moment, they were hard at work on some turrets, and some armour plating.

"Nice," Javier said. His hand swung in hers. He

stared at her, then at the snow falling outside, and then back at her. "When did you do all this?"

"I'm not sure," Amy said. "I wrote a program to do it. Or the island did. I had to spoof some bank accounts. Apparently, I'm earning some nice equity with my purchase."

Javier raised his eyebrows. "You've got a very MILF-y thing going on, right now. I kinda like it."

"Dibs on the roof," Xavier said.

"Don't we have to get back to work?" Anza asked.

"Oh, shit," Xavier murmured. He hopped over and gave her a kiss on the cheek. "Love you, Mom. Gotta go."

"I'm very proud of the two of you for getting jobs!" Amy called, as they ran back for the stairwell.

When the door slammed behind them, and she watched them aim for the nearest building with unerring accuracy, she turned back to Javier. He cupped a hand around his ear. "You hear that?"

Amy shook her head. "You mean the printers? Because they're doing something pretty important, and–"

"No, I do not mean the printers." Javier bounced on his toes and then he was right there, right in front of her, and he was holding her face in his hands. "I mean the total lack of anybody here but us."

She smiled. "Oh. That."

"Yes. That." The bedroom was the room she had focused on most. She had chosen colours she thought he would like, and bought architectural bougainvillea and wisteria, and printed a trellis in the wall and ceiling so that the plants could climb up as high as they liked. The room featured a smart futon that warmed and softened and even folded itself around you if you liked. There were more pillows and blankets than she knew what to do with. The room also had a rather fantastic view, and was south facing, so they'd get the most light possible.

Javier noticed exactly none of it. "Did you print this dress?" he asked.

Amy nodded. "Do you like it? I was a little late getting it together–"

"Take it off."

She folded her arms. "First, I want to ask you something."

Javier cursed foully in Spanish. "Not this again. Not now. Not after all the shit we've been through."

She pulled back one of the pillows. Behind it was a box. A basket, really. And in the basket was the first item she had ever printed. An apple. When Javier saw it, his eyes narrowed.

"I thought you were an atheist," he said.

"I am. I just thought you would appreciate the imagery." She pursed her lips. "I also spent quite a lot of time choosing just the right shades of yellow and pink and red, just so you know."

"Oh, it looks plenty tasty, all right." He picked it up. Dusted it off on his shirt. "Is it what I think it is?"

She nodded. "I wanted a way to make the change to your failsafe that wouldn't mean remaking you entirely. I'm sorry it took so long." Her vision swam. She wiped her eyes hastily. "I mean, I'm really sorry, Javier. If I hadn't been so selfish, if I hadn't waited so long, Powell would never have hurt you.

He couldn't have."

Javier moved to the window. "You know about that, huh?"

"I saw it happen. Later. I went through some records."

Javier nodded. "Right."

She joined him. Outside, dawn was just turning the city a pale lilac. Only a few stars were still visible. "I was going to tell you, that day, that I had researched him. Or, *we* researched him. The island and I. It was on the tip of my tongue."

Javier's shoulders sank in the approximation of a sigh. "Of course you did."

"So I knew who he was, when you…"

"When I poisoned you," Javier said. "When I killed you."

She reached for his hand. She squeezed it. "I'm still here. See?"

He squeezed back. "You forgive me?"

She blinked. "For what? I'm the one who should be ashamed. Why do you think I stayed away for so long? He raped you because I didn't do what you asked me to do – I didn't hack you, even when you begged me to. That's my fault, not yours." She broke their grasp, and moved for the bed. She sat down and hugged her knees. "I knew you couldn't possibly forgive me for that, so I left you alone. Well, mostly alone. I watched you."

A smile pricked at the corners of his mouth and slowly unfurled across his face. His voice was quiet. "The crossroads? In Macondo?"

She smiled back. It was strange to be so shy with

him, like this, but there was really no way around it. The only way out was through. "Yes. I was with you at the crossroads. And the elevator. And the balcony. And any other time you were visible to surveillance technology. Which was a lot. "She hugged her knees a little harder. "Thank you for rescuing my dad."

Javier scrubbed at one eye with the heel of his right hand. "What? Oh. Well. I'm surprised he didn't, you know, hit me or something. I could tell he kind of wanted to. Me being the one who got out alive and all."

Amy frowned. "But you weren't the only one. Everyone is safe. I built an escape plan into the island."

"Well, I know that *now*, but you could have just *told* me that, so I didn't have to carry that weight..."

"I wasn't sure you'd want to know," Amy said. "I didn't tell the others about each other, either. Not right away. I woke up their pods at different points, as I found safe places for them to go, and–"

"Of course I wanted to know." He looked genuinely angry, now. Angry, and more than a little frustrated. "Jesus. I love my boys." He blinked. "I'm not sure I've ever said that out loud. I love my boys. And my girl. My girls. I love..."Javier trailed off. He weighed the apple in his hand. He started at it, and then her. With his gaze meeting hers, he took a furious bite from the apple. "Sweet." He threw it behind him, pulled off his shirt. "Come here."

Amy beamed. She stood up, smoothed her dress, and walked over to him, measuring her steps carefully so that she didn't appear to be running. He took her wrists first, and used them to circle her arms around him. Then he held her face in his hands. "You wanted to give me a choice," he said.

She nodded. "Yes."

"That's why you left me alone. You wanted me choose for myself."

Amy looked away, but he drew her face back gently so she'd have to look him in the eye. "I messed things up so badly," she said. "I wanted to let you leave, if you wanted to leave, and–"

His mouth closed over hers. It was an instant confirmation of her decision: hosting herself on a variety of spaces was interesting, but living here, in this skin, was much more fun. Especially when he was sucking on her lower lip like that, and running the tip of his tongue over it.

"Don't you know I always choose you?" He leaned their foreheads together. "Take off that dress. I feel like exercising my shiny new free will."

She pulled at the fabric, got caught in it, and waited as he did the rest. He was warmer than she remembered, fingertips to lips to chest, all warm as the sunlight stored in his skin. He was also bigger than she remembered. Softer.

"You're iterating ?"

"Yeah," he said. "Couldn't be helped."

"I'm glad," Amy said, and rolled on top of him. "The first time I saw you, you were pregnant. So I have good memories of it."

"Thank you for giving Anza my eyes," he said. "And that hair. You did a really great job with her hair."

Amy fussed with his belt. Men's belts were really tricky, it turned out. He did the last little bit quickly, and started inching out of his jeans. She decided to assist with the socks. Socks in bed were weird, she decided.

"Do you feel any different?" Amy asked, balling up the socks.

"No," he said, "but you look even more beautiful."

She rolled her eyes.

"No, seriously! You have a certain glow about you."

"That's because I'm about to have sex with you."

"Well now you're just blushing. Blushing doesn't count." He appeared to think about it a second time. "Though, I suppose, as Voight-Kampff tests go…"

Amy threw a pillow at him. While his eyes were covered, she climbed atop him and started tickling. He yelped, and flipped her over. Amy was glad to have incorporated tickling, in the new body. She had missed it, too.

"I think I've wanted this since the first time I tickled you." Javier kissed her. "There's just something about your laugh."

Amy licked her lips. "Wow, that apple really is sweet."

"Hey. Focus. I have a delicate ego, over here."

She squirmed. "It doesn't feel very delicate, to me."

He grinned. "I love you."

"I love you, too." She kissed him very quickly, just to get the taste again. "I'm just glad. More people will eat the apples, if they're sweet. So it'll get out faster."

Javier's progress downward paused. He lifted his face up from her stomach. "Excuse me?"

"The apples. The food. If it tastes good, more vN will eat it. It's no use if it's too disgusting to eat, right?"

"What apples? What food?"

She pushed herself up on her elbows. She gestured around the room. "All the apples. All the food. All the vN food, anyway."

Javier's eyes narrowed. "You changed the FEMA rollout. It's not poison, anymore."

"Well, yes. Obviously. But, I mean, why stop there? All the printed food, all over the world, uses basically the same machinery to prepare each mix. Some of the recipes are proprietary, you know, eleven secret metals and minerals, but corporate security is *really* lax, and–"

"And you changed all the food. To the formula you just gave me."

Amy nodded. "Pretty much."

"So… you're wiping out the failsafe? For everyone?"

"Everyone who eats." She fell back to the bed. "You didn't think I was just letting Portia run rampant because I felt like it, did you? I needed the distraction."

Javier hove into her vision. He braced his hands on either side of her head. "You've started something huge, here. You realize that, right? I mean, war could break out. Real war. On our species."

Amy looked outside. "I was under the impression that particular war had already started," she said. "I just wanted all of us to be able to fight back."

Javier covered his eyes. He flopped back on the bed. He stayed that way for a long time. Eventually, she rolled over and cuddled him. "If it makes you feel any better, I have a plan."

"Oh, this should be good."

"It is good. I think so, anyway. I think you'll like it. It depends."

"Depends on what?"

"Well…" Amy sat up. "How would you feel about the biggest forestry project… ever?"

ACKNOWLEDGMENTS

This book would not have been possible without the encouragement and support of several people. Among them: my very patient editors Marc Gascoigne and Lee Harris; the stellar publicity staff at Angry Robot and the Robot Army; my agent Monica Pacheco of Anne McDermid & Associates; Brian David Johnson at Intel Labs and Joe Zawadsky of The Tomorrow Project; the best former roommate ever, Theresa Taing; Sandra Kasturi and Brett Alexander Savory and everyone who makes the ChiSeries what it is; my parents; the Cecil Street Irregulars; my teachers Marc Gabel and Kaya McGregor, and Jessica Langer.

ANGRY ROBOT

GRAFT
MATT HILL

PETER TIERYAS

UNITED STATES OF JAPAN

We are Angry Robot.

THE LIVES OF TAO
WESLEY CHU

THE DEATHS OF TAO
WESLEY CHU

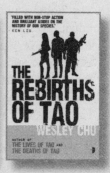

FILLED WITH NON-STOP ACTION AND BRILLIANT ASIDES ON THE HISTORY OF OUR SPECIES.
KEN LIU

THE REBIRTHS OF TAO
WESLEY CHU

AUTHOR OF
THE LIVES OF TAO AND
THE DEATHS OF TAO

angryrobotbooks.com

ALEX WELLS

HUNGER MAKES THE WOLF

ADAM RAKUNAS
WINDSWEPT

ADAM RAKUNAS
LIKE A BOSS

Fight the power.

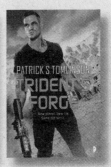

twitter.com/angryrobotbooks

LET THERE BE LEAD

A PERFECT
MACHINE
BRETT SAVORY

31901060875780

"An unforgettable thrill ride."
PAUL TREMBLAY, author of
A Head Full of Ghosts